Counterpoint: A Novel of Music & Murder

SummerFest Series Book Two

Barbara Burt

Bent Tree Press

Book Cover by Bailey McGinn

First edition 2025

Also by the Author

Dissonance: A Novel of Music & Murder
Book 1 in the SummerFest Mystery Series

For Young Readers
The Eve of the Revolution
Colonial Life: The Adventures of Benjamin Wilcox

Anthologies from the Memory2Memoir Workshops
(Barbara Burt, editor)
Stories That Connect Us
Things We Know
Writing Our Secrets

In memory of Lee Burt (1927-2012), lover of music and books, especially mysteries.

"I think of it all as exploration. Exploration outside oneself, exploration outside one's being. I don't want to have an idea of what something will always be."

—composer Annea Lockwood, in an interview in The New York Times with Joshua Barone, June 4, 2025.

Contents

Prelude

The door to cottage number three was locked, but faint strains of music[1] could be heard above the bob-o-links' songs in the meadow. Tanya shook the handle again. Nope, the door was definitely locked. She was annoyed. After several years of renting this cabin, this summer tenant certainly knew that Thursday was cleaning day. Tanya sighed and picked up her pail of cleaning supplies. After 25 years of cleaning summer cottages, she was disappointed the vacationing tenants hadn't gotten any smarter. She'd have to let RuthEllen Cox, owner of the Kennimac Inn and her boss, know that she wasn't able to get into the cottage to clean. That would probably mean she'd have an extra heavy day tomorrow. She trudged up the hill to the inn's back entrance and opened the screen door.

"RuthEllen, there's a problem with Cormorant," she shouted. "It's locked. I can't get in to clean."

For cripes' sake, RuthEllen thought. What now? Tanya was a sullen worker at best, and she managed to find something to complain about daily. Once Tanya set to work, however, RuthEllen had to admit that she did a thorough job. Having to put up with her negative attitude was worth it. Good cleaners were hard to find.

The Kennimac Inn was a big old house set in fields overlooking Kennimac Bay. Seven small cottages set closer to the water's edge were part of the property. Originally built in the 1800s, the cottages had been moved, renovated, and upgraded until they became charming places worthy of spending a summer vacation in. And this summer's occupants did just that. Three were occupied by members of the Kennimac SummerFest Symphony. They enjoyed the six weeks they spent in the cottages, where the breezes from the bay kept them cool, and RuthEllen's wonderful muffins and sweet breads kept them well fed. RuthEllen patted the cinnamon raisin bread dough she'd been kneading, rinsed off her flour-covered hands, and met Tanya at the door. "Are you sure the cottage door was locked?" she asked. Tanya nodded. "Did you knock and shout?"

"Of course I did. And I heard nothing, except some music. So I thought someone was in there. But no one answered the door."

RuthEllen wiped her forehead. "Well, skip Cormorant for now. I'll try to figure out what's going on." She took off her apron, grabbed the huge ring of keys hanging by the back door, and headed down the driveway toward the cottage. She noticed the renter's car was parked in the cottage driveway. Strange, she thought. As she stepped onto the porch, she also heard music. Strings. Maybe a quartet is rehearing inside. And they're so engrossed in the music that they didn't hear Tanya knock.

"Hello?" she said while knocking on the door. There was no answer. "Hello?" she tried a little louder. "HELLO!" Convinced that if there were someone inside, that person would have heard her, RuthEllen fumbled through the keys on her ring until she came to the one labeled "Corm." Slipping the key in the lock, she opened the door slowly, in case someone was actually inside.

From the doorway, everything looked tidy. RuthEllen stepped into the room. Her eye caught something by the couch, and she took a few more steps to investigate. Sunddenly, she gasped. "Oh my lord!" She fumbled for her phone, and her hands shook as she punched 911. She'd never seen a dead person before.

As she stood on the porch waiting for the emergency responders to arrive, the somber second movement of Schubert's string quartet, "Death and the Maiden," started up once again.

I: Allegro

"Music is the divine way to tell beautiful, poetic things to the heart."
—*Fanny Mendelssohn Hensel (German composer, 1805-1847)*

One

Allegra Brewster, assistant managing director of the Kennimac SummerFest Symphony, executed a few deft dance moves as she walked to the printer to retrieve the stat sheets she had just completed. The Bangles[1], she thought, now they knew how to get you dancing. This year's festival was turning out to be one of its most successful ever despite its tragic beginning in the spring, and Allie saw nothing on the horizon to change that. She adjusted her ear buds, grabbed the sheets from the printer, and hit repeat on her phone so she could dance back to her desk.

"Hey, Allie." George, her boss, croaked from his office. "Can you come here for a moment?" George had been injured in the troubles that started off the season. In fact, he'd almost died. But now, in July, with the festival in full swing, he didn't exhibit any lingering damage except for his hoarse voice. The small, still-red scar on his neck wasn't noticeable unless you knew where to look.

Allie took out her ear buds and walked into George's office with the papers. "Look at these numbers, George," she said. "We are sold out for all but the last concert."

"That's great," he replied. "Except I hate to disappoint people who didn't know they needed to buy tickets ahead of time. We suffer enough from classical music's snobby reputation."

"Do you think people in Kennimac have that feeling about us?"

"Probably not, if they've been here long enough to see how we operate. But people from farther away..."

"Right," agreed Allie. "I mean, we work hard to put musicians out into the community. You can't go downtown without running into a small group playing somewhere." She laughed. "I even saw the bassoon section sitting at the transfer station last Saturday, playing silly arrangements of kids' songs like 'Pop Goes the Weasel.' The line of cars moved pretty slowly because everyone was listening to the tunes."

George chuckled. "I wonder if Ruben did the arranging? It's amazing how he can whip those things off." George shook his head.

Ruben Perrotta was the orchestra's composer in residence this summer. He came at the insistence of Tony Bainbridge, the festival's music director. Ruben was a flamboyant character, full of laughter and practical jokes, who seemed to have music bubbling in his veins.

"I know," agreed Allie. "I can't wait to hear his new cello concerto. Aren't they supposed to start reading it next week?"

"I think that's been put off for a week. He's having trouble finishing up. Tony is working with him." George didn't seem to have any serious worries about the new piece being finished in time for its scheduled premiere.

"Here's an idea," said Allie. "What if we open the barn doors during the sold-out concerts and put some folding chairs on the deck outside? I bet we could fit another fifty chairs there."

"Hmmm. Not a bad idea," said George.

"And we could sell those outside seats at a cheaper rate on the day of the concert. That way, if the weather is threatening, we can cancel selling the deck tickets. Would that work?"

"It's worth a try. I'll pass the idea by the board and see what they think." He turned to his laptop, preparing to write an email to the board.

"Wait, George," Allie interrupted. "I wanted to show you the latest numbers. We're keeping within the budget, mostly, and the ticket sales are really high, as you know."

"Which budget items are over?" George had picked up on the small bit of less wonderful news.

Allie pointed to several lines of numbers on the spreadsheets. "Tony is overspending just a small amount. I think it's due to transportation costs getting both Ruben and Thomas here in June."

"Oh, right. I approved those changes. I can't imagine it's more than $1,000, is it?"

"Actually, $1,560."

"Well, we can handle that. But let's keep an eye on the budget going forward. It would be very nice to end up with a surplus. Especially after giving the orchestra musicians that three percent raise." George wanted to keep the board of directors happy. There were a few members who had been skeptical of the need to raise the musicians' wages.

"True." Allie put her earbuds in and danced back to her desk.

The SummerFest Symphony was made up of professional musicians from around the country (and the world) who came to coastal Kennimac, Maine, for six weeks in the summer. Some hailed from top orchestras, some taught in university music departments, and some were young virtuosi just beginning their career. Many of those who came from top ensembles had started at the festival as young players years ago. They fell in love with the vacation-like setting, the welcoming town, and the opportunity to play music for the sheer love of it. British music director Anthony Bainbridge was aware of the special nature of the orchestra's musical experience, and he tried to enhance it by choosing up-and-coming young composers and assistant conductors to liven the musical offerings. He'd often sandwich a wild contemporary piece between two familiar stalwarts, stretching the audience's and the musicians' appreciation of musical possibilities.

This year, he'd brought in Thomas Ramirez, a dashing young conductor who was gaining a reputation for his interpretation of late 20th century compositions, and Ruben Perrotta, whose avantgarde compositions spanned musical genres. Allie already knew Thomas from their time together in the spring. She and Thomas were both cellists, though neither had much chance to practice the cello these days. But back in April, they had rehearsed a movement of a Vivaldi piece they planned to perform at a benefit concert for the festival. Board chair Sylvia

Abbott was to play the harpsichord accompaniment along with the two cellos, but her murder put an end to their performance plans. Allie was quite taken with Thomas at the beginning of their collaboration until his intentions became clear. His affections seemed to be as superficial as his air of sophistication, she decided. After that, Allie was fine with just calling him a friend.

While Thomas was tall and handsome in a traditional way, Ruben was wiry, short, and in constant motion. He reminded Allie of a leprechaun, practically dancing a jig as he spoke with enthusiasm about his cello concerto commissioned by the Kennimac SummerFest. Allie was excited about the project, too. As a cellist herself, it was exciting to be a present for the birth of a fresh addition to the repertoire. And it was especially thrilling that her beloved teacher, Anne Kirschner, would be the soloist. Ruben seemed to move at twice the speed of most people. He smiled quickly, too, and as Allie had soon discovered, he reveled in practical jokes and ribald humor. At 5'9", Allie was a good two inches taller than Ruben, and when he met her, he looked up at her and said something like he envied that cello that lay between her legs when she played. "How intimate!" he had said, waggling his eyebrows in a Groucho Marx imitation. Allie had frowned, and Ruben caught her arm and quickly said he was sorry if he was out of line. He'd just meant it in fun. "You're quite a beauty," he had added. "That's all I was thinking."

So, Ruben could be a bit of a jerk, but most of the time his was a lively, light-hearted spirit added to the festival. He came with a pile of compositions silly and serious for small ensembles to play, and he generously passed them out to anyone who wanted to give them a try. He claimed to be only a middling violist and terrible pianist, but his pieces demonstrated a mastery of instrumental color and inventive rhythms borrowed from many musical genres, with special affinity to late 20th century composers. After a couple of weeks, he had become a well-liked member of the festival.

Two

"Hey, Al, did I catch a glimpse of you walking like an Egyptian?" Lucas O'Donnell breezed into the office, trailing a scent of sawdust and machine oil.

"That you did," Allie answered. "Watch it, you're getting sawdust all over the office. Let me brush you off outside."

The two stepped out the door of the converted milking shed, one of several former farm buildings that made up the campus of the festival. Allie ran her fingers over Luke's brown curls until he caught her hands and kissed her.

"Not here, Luke," she protested, laughing. "You'll ruin my reputation as a serious nonprofit arts executive."

"Aww, there's no one around to see us, Ms. Brewster," Luke answered and stole another kiss.

Allie pushed him away. "What did you want, anyway?" she asked. "I doubt you came just to get your hair styled."

"I came for a kiss. And to find out how much I can spend on the backdrop for Ruben's concert."

"What?" Allie stepped back in surprise.

"Yeah. Ruben has this cool idea of creating a specific backdrop when his cello concerto is performed. I'm not quite sure what he has in mind. Something that can be wheeled out, I guess."

Allie hadn't heard about this additional request. It would have to be approved by George; she didn't have that fiscal authority. But she guessed the plan would have to be more fleshed out before George could assign a number to it.

"You'll have to bring that up with George. Do you have any drawings or an estimate of the cost, or anything specific?"

"Nope. I've told you all I know. Sounds like it could be a fun project to work on, though. Ruben's full of cool ideas."

"Guess you should run it by George and find out what he wants to do," Allie suggested.

Lucas O'Donnell worked in the festival's wood shop, doing general maintenance and creating needed items like conductor podiums and new shutters for the barn. He and Allie had known each other for a long time, first as children who sailed together, then as boyfriend and girlfriend. A "summer kid" from a wealthy family, Luke had decided to stay in Kennimac the previous year instead of going to law school or business school like his older siblings. He'd gotten the job at the festival and was happy creating the various items that helped the festival run smoothly. Though he and Allie had been romantically entwined for a number of years, their relationship foundered two years earlier when Allie felt he was disloyal and unfeeling as she went through a difficult time. But, although Allie still harbored misgivings, they had become close again since the shocking events around Sylvia Abbott's death.

"Can I come down to the cottage tonight?" Luke asked. Now that the weather was warmer, Allie had moved from her father's house to the family cottage they owned by the water. Rustic and heated only by a wood stove, the cottage was perfect for a romantic rendezvous, just as it had been for Melissa and David, Allie's parents. Unfortunately, her parents' relationship hadn't lasted, and while David remained in Kennimac, Melissa now lived far away in Switzerland.

"I'm having dinner with Dad," Allie said. "Want to join us?"

"Nah, that's ok. I'll let you have a bit of family togetherness," Luke answered.

"Right. Like that's something you would enjoy..." Allie knew Luke didn't care to spend much time with his father. Mr. O'Donnell couldn't understand how this son turned out to be so different from his other two sons.

Three

David Brewster whistled along with a Mozart piano sonata[1] as he put the finishing touches on a pot of vegetarian chili with a dash of spice. A champion whistler, David was also a fine violinist and one of the founders of the Kennimac SummerFest Symphony. He twirled around and took a pan of cornbread out of the oven, centering it upon a G-clef-shaped trivet on the table. Then he stepped back and surveyed the kitchen. Everything looked ready and smelled delicious. The two place settings were colorful, with navy blue pottery bowls and bright red linen napkins. The two glasses of wavy Mexican hand-blown glass sparkled with ice and fizzy water. He looked down at Archie, his 20-pound West Highland White Terrier, who wagged his tail enthusiastically. "Ok, Archie," he said, "Where's your pal Allie?"

The sound of a car door slamming announced the answer.

"Hi, Dad. Mmmm, smells good in here!" Allie bent down to pat Archie. "Sorry I'm a little late. Pablo was slow to start again." Pablo was Allie's ancient and increasingly unreliable Volvo station wagon. "Hey, sounds like you're listening to a Mozart piano sonata. Are you playing again or just enjoying being a fan?"

"I've been working on the earlier ones. They're easier. But I do love this one. It just bounces along." Though he was an accomplished trained classical violinist, bluegrass fiddler, and whistler extraordinaire, David was constantly searching for new musical experiences and learning new instruments. The piano, however, was his biggest challenge. Keeping at least four lines of music moving together but independently was difficult for someone trained to read just one line of music. "As you know," he said to his daughter, "listening to a piece to get it in your ear really helps you play it. I'm hoping that someday I'll be able to master this sonata. But probably never at this tempo."

"Dad, you don't give yourself enough credit."

"Not so. I've heard enough great pianists to know I'll never be a tenth as good. Not even one hundredth. I'm just doing it for my own pleasure. Or maybe it's more like my own torture." He smiled.

"Right," agreed Allie. "Well, you can't be a virtuoso at everything."

"Speaking of knowing what you're good at..." David paused while he ladled out the chili into the bowls, while Allie cut the cornbread into squares. "I have decided to resign from the board of the festival."

Allie looked up but didn't say anything.

"It's been a long time, and with you a paid staff member..."

"But no one seems to feel that's a conflict, Dad."

"Well, I think it is. And you're doing a fabulous job, no question. But I need a break from the board. I don't think they need me, either." He paused while taking a spoonful of chili. "And I don't think they'll miss me."

"Don't be silly. Of course they will. You hold the institutional memory of the board—you know the history of the festival better than anyone else."

"Except some of the orchestra members, who've been around as long as I have. In fact, I have an idea. I'm thinking that it would make sense to bring one or two of the orchestra musicians onto the board."

Allie nodded. "That's a fantastic idea. Would you nominate someone? Who do you have in mind?"

"I can think of a couple of people who would be good. It needs to be someone who's level-headed, who can see the needs of the organization from both the musicians' point of view but also from a business perspective. Someone who can stay calm when the discussion gets heated." David was thinking back to the spring when the board went through leadership turmoil because of the board chair's murder.

"I guess that would rule out Karin, then." Allie said, laughing. Karin Anders was the hot-blooded representative of the musicians' union who'd fought to keep the board from cutting the musicians' pay during the troubles in the spring. Also the orchestra's principal horn, she was outspoken, blunt, profane, and respected. Her emotional support of the musicians' welfare was mirrored by her expressive and collaborative approach to playing music.

"You're right, she's not on my list." David smiled. "But I was thinking of Anne, perhaps. Do you think she'd be willing?"

Principal cellist Anne Kirschner and Allie had a long relationship, starting when Allie first began taking cello lessons with Anne. Over the years, they had gone beyond their student-teacher relationship to become friends. Anne often counseled Allie on non-cello questions, and Allie considered Anne her mentor.

"She would be awesome. She's so thoughtful and calm. And now that Cara and Andrew are off on their own in the summer, she probably has the time."

"I had a few other people on my list, but Anne is my top choice." David sighed. "Of course, it all depends on the board going along with the idea."

"It's definitely worth a try. I think it's a great idea. But do you really feel as though you need to get off the board?" Allie wondered to herself if her father's departure might leave her more vulnerable to the board's whims. Her position was a fairly new one, and she'd only been the assistant managing director for a few months. The festival was in fine shape financially this summer, but that could change. A summer of bad weather, a few hiccups in scheduling, competition for donors from another arts nonprofit, a change in audience interest, a pandemic—Allie quickly totted up a list of calamities that could befall a nonprofit arts group.

"I can feel my blood pressure drop just by contemplating life without the board. Who knows, I might even have enough time to master the piano."

"Or finish work on Calliope, more likely." Allie put down her spoon. "Where are you with getting her ready to launch? I'd like to go for a sail every now and then, and it's already July."

"Ho! You're a wicked taskmaster, just like your mother," said David. "Paint is drying as we speak. So I plan to dump her in the water tomorrow."

The two ate in companionable silence for a few seconds. Through the kitchen windows, the sun was low, bringing a golden glow to the worn table. Archie slurped from his water bowl, then stopped, listening. A faint popping sound was audible.

"What's up, Arch?" asked Allie. "What do you hear?"

"Oh, that damn Roger Hylie," said her father. "He must be out in his field doing target practice again."

A barrage of shots followed David's pronouncement, their origin heard more clearly now. Archie whined softly.

"That man sure knows how to break the atmosphere. And for some reason, Archie is very sensitive to the sound. It's weird, because fireworks don't bother him in the least. But Roger's guns seem to set the dog off."

As if in agreement, Archie gave a little yip.

"Oh, Arch," said Allie. "Don't worry, puppy. He's not going to come here and shoot us." She bent down from her chair to scratch the Westie between the ears. "But, Jesus, Dad, why does Roger spend so much times shooting off his guns? It's creepy."

"Especially after what happened in Lewiston," said David. "You know, Roger's always had guns. And been a little strange—unfriendly. Remember that time you were trick or treating?"

"OMG! He scared me half to death! I never went back there again."

"And you were the cutest five-year-old firefighter ever. That was such a great costume."

"Yeah, brilliant using the vacuum cleaner hose." Allie laughed, then became serious. "Is Roger shooting his guns more often these days?"

"It sure seems like it. I think he's bought some new ones. They sound different, louder, faster." David sighed. "I'd like to ask him to cool it, but he's so unpredictable..."

"Right. You might be taking your life in your hands by making a suggestion like that. Isn't there a law or something?"

"Not here. Roger's on his own land and I would guess he has a permit for whatever weapons he's using." He shrugged. "Not much we can do about it."

"Ugh, let's think about something else. And it sounds like he's stopped, anyway."

Allie left the house after she and David had demolished a bowl of chocolate mousse, one of David's specialties. Allie suspected it contained some mystery ingredient like silken tofu mixed in with the dark chocolate, but she decided it was delicious, anyway. Best not to know.

As she drove down the dirt driveway to the cottage, she mused about her father's news that he was retiring from the SummerFest board. She had to admit that he looked and acted more relaxed than he often did. He hadn't appeared to have smoked any weed, either—his usual method of dealing with anxiety. His leaving the board was probably the right thing; she would just have to stop worrying about her own position. After all, she didn't feel she'd gotten the job through his influence. They hired her on her own merits, right? And her degree in arts management, and her long history with the festival, and her great recommendations, and..., and..., well..., maybe her father's reputation, too. It would be strange not to have him so closely connected with the festival.

Four

Allie opened the double set of French doors out to the cottage's deck, leaving the screens closed so the mosquitos couldn't enter. She inhaled the familiar scents of the cottage: old pine woodwork mingled with the faint aura of smoke from the wood stove; musty furniture; ancient paperbacks with yellowed pages and curling covers lined up across sagging bookshelves. These all met the salty tang of the ocean air outside. It was peaceful; the only interruption to the quiet was the occasional rustling of small rodents scampering through the underbrush. In the background, Allie could hear the rhythmic lull of wavelets on the stony shore.

She nestled into the ancient sagging wing chair that had occupied a space by the doors for as long as she could remember, and closed her eyes, letting the calm wash over her. A melody began softly playing in her head. A-C#-A-D-A-D#-A-E-A-A... Where did that come from, she wondered. Then she remembered hearing Anne play through the opening melody of the new cello concerto that Ruben was composing for the festival. Anne would be the soloist in the premiere concert. What she had heard of the theme sounded haunting, Allie thought. She knew Anne could wring out the most possible emotion, whatever it was. She was an introspective player who dug into the joys and tragedies of her life to fuel her expression. When Anne's husband, Mark, had died unexpectedly at a young age, Allie knew it had been rough; Anne had looked haggard and thin during those first years as a widow. But she had come through those times—not unscathed—but strong and newly vibrant. And she'd hauled her two children through it as well.

Allie's phone pinged as she sat, signaling a text.

It was Luke:

home now? can I come over?

Allie paused before answering. She and Luke were falling into an old familiar pattern: affectionate and solicitous friendship, comfortable sex. But where was their relationship headed, she wondered. Everyone around them, including her father, seemed to think they were headed for marriage, but Allie wasn't so sure. And she liked to be sure of things. Always.

Still, the thought of another night with Luke was tempting.

She replied with the thumbs up emoji.

Luke's jeep sprayed gravel as he tore down the cottage's driveway. Allie imagined all the night creatures scurrying away in terror before his approach. She met him at the door.

"In a hurry?" she asked with a smile.

"Always, if it's for..." And he kissed her hard. "This," he said, coming up for air.

Holding tightly to each other, Luke walked Allie backwards into the bedroom. They fell onto the mattress, the bed's rusty iron frame squeaking in complaint.

The next morning, Luke shook Allie's shoulder. "Al, where's the coffee?"

"Oh, crap. I meant to buy some. I ran out yesterday." She brushed a strand of her long caramel-colored hair from her face and yawned. "Ok. I guess we can stop at Dunkin's to get some on the way to the office."

"How about hitting the Green Reaper? They have the really good coffee and baked goods, too."

"As long as we don't take too long. I don't want to be late for work. Lots to do."

"We've got an hour. Should be enough. But first..." Luke bent down to kiss Allie, but she rolled away.

"Not this morning, mister. Too much to do." Allie sat up and gathered her clothes, still scattered over the blankets.

"If you say so." Luke smiled. "But if you change your mind, Al..."

Allie swatted him with a shirt.

Five

Assistant conductor Thomas Ramirez was in the Green Reaper's small dining area, drinking a cup of coffee and looking over a music score while waving his hands in tiny conducting motions. Luke pointedly ignored him, carrying his coffee and muffin to the table farthest from where Thomas sat. But Allie smiled and said hello to Thomas, motioning Luke to come sit at Thomas's table. He grudgingly complied.

"Thomas," said Allie. "How are things going? Oh, is that the score to the Grieg?"[1]

Thomas nodded yes. Luke sat mutely, wearing a sour expression. He'd suspected correctly that Allie had been romantically interested in Thomas a few months ago, before the terrible occurrence at the benefit concert. She assured him that her interest in Thomas had quickly dissipated, but he was still wary. He busied himself with spreading butter on his blueberry muffin.

"I love the way she plays the opening," Allie said. "It's such a warhorse, but it sounds completely new when she holds out those chords. So dramatic!"

"Yes, she's good," said Thomas. "I've got to get this up to speed—Tony's asked me to fill in for him this afternoon. He's working with Ruben to finish up the cello concerto." Thomas took a long sip of coffee and looked down at the score. "I've heard this a thousand times, but I still feel like I don't know it well enough." It was clear that he didn't want to be disturbed.

"We'll leave you to it," said Luke, picking up his muffin and coffee and moving to the far table.

"Yes," agreed Allie. "Hey, I'm sure you'll do fine, Thomas."

"Wish I were so sure," he said.

Allie was surprised that Thomas seemed so nervous about filling in for Tony. Usually, he was more than confident, almost cocky. The guest soloist was young and just starting out on her solo career. Hmmm, she was also strikingly gorgeous and very exacting and self-assured, Allie thought. Maybe that's what had Thomas twisted in knots.

"I think there's a backstory there," she whispered to Luke.

"What? That Thomas is an ignorant egotist and is finally realizing it?"

"Oh, shut up. No, maybe he and Julia know each other from earlier. Or maybe he would like to 'know her better'." Allie used air quotes around the last three words.

"No doubt. He seems to want to know all attractive young women 'better.'"

"Lucas O'Donnell, your green monster is showing. Thomas is not a bad guy. Just a bit superficial."

"Yeah right, Al, whatever you say. Hey, want a coffee refill?" Luke gathered the two mugs and headed to the coffee station.

Allie looked at her phone, then got up and headed toward Luke. "It's too late to drink another cup here. Can you put it in to-go cups? I'll head to my car."

Allie checked her email while she waited for Luke to bring her coffee. There was a message from George, saying he'd be a little late. A good thing, since it looked like Allie would be a little late this morning, too. There was a voicemail, too, from a number she didn't recognize. I'll listen to that at the office, she decided.

When Allie arrived at the festival's parking lot, she saw that George's gray Prius was already there. Not good, she sighed to herself.

"Allegra, there you are," George greeted her in his croaky voice. "Listen, Grant and I are in the middle of a serious discussion. So don't let anyone disturb me until I tell you it's ok."

"No problem," she replied. She wondered what was up; George looked disturbed. He closed the door to his office, but Allie could hear the two of them talking in low but emphatic tones. It was obviously something personal. Allie hoped it wasn't anything too serious. She liked Grant; George was much happier and lighthearted since going public with their relationship. She turned on the office radio to the classical station to cover their voices.

Allie got to work, organizing the invoices that had arrived the day before. While she couldn't authorize the payments, it was her job to enter the invoices in the accounting program and let George know about them. She also had to check the invoices' amounts against the amounts previously agreed upon, as well against the amounts budgeted. Oddly, it was satisfying work—not creatively challenging, but a welcome respite from trying to solve housing complaints or schedule conflicts. Of course, she thought to herself, it didn't hurt that the SummerFest was in good financial shape right now. She knew it would be a different story if funds were short.

Allie clicked on the voicemail from an unknown number. She listened as an officious caller told her that Senator Crandall McGregor would like to attend the concert that Friday and would require three tickets.

"Crap," Allie muttered. That concert was sold out. She hated to do it, but she was going to have to dislodge some faithful concertgoers to make room for the senator. She remembered his smug, self-satisfied smirk. Senator "Crank" McGregor prided himself on being an "independent, free-thinking moderate." Allie and some of her high school classmates had visited him in his Portland office when she was a senior in high school. They had been horrified by the massacres of fellow students across the country by killers wielding high velocity rifles and went to his office as a group to urge him to vote for gun safety laws. Instead, he had lectured them about Maine's hunting tradition and the U.S. Constitution's 2nd Amendment. He hadn't asked them one question, insisting that mass murder by guns in Maine would never happen and they should stick to their studies instead of worrying about something that would never happen. Yeah, how'd that work out, Allie thought. Her stomach roiled, remembering the shock and horror of the shooting of 18 people in Lewiston, Maine, just an hour's drive from Kennimac. The entire state had been traumatized. Allie had sent the senator a heartfelt email then and received a form reply.

After an hour or so, the door to George's office exploded open and Grant stalked out. George followed more slowly. He stopped at Allie's desk.

"Allegra," he said. "I guess I'm available now."

"Ok. There were just two phone calls for you. Nothing very important." She handed him the slips with the messages. "And I've got the latest invoices up, if you want to take a look. We're still right on track. Actually, even a little better than on track. Oh, and by the way, we'll be 'blessed' with Senator McGregor's presence at Friday's concert. Whoop-de-do."

"Thanks, Allegra." George ran his hand over the top of his balding head and seemed lost in thought for a few seconds. Then he turned and went back into his office, leaving the door open.

Six

Anne Kirschner stepped out on the porch of her cottage and shielded her eyes. The sun hit the top of her head, causing the silver threads in her hair to shimmer. Yup, there by the steps was a basket with a lemon poppyseed muffin, a slice of banana bread, and a croissant. RuthEllen had been busy. How she expected Anne to eat all those baked goods, Anne didn't know. Once again, she'd tell RuthEllen that it wasn't necessary. And she'd wrap up the two items she didn't eat to bring to rehearsal to share with other cellists.

Anne stretched and looked around the field. Tony's car was still parked at his cottage, and faint strains of music could be heard above the breeze and the screeching gulls. Tony's cottage was about twice as big as Anne's and much grander. It had lots of glass facing the water and three bedrooms. Anne's cottage had only one bedroom and a foldout couch in the living/dining/kitchen area. She loved her cottage's quirky cosiness and didn't mind taking five-minute showers or washing her dishes by hand in the chipped white porcelain sink. The big room had a high ceiling, which gave the acoustics a nice resonance, making her hours of practicing more fun than a chore. She'd already put in an hour this morning.

The cottage—cabin, really—wasn't built as close to the water as Tony's, and an acre or more of mostly evergreen trees marched right up to the back door. Anne loved the mix of the sound of the pine boughs swishing in the wind and the waves on the shore. The piney scent was just like those souvenir balsam pillows tourists buy to remind them of the Maine woods. Anne had rented this cottage for five years and thought of it as her summer residence, even though she knew other renters occupied it when she departed.

She glanced at the other cottage close by. This summer, Thomas Ramirez, Tony's assistant conductor, and Ruben Perrotta, the SummerFest composer-in-residence, occupied it. Both of their cars were gone, so Anne assumed they had already headed into town. She brought RuthEllen's basket into the cottage and absentmindedly munched on the slice of banana bread, while gathering her music and nestling her cello in its case. Then, stowing everything in the back of her station wagon, she headed to town herself.

Seven

As Anne pulled into the festival's driveway, she saw Allie emerging from her car, hauling a canvas bag full of photocopies. "Hey, Allie, do you have time for a cup of coffee before you get started? I have a few minutes before I need to warm up for rehearsal. I'd love to catch up."

Allie crossed the parking lot to Anne. "Sure! I just got back from the post office. We have some decent coffee in the office. Shall I make us a pot? We can sit outside and chat. I'd love to hear what Cara and Andrew are up to this summer. I miss having them here."

Anne strapped her cello case on her back and held up an insulated coffee mug. "I've already got a full cup of coffee here. I'll meet you at the picnic table under the apple tree."

Allie hurried back into the office with the bag of papers. Ah, George had made another pot. Good! She looked in on him to say thanks, but he seemed occupied with writing on his laptop. Allie decided not to disturb him. She poured herself a mug of coffee and joined Anne at the picnic table.

"What I want to know," started Anne, "as your former cello teacher, are you finding any time to practice since you're so busy with work?"

"A little," said Allie. "I really had to practice the Dvorak[5] for our opening concert—I'd forgotten how many notes there are in that symphony!"

"You did a great job. You fit right in with the section. We were happy to have you with us."

"But if Tony wants me to play in any other concerts, he'd better tell me now. I'll need to start practicing the part ASAP."

“Do you miss playing? I miss giving you lessons. You’ve always been my best student.” Anne smiled.

“Aw, thanks, Anne. I don’t miss practicing that much, to tell you the truth. It’s boring! But work can be equally tedious, for sure. You know what I really do miss? Playing duets with you.”

“Maybe we can do that. Let’s try to find some time. I’m pretty swamped with Ruben’s new cello concerto right now. It’s hard.” Anne grimaced. “And it doesn’t help that he keeps changing it. I have a premonition that I’ll be playing off scribbled manuscript pages at the concert.” A thought struck her. “You know, it would be great if you could listen to me play some of it—I’d like to get your opinion on a few technical things.”

“I’d love to do that!”

“So, you were wondering about Cara and Andrew. They are both doing exciting, fun things this summer. I think I’d mentioned that Cara is a counselor at Camp Tamarack this summer.”

“Oh, that’s right. She’s helping to guide the kayaking trips, right?”

“Yes, and also the hikes. She’ll be in great shape by the end of the summer.”

“And what about Andrew?”

“Andrew’s doing an art camp at Exeter during July. Then in August, he’s going on a trip to Bulgaria, of all places. I’ve never been, so I’m eager to hear what he thinks. You can check out their photos online; they’re both on Instagram.”

“Wow. I remember when they were such little kids. Now they’re almost grown up.”

“I wouldn’t go that far, Allie,” laughed Anne. “They are turning into very interesting people, I will say.”

“I’m sorry I won’t get to see them this summer.”

“They may both try to make the cello concerto concert. It’s before Andrew goes to Bulgaria, and Cara is going to try to get away from Camp Tamarack for that weekend. So maybe you will get to see them after all.”

“Speaking of that concerto, I’m happy to listen in as you practice it, if that would be helpful.”

"Shall we set a time? Let me look at my rehearsal schedule. And you check yours. Maybe some evening coming up?"

"That would be great. I do have free time occasionally, though this job is pretty much 24/7." Allie smiled ruefully. "Speaking of which, I'd better get into the office."

"And I'd better go warm up for rehearsal," said Anne.

Eight

Allie looked out the office window. Cars were arriving; rehearsal was scheduled to start at ten o'clock. She watched Anne lug her cello toward the concert barn. Anne looked good, thought Allie. She walked with energy and was smiling. Anne and Ruben met up and continued to walk down the path to the barn together. Ruben waved his hands about while Anne listened intently. Soon they were out of sight.

"Allegra." George's voice intruded in Allie's reverie. "Can you find a time for me to meet with the executive committee? There's something urgent I need to discuss with them."

"How much time do you need?"

George paused. "An hour should be more than enough."

"Will do," said Allie, returning to her laptop. She checked George's calendar, found a time that afternoon, the following morning, and tomorrow afternoon, and sent off an email to the committee members asking them to let her know which times worked best for them.

"The sooner the better," George added from his office. Allie smiled to herself. In George's hoarse injured voice, it sounded like a mobster's threat.

In a moment, board member Esther Swift was on the phone to Allie. She was a longtime supporter of the SummerFest and had been cycling on and off the board for years.

"Allegra," she said in her quavery voice, "What's up? Is there some sort of emergency?"

"Not that I know of, Esther. George hasn't shared the subject with me. But he does seem to think it's urgent. Do any of those times work for you?"

"Oh, all of them are fine, my dear. I was just planning to be puttering in my garden the next few days. You know how it is with us retired old ladies." Esther laughed. "We're either gardening or having lunch. Right?"

Allie laughed, too. Esther's depiction of herself was deceptive. An energetic 80-year-old, Esther still sailed her own dinghy in the Wednesday races, taught knot-tying to the sailing classes, and helped keep the festival on an even keel. Her gardens were legendary, and she did all the work herself. Her organic vegetable rows were so productive that she supplied baskets of zucchini, tomatoes, cucumbers, lettuce, and other vegetables to the food pantry every week. Lunching with friends, at least in the summer months, was not something Esther Swift had much time for.

"Right, Esther," Allie smiled. "You don't fool us—we know you put the rest of us to shame with all the work you do." She paused. "I'll let you know when a time is set. Will you be available by phone the rest of the day?"

"I'll keep it by my side."

"Thanks, Esther. I'll be in touch as soon as I know."

A new email message popped up on Allie's laptop as she set her phone down. It was from Ken Henson, saying he could make this afternoon and tomorrow afternoon but not tomorrow morning, as he was "playing a round of golf with Ron Hartford, former head of Merrill Lynch's Northeast Division."

Blah, blah, blah, thought Allie. As if Ken's golf partners impressed her.

Her dad chimed in next, with a text:

> Anytime is fine for me.

The only person left was Professor Shimmler. But he was away for the week, a trip to France, thought Allie. She walked into George's office. "Looks like they can meet this afternoon, George. Dr. Shimmler is out of the country, but the other three are available."

"Excellent. Thanks for setting that up so quickly."

Allie emailed Ken Henson, texted her dad, and called Esther Swift. The meeting was set for half past four.

At quarter past four, George stopped at Allie's desk and asked her to head down to Portland to pick up some posters being printed.

"You don't need me at the meeting? To take notes or anything?" Allie asked.

"Nope, not this time. Take some money from petty cash for your gas money."

Puzzled, Allie looked up the address of the printing company and headed to her car. Before setting off, she texted Luke:

> off to pland to pick up posters cu tomorrow

Luke didn't reply immediately, which meant he was probably in the middle of a project.

As she pulled out of the festival driveway, she mused about the strange meeting. Something's up, she thought. But what?

Nine

SummerFest conductor and music director Anthony Bainbridge looked at his watch and sighed. Four o'clock already. Christ, he was knackered. Thank goodness Thomas was able to take over the morning rehearsal. He was turning out to be a fine addition to the festival, Tony thought. Glad I found him.

But the Adams piece[6] they were performing in two weeks was giving him fits. He had fought like hell to get it on the schedule. With its six percussionists, keyboard sampler, and amplified steel-string guitar, the piece was a budget-breaker, and George had complained about the cost. But Tony was sure the audience would adore it, and it was another contemporary piece—1999—to add to their repertoire.

We have to play it perfectly, though, he mused. It simply had not yet jelled. The tempos were off in the third movement, and in that movement, the tempos were everything. That movement wasn't titled "Chain to the Rhythm" for nothing.

Tony ran his hand over his spiky white hair. He knew that there would be reviewers at the concert that Saturday. "We'd better bloody well perform," he said out loud. "And that includes me."

"What's that?" said Ruben through the screen door. "Talking to yourself again, Tony?"

"Ah, Ruben, it's you." Tony let the composer into the cottage. "Did we have another appointment?"

"Well, no. But I was hoping you could listen to this bit of my second phase." Ruben glanced at the score that was open on the table. "Studying up on the Adams? Thought you had that well in hand."

"It's not clicking yet. I can't put my finger on what's missing."

"Maybe a question of rehearsing? You've got lots more chances before the concert. Don't you think that will do it?"

"Bloody well better do it." Tony grimaced. "At least the Grieg is fine. Soloist is great and the orchestra practically know the piece by heart anyway." He turned to the large iPad that Ruben had carried in with him. "So, let's have a look. What's bothering you about the second movement, erm, second *phase*, as you call it."

"I'm not sure how to resolve this part." Ruben pointed to a section of the score. He hit "play" and a stream of complicated music poured out.

"Hold on." Tony brought a portable speaker to the table and attached a cord. "Let's listen with the soundbar so we can really hear all the nuances." The agitated sound filled the room.

"Ruben, why not have the horn echo the cello solo here," suggested Tony. "Then have the entire cello section respond. Like an army. Full bore."

Ruben winced. "Might be overkill. What if it's the bassoon instead of the horn? Or the English horn?"

"Or voice it in a completely different range," Tony replied. "Try it with the piccolo." Ruben looked at him in surprise. "I'm not joking, Ruben. Try it."

Ruben quickly changed a few things on the score and played the result. "I'm not sure about that..."

"I like it," Tony replied. "And you could pick it up here again," he said, turning a few pages on the iPad.

The two of them tussled with the composition, and they didn't hear the footsteps on the porch. "Tony?" said Anne Kirschner through the screen. "Are you busy?"

"Anne, hold on for a bit. We're just working out a difficult part of the second movement. Say, would you like to take a look?"

"Definitely." Anne was concerned about Ruben writing an unplayable cello part, as sometimes happened. Composers who were writing for an instrument they didn't play themselves sometimes asked for impossible effects. These musical requests might stretch the soloist's skills, or they might prove to be an insurmountable challenge.

Anne didn't mind the former, but she was wary of the latter. She looked at the score and noticed that there were big jumps that she would have to perform quickly. Difficult but doable. Then she saw these instructions:

SOLOIST STANDS AND SHOUTS "STOP" THREE TIMES

Anne laughed. "Ruben, I will love to do that! But you have the soloist playing too soon afterward. Can you give me a little breathing space? Especially if you're going to have me playing so high on the G string."

"Can do," agreed Ruben. "I'll just have the first violins continue their tremelo for a few more beats. Is one more measure enough time?"

"I think so." Anne turned to Tony. "Shall we postpone our dinner date to another time? You seem pretty busy here."

"Please don't," Ruben said before Tony could answer. "I'll go back to my cottage and wrestle with it some more. I've also got more to do on the last phase. You've given me enough help for today, Tony." Ruben unhooked his iPad from the speaker and prepared to leave. "Thanks, again," he said to both Tony and Anne as he left, the screen door banging behind him.

"Are you still in the mood for the lobster dock?" Tony asked Anne. He noticed that she was dressed for the outdoors, with a fleece pullover around her shoulders and a green baseball cap that said "A# Team" on it.

"Yes, it's a gorgeous afternoon. The sunset will be dramatic, with all these puffy clouds." Anne pointed toward the door. "I left a basket on the porch that has a nice bottle of wine and two glasses. Hope the wine's not getting baked in the late afternoon sun..."

"Let's scoop it up and head right out, then." Tony grabbed his sunglasses and opened the screen door for Anne. "After you," he said with a flourish.

Ten

"I'm all about that bass, 'bout that bass, no treble..." Allie sang at the top of her lungs to the old Meghan Trainor song[7]. Allie's ancient Volvo wagon zipped along the highway on the way to Portland, windows down and sunroof open. Funny, she thought to herself, I used to think the word was no *trouble* instead of *treble*. But I got the double entendre right away, even if I got the lyrics wrong. She continued singing as the low sunlight glinted off Montsweag Bay. She loved the drive to Portland—there were so many glimpses of the ocean: the high bridge in Bath over the Kennebec, where the huge military vessels lined the wharf at the Bath Iron Works; the marsh in Woolwich that connected to the bay she was passing; the low bridge in Wiscasset crossing the Sheepscot River, where her father said there'd been the rotting hulls of two large sailing ships not long ago. A while later on I-295, she saw the open waters off Portland and the low tide mud in Portland's Back Bay. Mud tide, flood tide, Allie thought, it's all beautiful. She loved being in Maine in the summer.

And she loved her job. She'd grown up around the SummerFest, so it was deeply satisfying to have a place there. George wasn't bad as bosses go, and it was great to have an adult relationship with many of the musicians she'd known since childhood. The bonus was that Tony invited her to play with the orchestra when a piece called for a large cello section. Really, thought Allie, it couldn't be any better.

Her euphoria dimmed a bit however, as her thoughts turned to Luke. He was part of her history with the SummerFest, or at least, her summers. They had started as summer friends in elementary and middle school, sailing and swimming and hiking together with a group of kids who were a mix of "locals" like her and "summer people" like Luke. Their relationship had grown into something more in the latter years of high school. By the time Allie went to Bowdoin College in Brunswick, everyone in town considered the two of them a couple. And Allie had been fine with that back then. It was comfortable, she had fun with Luke, he was a good person. He got along with her Bowdoin friends, who appreciated his sense of humor and generous attitude.

To his parents' dismay, unlike his older siblings, Luke hadn't really been interested in college. He ended up attending the University of New Hampshire as a studio art major concentrating in sculpture. Although the program was a strong one, Allie figured he'd chosen UNH because he would still be close to Kennimac and Bowdoin College. There was even a train that ran between Durham, New Hampshire, and Brunswick, Maine, making it possible for the two of them to get together frequently. Luke came to Allie's recitals and orchestra performances and Allie traveled to Luke's gallery shows.

The summer after graduation, they had both returned to Kennimac. Luke continued in his summer job as head of the sailing program, where he was respected by parents and adored by the young kids and his assistants. But Allie felt adrift that summer. She occasionally subbed in the cello section of the orchestra and waited tables at the Watering Hole, but it felt like she was marking time. She and Luke quarreled uncharacteristically over little things.

And then came the disastrous sailing accident. Toby, the young son of Allie's close friend, Kate Zeller, had drowned in a small boat during a thunderstorm. Toby's death devastated Allie. Luke was sad, too, but to Allie he seemed much less affected. She accused him of callousness and said she wanted a break from their relationship, which a puzzled Luke granted her.

Her grief turned to fury when she caught Luke kissing a local girl. She attacked him for being unfaithful, even though she had been the one to break things off. He was angry in return. He protested that Tiffany had kissed him, not the other way around, and the kiss meant nothing. Allie and Luke retreated to a frosty distance.

That fall, Allie had gone to Switzerland to visit her mother for a few weeks. While the two of them didn't exactly bond, they got along better than in the past few years. Melissa recognized Allegra needed to figure out her future path and get over the tragedy of the sailing accident, so she held back from offering her usual "helpful" suggestions. The new setting and distance from Kennimac and Luke gave Allie a chance to breathe. She left Europe vowing to apply to business school with an emphasis in arts administration.

And here she was, Allie thought, assistant managing director of the SummerFest Music Festival. Her two years at Boston University went quickly; she landed an internship with the Boston Symphony during that time, which strengthened her resume. She was thrilled when offered the job at the SummerFest, though she figured that such a small organization—though beloved—wouldn't satisfy her ambition for too long. But it was a wonderful jumping off point.

When she realized Luke had taken the job as maintenance manager with the festival starting in the spring, Allie felt conflicted. She thought he'd do a fine job—that wasn't the problem. But she would see him on a daily basis. Awkward.

When he arrived, Allie didn't quite know how to act toward him. But his genuine friendliness and good humor warmed her up. Maybe they could just be friends, she thought.

In April, the horrifying murder of the SummerFest's board chair, Sylvia Abbott, changed their relationship. Luke was a steady supporter, comforting Allie through the trauma of discovering Sylvia's body and defending her father against false charges. He understood Allie's horror when she discovered the murderer was her dear friend Kate, who had become unhinged after the death of Toby, her son, and blamed Sylvia.

Slowly, Luke and Allie floated back into their earlier relationship, but Allie had a niggling feeling. Was this really what she wanted? She exhaled. Look at her parents. They had been sure they were "made for each other," and now they were divorced and living on different continents. How sure was *really* sure? How much love and what kind of love did a marriage need? Of course she loved Luke, but forever?

She just couldn't see it. They didn't share the same hopes for the future. Allie wanted to work with the best orchestras and musicians in the world, wherever that might take her. Luke was happy staying in Kennimac. That seemed like a bad way to start a marriage—giving up dreams right at the beginning. Plus, Luke wanted to have kids someday. Allie, not so much. Shit! She just wasn't sure about anything...

Eleven

David Brewster, Ken Henson, and Esther Swift looked at George Park in shock. Ken sputtered something profane, unusual for him.

"I know this is hard," said George. "Believe me, I've thought about it for weeks and have gone back and forth. But I'm at peace with my decision, and it's final." He looked each of the board members in the eye.

"*You* may be at peace," exclaimed Ken, "But Christ!"

"Let's all take a breath," interrupted David. They sat for a moment, looking at each other and at George, who wore a defiant expression.

"Like I said, this is a final decision," he said.

"What if we just gave you a few days, or a week off?" tried Esther. "It's just such a crucial time..." Her voice petered out and she looked to David for help.

David Brewster was looking down at his hands splayed on the table as if holding it down in an earthquake. He took a deep breath.

"It's not as bad as you think," said George. "Basically, the whole season is set up. Allegra has," he nodded to David, "been a huge help. She's incredibly capable. She thinks of things before I do and she's an excellent problem solver. The program is set, the publicity is in motion, everything is running well. My absence will not be the disaster you are contemplating."

"But why leave now?" Ken's voice had taken on a definite whine. "Why not wait until the end of the summer when the festival is over? Why not..."

Esther interrupted him in a calm voice. "George, we understand that you are still suffering in the aftermath of an attempt on your life. Perhaps this is a form of post traumatic stress? Have you seen a therapist?" She cleared her throat. "Of course, that is your private information, I shouldn't ask..."

"I don't mind telling you that I have been working with a therapist. And I think it has been very helpful. But the main reason for my decision is that my near-death experience, as it were, along with the other terrible things that happened a few months ago, made me see my life ahead with greater clarity."

Ken Henson was doodling on a pad of paper as George spoke, but Esther Swift and David Brewster nodded their heads in response. They knew that George's damaged vocal chords weren't the only collateral damage caused by Kate Zeller's murderous attacks.

"It's been a blessing, in a way," George continued. "I've come to realize that my work and my career aren't the most important things in my life. I don't want to go to the grave having been a successful arts organization manager with no private life." He twisted a ring on his left hand as he spoke. "Grant and I have decided to get married, and we want to do that as soon as possible."

"But for Chrissake, you can do that and still continue on here for the summer!"

"No, Ken, there's more. Grant's just accepted a job in Minneapolis starting the end of August. We want to get married, travel a bit, and get moved in so he can be there in time to start."

"Wow," David said in surprise. "That's some major change."

"Are you sure about this?" asked Esther.

"I know, I know. I'm not a person you would have thought would be so, um, venturesome."

"I'd call it impulsive and foolhardy," said Ken.

"As I said, it's not a decision I made lightly. But it's the right decision. Grant and I are very excited." George took a big breath in. "And I know the Kennimac SummerFest will do just fine without me."

"So, when are you proposing to leave?" asked David.

"Get ready for this," said George with a wry smile. "I'm giving you two week's notice. As of right now."

The three board members looked at each other.

"How the hell will we find a replacement manager in such a short time?" Ken's face was turning red.

"I've thought it all out," said George. "First of all, after Sylvia's death and my, uh, injury, this spring, two things happened. One, some fine volunteer help stepped up—you three among the volunteers. Two, Allegra handled the office and all the managerial responsibilities with great success. She knows everything about the running of the festival and will make an excellent interim manager. I have no qualms in recommending that you promote her."

David Brewster grimaced. "You really think Allie could handle it?" He thought of his daughter, only 25, shouldering that level of responsibility.

"What about the financials?" demanded Ken. "Who will manage that aspect?"

"Allegra is fully knowledgeable about the festival's accounting, and I'm sure that our CPA will be there to help if any questions arise. Ken, she is fully qualified. And I'll be happy to be consulted if and when questions arise. Really, Allie is the best choice for the festival at this point. The board can do a full search for a new manager at the end of the summer."

Esther smiled. "I certainly agree that Allegra has the ability to manage the festival through the end of this season."

"We'll need to bring this to the entire board," said David. "And I will recuse myself. I certainly can't weigh in on whether my daughter should be promoted." Esther nodded in agreement and Ken rolled his eyes. "We'll need to convene an emergency meeting as soon as we can," continued David. "George, can you set that up?"

"Thank you. Of course." George and the three board members ended the meeting by discussing possible dates and times for the emergency meeting.

"I'll let Tony and Allegra know about this," said George. "They're the people most directly affected by my resignation."

"Don't make any promises to Allegra," said Ken. "The board hasn't weighed in on any decisions regarding your replacement."

"Right," said George. No promises, he thought to himself, but I will let her know that I'm suggesting she take over.

Twelve

The sun was getting lower as Allie sped along Route One through Brunswick and Bath. Soon it would be dusk. There was a golden glow over the fields, and the water was glass-still, mirroring the gold shimmer. Her cell phone rang as she passed Montsweag Bay again, on her way home. Caller ID recognized the call as coming from Ruben Perotta. Allie answered with, "What's up, Ruben?" as she pulled over to take the call.

"Hey, Allie, I have an important question for you."

"Ok?"

"How does a violinist keep their violin from being stolen?"

"What? Why are you asking?" Why would Ruben would call and ask her that?

"You don't know how a violinist keeps their violin safe from thieves? They store it in a cello case!" Ruben laughed.

"Oh, ha, ha," Allie answered. "Pretty weak, Ruben."

"Ok, hit me back."

Allie thought for a moment, running through her repertoire of jokes about composers. "Let's see. Ok, this is an easy one. What did Arnold Schwarzenegger say when the casting director asked him which character he wanted to play in a movie about famous composers?"

"Super easy," Ruben responded. "'I'll be Bach.'" He said it in an imitation of Arnold Schwarzeneggar. "That's one point for me, none for you. See if you can answer this one: What is the range of a cello?"

"Oh, I hate this joke," said Allie. "'As far as you can kick it.' I've heard that joke applied to other instruments, too, and it always sucks. Ok, now we're even. Hm..." Allie wracked her brain for another composer joke. “Here’s one: What do you call a Hungarian composer with one leg shorter than the other?”

“Wow, I don’t know this one. Umm, Bartok?”

“Nope. Liszt.”

“I don’t get it. Liszt, list? One leg shorter?”

“If you were a sailor, you’d know that when a vessel tilts to one side, you say it has a list or is listing. Now do you get it?”

“Guess so. Don’t know how to sail but I wish I did. I’ve never been around boats very much.”

“Well, I’ve been around sailboats my whole life...”

“Hey, maybe you could teach me! “

“Actually, Lucas O’Donnell used to be a sailing instructor. You know Luke, right? From the wood shop?”

“Oh, yeah, Curly hair. Work pants spattered with paint. He’s a sailor?”

“Yup. A damn good one, too.”

“Maybe I’ll cajole him into giving me a few lessons.”

“Good luck with that. He’s pretty busy these days. Look, Ruben, I’m on my way back from Portland. I really need to get going, and I’m not going to drive and talk on my cell.”

“Oh, darn, I wouldn’t want to get you in trouble. ‘Orchestra administrator jailed for making bad jokes on cellphone while driving.’ Wouldn’t look good.”

“Yeah, yeah. Well, we’re even in the bad music jokes department. And I’ll get you next time.”

“Highly unlikely. Bye, All-leg-hurrah.”

“Ok, now *that* was pathetic.“ Allie laughed. “See ya.”

Allie smiled. That Ruben was a character. I’ll have to pull together some good composer jokes, she thought.

Allie turned the radio on and was met with a news broadcast. Not in the mood, she said to herself, and turned the knob to an oldies station. Alanis Morrisette’s voice filled the car with “Ironic,”[8] and Allie sang along at the top of her lungs.

Thirteen

At a few minutes past eight o'clock, a flurry of texts and phone calls filled the air over the town of Kennimac.

Allie's phone rang as she drove through the town of Bath. She glanced at the phone's screen; it was her father calling. That can wait, she figured. She let it ring, and eventually the call went to voicemail. I'll look at it when I'm back at the cottage, she thought.

George had decided he would talk to Allie about his news in person. He texted her a few minutes after Allie's dad had called.

Can you come in early tomorrow morning?

sure — what time

7:30 am ok?

yup

Allie thought nothing of it. Must be some minor issue that's come up, she thought. Jeesh, hope it wasn't something I did...

Meanwhile, Tony noticed his phone buzzing as he ate his boiled lobster on the dock. He looked at the phone, then looked at his butter and lobster-covered hands and said to Anne, "It's George. It'll have to wait." That call, too, went to voicemail.

Still in the office, George sent an email with the subject line "Emergency Meeting" to all the board members. It suggested several times for a meeting and asked for a quick response.

Ken Henson saw George's email to the board and followed with a message to a few of his friends on the board. "Still more SummerFest troubles" was the subject line of his email.

Finally, George made the call he had been anticipating all day. "Grant," he said, "I did it. I told the executive committee that I'm leaving in two weeks. I can't believe it. I did it, Grant. They were surprised—or shocked, really. But it's going to happen. I'm so happy!"

Fourteen

The Lobster Dock jutted out into a small cove filled with anchored boats, about half of which were lobster boats. This cove opened out to a wider bay, and in the low light of the summer evening, the sun picked up the lobster buoys scattered across the water. The breeze had died down, and the bay's surface was glass smooth. One lone lobsterman pulled traps in the dying light; his rough engine roared loudly, then idled, then roared again as he made his way from lobster buoy to lobster buoy.

The wharf held a shack at one end. Several large metal tanks held live lobsters, and the customers at the front of the line could watch as the lobsters for their meal were plucked from the tank. Salty steam curled up from the boiling pots in the back of the shack. The high school and college students who ran the operation dunked mesh bags of clams or mussels, unhusked corn on the cob, and lobsters in the boiling water, setting timers to announce when the food was cooked.

Picnic tables were scattered over the wharf. The ones lining the wharf's edge had the best view of the water and were the coveted choices, but it was first come, first served. On each table sat an empty wine bottle holding field flowers, along with a roll of paper towels. Seagulls sailed lazily overhead but rarely bothered the diners, unlike at other outdoor restaurants that featured French fries. On a beautiful evening like this, the picnic tables were crowded with customers sporting brightly colored tee shirts and sweatshirts with LL Bean or Patagonia insignias, shorts, summer dresses, and Birkenstocks or Teva sandals. The teenaged servers wandered among the tables, carrying trays laden with lobsters, calling out a customer's first name.

Anne Kirschner handed Tony the paper towel roll. Their table held the detritus of a lobster meal: lobster carcasses, a pile of empty clam shells, two corn cobs, cooling melted butter in paper cups. "Do you need to call George back, do you think?" she asked.

"I doubt it. I'll listen to his voicemail later. I'm quite sure it's nothing terribly important. Things are running smoothly this summer."

"I know. I'm so proud of Allie. She's a great addition to the management team. It's such a treat to see her take on so much and do it so well. I remember when she was a skinny little kid with braids hanging around the festival..."

"Everything would be brilliant—if we could just get the last movement of the Adams to tick along. Right now it feels like the orchestra lacks conviction." Tony finally tore a sheet off the paper towel roll and wiped the butter and lobster off his hands. "And I know that there will be at least two reviewers in the audience for that concert."

"You can't possibly be worried about that, are you? I've never read a negative review of one of your concerts."

"There's always a chance for a first." Tony shook his head.

"What I'm concerned about is Ruben's piece," said Anne. "I need to get the solo part down, and he keeps changing it. The premiere is three weeks away. Can you please tell him to call it quits and go with what he has written?"

"What do you think of it so far, Anne?"

"I like it. It's a challenge, but great fun to play. But I wish I could see a finished fourth movement. I mean, he's given me a few sketches, but I don't have the whole thing."

"I know," said Tony. "It's worrisome. I think he's calling that movement "Unhinged" because that's how he's made us all feel about it."

"Right. Although he'll say it's the listeners who he wants to feel unsettled, upset, anxious, twitchy—whatever adjectives come to mind."

Tony got up from the picnic table and loaded the tray with the paper, plastic, and cardboard refuse left over from their meal. "Shall we wash up?"

A large washtub was located on the wharf, where customers could rinse off the butter, lobster, clam juice, and other coatings that coated their hands when they ate the labor-intensive offerings. Tony and Anne splashed water on their faces and rinsed off their hands, toweling off once again with the paper towels provided.

"Thank you, Tony. That was lovely. Are you up for an ice cream? We can stop at the little store in the village."

"Perfect. And thank you for bringing the wine, Anne. A brilliant addition to the meal."

There was a line at the ice cream window, so Tony decided to listen to George's message while they waited. Anne studied the list of flavors, trying to decide between Moose Munchies and Blueberry Fields, when Tony grabbed her arm. He was still listening to the message but had a shocked expression.

"You won't believe it," Tony said when he finished listening.

"Believe what?"

"George is leaving SummerFest."

"Well, I think everyone knew that was happening. I mean, he's been here for quite a few years, and after what happened... In fact, didn't he announce that a few weeks ago?"

"No, I mean he's leaving now. Or in a couple of weeks. In the middle of the season."

"Holy cow. Poor guy. He must be suffering more than he shows."

"Bollocks! He's leaving us high and dry! I can't believe it." The people in line in front of them turned and looked at Tony.

Anne shushed him. "As you would say, Tony, 'keep calm and carry on.'"

"You might say that, but I wouldn't." Tony made a face. "This is all I need."

"It'll be fine. Don't worry." Anne thought Tony was overreacting. "I'm sure there is a plan to keep things running smoothly to the end. Did he say why he's leaving?"

"He's getting married or some such rubbish."

"That's wonderful! I'm happy for him—he deserves it. We'll all be fine, Tony. The board will handle it."

The two placed their orders for ice cream cones. When they got the cones, Tony said, “Look, I was going to suggest a walk on the beach, but I think I’d better get back.”

“If that’s what you need to do, that’s fine. But don’t worry, Tony. I’m sure the rest of the season will go smoothly.” She paused. “If Ruben would finish his damn concerto,” she added under her breath.

“Right,” added Tony. “Sorry to cut this short, my love...”

“Oh, no problem,” Anne quickly added. What was this “my love” stuff? “I’m happy to get back to do a bit more practicing.”

Fifteen

Allie slowed down as she entered Wiscasset, the small town that was the county seat. Three- and four-story buildings lined the two-lane road through the village, flowing down a hill and ending at the bridge over one of the many rivers that cut into this part of the Maine Coast. Most buildings had street-level shops with offices or apartments above. The shops were owned by locals, and ran the gamut from an unassuming pizza parlor to a very exclusive art gallery. In between were clothing boutiques, gourmet food vendors, and antique dealers. Traffic often slowed through this stretch of the road, and Allie wasn't surprised to find herself stopped in traffic. She opened Pablo's windows and listened to the chatter of people on the sidewalks, but a whiff of cigaret smoke from the car ahead caused her to close the windows and turn on the radio instead. It had been a humid afternoon, and the car felt stuffy.

As she slowly inched down the hill toward the bridge, Allie's thoughts turned to the two men who were sharing a cottage during the festival, Thomas and Ruben. They seemed like a bit of an odd pair; Ruben was short and elfin, and Thomas was tall and serious. George had worried that they might not get along as forced roommates, but their boss, Tony, said, "They're grown men, for God's sake; they can hash it out." Allie guessed he was right, although she had heard some grumbling by Thomas in the last couple of days.

"If I hear another version of that damn last movement of his concerto," Thomas had confided in Allie in the office, "I'm going to erase it from his iPad! He's constantly asking me to listen to the latest version, and frankly..." Thomas cut short his comment as Ruben walked through the office door.

And Ruben did seem worried that morning—not so playful and puckish. It wasn't unusual to hear Thomas speaking honestly about worries and concerns, but Ruben was almost always sunny and ready with a joke.

Allie was developing a new opinion of Thomas in recent weeks. She was learning that he took things seriously, though he wasn't always somber or as self-important as she had thought. He was treating her differently, too. More respectfully, maybe. Though they had shared a harrowing experience in the spring—the murder and its aftermath—he didn't presume that the two of them were close. Allie shivered, remembering the kiss they shared on the beach. That had been... significant. But then Thomas had ruined it all by showing his true colors. Superficial, that is. He'd made it perfectly clear then that he looked at it as a simple hook-up, nothing more meaningful than that.

"Guys! Ugh!" Allie said out loud. Such a complication. There was Luke, who wanted more than she could give. Luke, she smiled wryly, thinking of the two of them as teenagers. That had seemed simple, not fraught with expectations. But that was a decade and more ago. She had changed. She wanted more than she had even known about back then. Her sense of her own abilities had expanded. Luke and she... they weren't on the same trajectory. Yes, she still loved him, but not madly, passionately. And she didn't want to hurt him, but she wasn't going to pretend that they were meant to be together forever.

"Maybe I'm as superficial as Thomas," she said to herself. Why couldn't relationships be straightforward? Why couldn't people be honest with each other, and understand what the other person was saying? And accept it. The rest of this summer was going to be interesting. I'm not going to let this stuff mess me up, she thought.

The cars in front of her finally started moving toward the bridge. Allie turned on the radio and laughed as "Confused in Love" by Keyshia Cole[9] blared out at top volume. As she drove across the bridge, she opened her window and let the music stream out into the air above the river.

Sixteen

Allie, please call me back. Something is happening and I think you should know about it. You may also get a call from George.

Allie listened to the message from her father as soon as she stopped the car. What a weird message, she thought. What the heck was up? She shivered, remembering how the police had focused on her father as the murderer that spring. Her panic, and her need to protect him, was still a traumatic memory.

Her light-hearted mood caused by the drive to Portland melted away. The darkness outside the cottage windows pressed in, and Allie turned on all the lamps to dispel it. Several moths fluttered around the bulbs, their shadows causing the light to flicker on the pine board walls.

Prone to depression and anxiety, David Brewster seemed much happier and stronger recently. He was back playing with the Summer-Fest Symphony, as well as gigging locally with his friends in the Celtic band. They'd played outdoor performances at three festivals in nearby towns, and Allie and Luke had made it to one. She'd been happy to see how her father threw himself into the music and played the jigs and reels with abandon, his fingers dashing faster and faster on the fiddle's neck and his bow winging over the strings. The tune to her favorite jig[1] filled her head momentarily, halted by her phone's ring. This time, it was George.

"Hey, George, what's up?"

"Hi, Allie. I guess you haven't talked to your dad yet." George's still raspy voice sounded strangely excited—not his usual subdued self.

"No, why? He left a cryptic message, but I haven't had a chance to call him back."

"Well," George drew out the word. "Are you sitting down?"

"Uh huh."

"Well," he began again, clearing his throat. "I have news. I was going to tell you tomorrow morning, but I couldn't wait."

"Ok?"

George took a breath and plunged in. "I'm going to be leaving the SummerFest at the end of two weeks." He heard Allie inhale sharply. "Whoa, not to worry."

"But who'll be in charge?" Allie imagined someone coming in who wouldn't know all the idiosyncrasies of the festival management, like when Tony was willing to talk with the press, or how to get the board to agree to necessary expenditures.

"Hold on to your hat," answered George. "I've suggested to the executive committee that they promote you to interim managing director. They'll be taking that up with the entire board at an emergency meeting."

"Are you kidding? Holy crap." Allie paused. "Wait, why are you leaving? Is everything ok?"

"More than ok. Grant and I are getting married. And moving to Minneapolis."

"That's great, George! Congratulations. You deserve to be happy. But why Minneapolis?"

"Grant got a terrific job offer there. And I figure that there is so much arts activity there, I can probably find another arts management job fairly easily. But I may take some time off first..."

"But you think I can take over the festival, running it, I mean? You think I know enough? I mean, that's flattering, but..."

"Look, Allegra," George said. "I have no doubt. You will do a great job and I'll be at the other end of a phone call or email if you have any questions. Of course, all this depends on the board approving my suggestion."

"Oh, yeah," Allie grimaced. "I bet Ken Henson is on board with that. Not."

"You might be pleasantly surprised. We shall see. I made a strong case for you. And they'll probably want to interview you. Of course, your dad will have to recuse himself."

"Yeah, of course."

"Well, look, I've got to go—lots to get organized for the transition. But I wanted to let you know. Don't be too freaked out, ok, Allie?"

"Freaked out is exactly what I am. OMG! My summer is certainly about to change!"

"It sure is. Call your dad back, have a relaxing evening, and I'll see you in the morning, early, remember?"

"Yup, of course."

David Brewster picked up Allie's call on the first ring.

"Hi, sweetheart. I assume you've heard by now," he said.

"Whoa, Dad, it's a shock. I mean, I'm happy for George; he deserves it, but I'm not sure..."

"George has total confidence that you'll do fine. And I'll pitch in, and I know other board members will, too."

"I know, I know. It's the thought of it—I just wonder if I'm ready."

"Think about the work you've done this year so far. When George was recovering, you basically ran the show then. This won't be much different. And it's only for the last four weeks. Everything is already in place; you just need to keep the machine running."

Allie was silent.

Her father spoke again. "Look, if this seems like the wrong thing, say the word, and I'll let everyone know that you're not comfortable with it. We'll find someone to step in for the last month of the festival." He paused. "Of course, that person will need you to explain everything about how things work, who does what, what to watch out for, etc. You'll have to hold this person's hand the entire time. In fact, you may find that bringing in a temporary manager creates more work for you than just taking over yourself."

"I know. I've been thinking of that." Allie took a big breath. "So, let's see if the rest of the board has the same confidence in me that you and George have."

"Esther is a big fan of yours. And Ken isn't onboard yet, but I don't think he's totally opposed. We'll all be meeting about it soon. I'll speak in your favor, too, even though I won't be able to vote."

"Ok, Dad. This is daunting but..."

He interrupted. "You know, Allie, you should talk to your mother about this. She's the management wiz. I'm sure she'd have some advice to give you."

"No doubt. I guess I should call her. Maybe tomorrow. For now, I'm going to do a little thinking. I want to figure out how I really feel about this. Right now, my main reaction is I'm excited, flattered, and scared. I'll need to dredge up some more of my own confidence if this is going to work."

"So have a quiet evening, listen to something calming, and do your thinking. We can check in tomorrow morning."

"Love you, Dad."

"Love you back, sweetie."

Something calming, thought Allie. Hmmm, maybe Debussy's Nocturnes[2]. She found the recording in her music and hit "play."

Seventeen

The Debussy ended and Allie still felt agitated. She considered calling Luke. He was always a good person to bounce ideas off. But then, she thought, he'll probably want to come over, and I really need to be alone and think this through myself. How do I really feel about it?

She remembered the exercises that Anne had taught her to do before a nerve-wracking performance. Slowly breathe in, hold for five counts, slowly breathe out, hold for five counts. After three rounds of that, Allie decided it wasn't helping very much. Another exercise: stand with your feet firmly on the floor. Swing your arms as you swivel from side to side, gradually letting your arms rise with the motion. Then slowly return to a still posture. Ugh, that was not making a difference.

Allie looked at the music on her phone. Maybe she should listen to Krishna Das like her father did when he was anxious. Usually she knew what she wanted when she opened her music library, but tonight she was open to trying something she didn't automatically think of. She scrolled through the genres listed. Hmmm, New Age, how did Apple Music decide that something she had added was New Age, a genre she typically avoided? An album cover that looked intriguing showed up: Andreas Vollenweider, "Cosmopoly."[12] She sat in the comfortable old chair, put in her ear buds, and hit play. The sounds of an electric harp and some sort of woodwind instrument filled her head. It was almost a Middle Eastern sound—but not quite. It was definitely soothing. The woodwind's tune was plaintive and gentle. Allie didn't know how this music had been added to her library, but right now it was just what she needed.

After a few songs, Allie noticed that her stomach was rumbling. She hadn't had dinner yet, and here it was eleven o'clock. She stopped the music and made herself a peanut butter and jelly sandwich. I'm turning into my father, she thought with amusement. A cup of chamomile tea finished her meal. It suddenly seemed too quiet in the cottage. Allie felt itchy, anxious, like she needed to do something. In the evening light, her cherry red cello case in the corner seemed to glow. Make some music, she said to herself. That's what I need to do.

She pulled the case out and opened it. She hadn't played her cello in a week; she'd been too busy with work and spending several evenings with Luke. Allie tightened the horsehairs of the bow and rubbed rosin on them so the hairs would grip the metal strings. She pulled a kitchen chair into the circle of light cast by a floor lamp, carried over her music stand, and settled the cello on its peg on the floor, resting it between her knees. Then she turned the cello's ebony tuning pegs to tune the four strings. I've neglected you, she said to her beloved instrument. She ran the fingers of her left hand up and down the fingerboard, feeling the smooth texture of the strings. The familiar and reassuring scent of old wood and varnish and rosin brought a sense of comfort.

On her music stand was a short piece by Mendelssohn, "Song Without Words."[13] She'd heard it on an old Yo-Yo Ma recording and liked how its mood shifted within its short length. As she played, she felt her shoulders relaxing. When she got to the faster, more assertive section, she could feel her heartbeat rising in tandem with the tempo. Then the return to the first musical theme was more uplifting and self-assured. As she finished the piece, Allie exhaled.

"I can do this," she said out loud. There was no answer but the rhythmic whisper of wavelets on the shore.

Eighteen

"So, honey, what's this all about?" The "Ride of the Valkyries" by Wagner[14] blaring from her phone—the ring tone she'd assigned her mom—had woken Allie up from a deep sleep at 6:15 am.

"Mom?" Allie mumbled.

"Allie, I got a cryptic text from your dad this morning. Well, he sent it last night. He said something like, 'Allie could use your managerial advice.' What's he talking about? Isn't your job going well? I'm heading into an all afternoon meeting in about 15 minutes, so I decided to call, even though I know it's early for you. I do want to help, if that's what you need."

Allie cleared her throat and spoke as she got out of bed. "Mom, it's nothing bad. I..."

"I was worried. I know this job is important to you. The last thing you want is to mess up on your first big job, so..."

"Mom! Slow down." Allie moved around the kitchen, putting coffee grounds into the French press and starting a kettle of water. "It's actually, potentially, possibly really good. I mean, great." She thought about the conversations she'd had last night with George and her father. "George Park, remember him? My boss? He's leaving the festival..."

"Oh, Christ, the place is falling apart. I figured that after what's-her-name's murder it would implode. It's taken longer than I expected, though..."

"No, no, you have it all wrong. Things are going well. Really well. George is leaving for personal reasons..."

"So, you'll get a new boss? Do you know who that is? Is it a problem? People thrust into the middle of an ongoing effort like an arts season can have a lot of trouble. Plus, they need serious handholding..."

"Mother, listen! The reason Dad thought I might like your advice is that George has recommended to the board that I replace him. Until they hire a new executive director, that is."

"Oh!"

"The executive committee will have to make a recommendation and the board will have to approve it. Dad won't be allowed to vote because of the conflict of interest, but he thinks the rest of the board would be in favor."

"Honey, that's exciting. Do you think you're up to it?"

Allie laughed briefly. "I guess so. I mean, I did take over from George while he was recuperating during the pre-season. That seemed to go ok; everyone was very helpful." She paused.

"First of all, Allegra, if you want this job, you need to be positive in an assertive way. When you talk to the board, don't emphasize how people helped you, be clear about the things *you* did to keep the festival on track. In fact, before you sit down with the board, take some time and write down all the things you did that would normally have been George's responsibility. Think of every little thing. If it helps, make a chart. Think about it from a board member's standpoint. Don't assume they know the inner workings. Be explicit. Now, who's going to be your biggest supporter and who's likely to be opposed?"

"Uh, I think..."

"I don't need to know their names. But you need to think about how to work with them. Who has influence in the group? Who would be best to speak up for you? Is there information you could get to them that they could use to argue your case? What are the objections that your detractors might have, and how can you counter them beforehand? Do you need to check in with any of the players to see where they stand? Can someone be your proxy? See if you can exert some control over the decision-making process to make sure you can present your case in the best possible light..."

Allie sipped her coffee as her mother rattled on. It sounded as if she were giving a lecture on "How to Work with a Board of Directors to Get What You Want," which she probably had done in front of international bankers and financial executives at some conference or other. Melissa ended up with, "I've got to run to my meeting now, sweetheart. I hope that was helpful. Call if you have any specific questions. You've got this, honey. Love you!"

Allie rubbed her eyes, yawned and stretched. Her mother's advice was good, if a little over the top. She tried to recall the various steps her mother had laid out: find out who would support her; get someone to speak for her; make a list of the things she had managed while George was out of commission. It seemed rather overwhelming at 6:30 am.

Outside on the deck of the cottage, the air was soft and a gentle breeze ruffled Allie's hair as she set her coffee cup down on the low table next to a weathered Adirondack chair. The birds were making quite a racket: phoebes and robins and barn swallows near the cottage, an osprey crying out over the river, the ubiquitous cawing of crows in the distance. The rising sun cast a rosy glow across the river. Lobster boats' engines rumbled in the distance.

It's so peaceful, thought Allie, as she sat down. I can do this, take this on. But do I want to?

She took a deep breath and thought again about the machinations her mother had prescribed. All that politicking! Was it really necessary? Figuring out who was against her nomination and trying to win them over? Etcetera, etcetera. Maybe she should just be her regular self—conscientious, positive, organized. Well, the part about listing what she'd already done, that was a good idea.

A loud crashing in the woods caught her attention. She stood up and walked to the edge of the deck. Through the trees, she could see a large dark form. In a moment, it crashed through the underbrush lining the driveway and ambled down the dirt road toward the shore, unconcerned about the broken twigs snagged on its hide. Allie had seen a moose once before, but that was from a car. This shambolic animal, with its wide rack, huge rounded horsey face, and loosely jointed body atop oddly spindly legs, was both majestic and foolish-looking.

Allie watched as it disappeared into the woods by the shore. A moment later, she thought she could see its head moving through the water. Wonder where he's going, Allie mused. What a great way to start what was sure to be a crazy day.

Allie picked up her coffee cup and returned to the kitchen. I might as well get started, she thought. What music would get her going this morning? She remembered hearing a Vivaldi piece on the radio the other day, something like Chamber Concerto in A Minor, with flute.[15] Light, but with a driving rhythm—perfect to get her brain moving. She found it on her phone and got it started.

Nineteen

From the moment she started teaching Allie, Anne Kirschner recognized that Allegra Brewster was no ordinary cello student. At nine years old, Allie approached her lessons with a serious and focused attitude. She asked questions and noticed details in a way that showed an unusual depth of engagement with the music. "When Bach plays that tune again, I like how he makes little changes." "Why is this part so much harder to play?" "Why is this piece like the other one we worked on?" She disdained the typical childish ditties that most nine-year-olds liked to play, asking instead for music by well-known composers.

Not that Allie didn't have a sense of fun. Together, they devised a series of games that became part of their lessons. In Follow Me, Anne would play a short excerpt or improvised tune and ask Allie to copy it by ear. Match Me was a game that required Allie to play with Anne and match her pitches exactly; Anne would play a little sharp or flat to test Allie's listening ability. As Allie became more proficient, the games got harder. In What's Wrong, Anne would show Allie a page of music and then play it, leaving something out or changing it; Allie would try to find the mistake. In Who Wrote It, Anne or Allie would play a page or two of a piece with the composer's name covered, and Allie would try to figure out who wrote it and when. Sometimes Anne would try to trick Allie by taking a popular tune by a performer like Katy Perry or Rihanna and "classicize" it, playing it in the style of a classical composer. The two of them would laugh and laugh over their games, often going over the hour deadline. Lessons usually took place on the festival campus, and other orchestra members would cluster outside the door, listening to the cello lesson for a few minutes with smiles on their faces.

As she progressed, Allie's intensity challenged Anne. Even though Allie demanded more from her teacher, Anne found the lessons constantly rewarding. Together, they reveled in Allie's growth as a cellist and as a musician. Even so, Anne knew it wasn't likely that Allie would become a professional cellist—and certainly not a soloist. She could probably earn a spot in a good orchestra, Anne thought, but she sensed Allie would find being an orchestral musician limiting and also stressful. When Allie pursued an interest in arts management after college, that fit with Anne's perception of her student. She knew that Allie's musicianship and passion for music would inform her management, and her focus and curiosity would lend itself to continual professional growth. Allie was on the right path, her teacher believed.

Walking past the SummerFest office windows on the way to rehearsal, Anne could see her former student sitting at her desk, staring into space and biting her lip. Anne thought back to news of the night before that George Park was leaving in two weeks. Did that put Allie in a tough spot, she wondered. Who would take his place for the rest of the summer festival? She checked her watch and decided to stop in for a quick chat with Allie.

Allie was surprised to see Anne come through the door, dragging her cello case behind her. Usually Anne was the first cellist to rehearsal, warming up on any hard licks in the piece on that day's schedule and generally reacquainting herself with the music.

"Hey, what's up?" asked Allie.

"That's what I was going to ask you. I saw you through the window, looking so pensive. I heard about George..."

"You did? Wow, news travels fast around here."

"Well, I had dinner at the dock last night with Tony and he got a call from George." Anne stood her cello up against Allie's desk. "So, what does that mean for you?"

Allie smiled and opened her eyes wide. "It means that George has suggested that the board appoint me the interim manager."

"That's wonderful, Allie!" Anne dropped her jaw in a show of awe.

"You think? I'm not so sure. For one thing, the board may not approve that idea."

"Well, your father..."

"Dad has to recuse himself..."

"Oh, of course."

"And anyway, he was about to step off the board." Allie pushed her hair behind her ears. "I know that some of the board members will say I'm too young."

"Do you want it? It could be a lot of hassle and responsibility." Anne was thinking back to the trauma of the spring, when the musicians' union was in revolt and Sylvia Abbott was murdered.

"No, I do want it. I mean, who else knows this place the way I do? If they bring in someone from outside, I'll have to train that person, and it'll be just as much work and a lot more frustrating. At least, that's what I'm guessing." Allie paused, adjusting the pens on her desk. She looked up at Anne. "It's just the getting from here to there. Convincing the board to agree. I'm not looking forward to that."

"Sort of like auditioning and waiting to hear if you made the cut. Ugh, it's the worst." Anne bent down to be closer to Allie's face. "Listen, if you'd like a break from thinking about this, why don't you come over to Cormorant tonight and I'll play some of the concerto. Like I said, I'd love to get your feedback..." Anne chuckled. "And you probably won't have time after today."

"I'd like that. After dinner?"

"No, come for dinner, too. I'll do a pizza on the grill—you like artichoke hearts, right?—and then we can look at the music."

"Ok, sounds great. I'll bring brownies from the Barnloft Bakery."

"Oh, yum, that'd be great. Now I'd better run to rehearsal! See you tonight. Around six?"

"Perfect."

"Hey, bring your cello," Anne shouted over her shoulder as she wheeled her cello case through the door.

Allie gave her a thumbs up and reinserted her earbuds. The sound of the fourth movement of Fanny Mendelssohn's Piano Trio[1] filled her ears.

Twenty

A few minutes later, Luke burst through the office door.

"Is it true, Al?" he sputtered.

"Is what true?" Allie was fairly sure she knew what he was referring to, but she wanted to know what he'd heard.

"That George is leaving. And the board will have to hire a replacement. In two weeks!" Luke rubbed his forehead. "That'll never happen. And we'll be left to fend for ourselves, without someone in charge."

"Where did you hear that?" Allie asked calmly.

"Tony's assistant, Ted, said Tony texted him last night. I saw Ted when I was getting a cup of coffee at the Barnloft this morning." He held up a paper cup of coffee. "I got one for you, too, but I got sidetracked by Ted. The coffee's probably pretty cold by now."

"Thanks anyway," Allie said as she grasped the cup. "I can always zap it in the microwave."

"So...?"

"Yes, it's true. But..."

"It's a disaster! First the murder and now this!"

"Lucas. Chrissake, calm down. It is not a disaster and I'll tell you why." Allie poured the coffee into her mug and placed it in the microwave. Turning around to Luke, she continued, "George and Grant are getting married."

"I know, I know. They made a big announcement. But they're not getting married until *after* SummerFest ends, right?"

"They were. But then Grant got a great job in Minnesota, so they decided to get married now and move together. I think they don't want to be apart." She looked toward George's office to make sure he wasn't there. "I think the trauma of Kate's attack on George really still bothers him."

"I get that." Luke nodded. "He almost died."

Allie closed her eyes as if to block the memory. "Yeah," she whispered. The microwave beeped and Allie opened the door to retrieve her coffee. She took a sip. "Yuck, what did you get me?" She stuck her tongue out.

"Maine maple—I thought you liked that. Sorry, Al."

"I guess I can suffer through one cup of it."

"Back to the story about George and Grant. Why is George's leaving *not* a disaster?"

"Because..." Allie drew the word out dramatically, "Because George is recommending that I take over as interim manager."

"What! That's awesome!"

"Cool, huh? Of course, the board has to agree to it. And that's going to be a challenge. Dad will have to recuse himself, which leaves Ken Hanson in charge. He's not a fan." Allie rolled her eyes. "And I'm sure Helen Davis and Alice Vogel will be right there with him. His little cheering squad..."

"Oh, I don't know," said Luke. "It seemed like everyone came around and pitched in while George was recuperating this spring. I mean, you basically ran the show then. They'll have to remember that."

"Right. Let's hope they do." Allie turned to her desk. "Anyway, I have work to do..."

She was interrupted by the arrival of Thomas and Ruben.

"Allie!" they both said.

Thomas looked at Ruben and continued, "Allie, what's the plan? If George is leaving, I mean."

"I see Ted is getting the word out. Who knew Tony's assistant was so good at mass communications," she said dryly. "Yes, the plan is for George to leave in two weeks. And he's suggesting that I be appointed his replacement. Temporarily."

Both men relaxed. Ruben smiled. "That's terrific!" He eyed Allie. "Now I'll be able to get what I need," he said, half in jest.

"Oh, no, you won't," Allie said, laughing. "I will run a tight ship."

Thomas nodded. "Yeah, Allie knows how this all works. She was great this spring, when the murderer was on the loose. This is an excellent solution."

"Now that you have that cleared up," said Luke, "I'll be on my way."

"Oh, Luke, didn't see you there." Ruben moved close to him. "Don't suppose you have a minute to talk about backdrop ideas for the concerto?" The two of them left, talking and gesturing.

Thomas sat down in the folding chair in the corner and crossed his legs. "So, Allie, how do you feel about that?"

"I think it's fine. If the board approves it. And that's a big if. Not all the board thinks I'm capable. At least, that's my guess."

"It's a great thing for the festival, actually." Thomas smiled with enthusiasm. "What a story! Hometown girl takes over the running of the festival after a series of tragic events. I should say, *talented, beautiful* hometown girl. You should capitalize on the story. I bet the ticket sales would go through the roof."

"They're already 'through the roof,' Thomas. Every concert is sold out except for the last one. We're even putting chairs on the deck outside the barn for extra seating. So I'm not looking at this as a big publicity stunt."

"But think of the PR value! It would make national news for sure."

"A lot of good that would do us right now," Allie said. "Remember the hassle of dealing with reporters after Sylvia's death? It takes a huge amount of time."

"Don't minimize the value. You may pull in some big money." Thomas stood up. "I should get down to the rehearsal." He turned toward Allie as he walked to the door. "It's a big chance for you, Allie. You should make the most of it."

Thomas left. Somewhat rattled by the interruptions, Allie put her earbuds back in. That Mendelssohn Piano trio no longer seemed like the right music to fit her mood. Her eyes lit on the B-52s listing. She felt like things were crazy enough to warrant their boisterous sound. She listened to "Your Own Private Idaho"[17] for a few minutes.

Twenty-One

Allie took her earbuds out when George came in.

"What were you listening to?" he asked.

"Oh, just the B-52s—"Private Idaho."

George smiled. "I loved the B-52s when I was younger. Hey, aren't you too young for them? How do you know about them?"

"Oh, my wild and crazy aunt went to school in Georgia. My dad's sister Lucy. She love, love, loves the B-52s and R.E.M. So I've heard a lot of them growing up."

"Sort of balances out the Bach and Bluegrass from your dad?"

"Yup. I'm a 'well-rounded music lover'." Allie garnished the phrase with air quotes.

"And that's just what the Kennimac SummerFest needs in its interim manager!" George smiled again. "Ok, Allegra, let's talk about how you're going to take over when I leave in 14 days." His voice got progressively louder as he spoke. Allie thought he clearly was happy about the prospect of leaving.

"Right. But first we have to convince the board."

"You're going to be great. I think your youth and energy are just what the festival needs. So let's make sure the board knows that. The first thing to do is for you to document all the work you did while I was recuperating from, you know..." George paused for a moment. "I think the best way for you to do that is to think about what you did each day. Make a comprehensive list of all the things that weren't in your usual job description."

"Ok. But that's going to take me a while."

"Of course it will. It would probably be easiest if you find a quiet place to work, where you can think without interruptions. Not easy to find around here. You'll need to get away to find that solitude. Where might that be?"

Allie thought for a moment. She looked out the window at the sunny sky. "Hmmm. What if I take Calliope out for a sail? Dad just finally got her in the water. The breeze is gentle today; just enough to move the boat along. I could dictate my thoughts into my phone."

"Yes, but turn the cell service off. No texts or calls or emails. Now, what are you waiting for—get out of here!" George made a pushing motion with his hands as if sweeping Allie out the door.

"Ok, ok!" Allie laughed. She stuck her phone in her backpack and headed for the car. As she drove to the sailing club, she called her father. "Dad? Is it alright if I take Calliope out for a sail this morning? George thinks that's a good way for me to put together my justification to the board."

David Brewster was walking Archie. "What? What do you mean, justification?"

"George wants me to write down all the things I did while he was in the hospital this spring. Like how I took on a lot of his work. He wants the board to know that I'm capable of taking over now."

"Oh, I see. Yes, of course, good idea. Archie, ignore that squirrel! Hang on, Allie." The call was suspended for a moment while David corralled the wayward Westie, then he continued, "But why the sailboat? How will you do that away from your desk?"

"I'll use the peace and quiet of a sail to remember all the things I did. George said to think day by day, through each hour, to remember. I guess I can check it against my calendar when I get back. But I'll leave my phone turned off so I don't get interrupted."

"When are you planning to do this? You'll need to have the information ready for the board soon."

"I was going to go out this morning, if that's ok with you. Were you going to use Calliope this morning? I'll only be gone for a couple of hours."

"No, no, that's fine. You'll need to stop by and get the iPad so you can navigate. It's in the usual place. I'll be out on a walk in the fields with Archie. Let me know how it goes."

"Thanks, Dad. Hey, I saw a big moose this morning. Walked right down the path to the water. He was impressive."

"Wonder if it's the same animal I saw in the fields a few days ago. He's a big guy."

"Sure was. Hey, love you, Dad."

"Love you, too, sweetie."

Allie ended the call and started her car. This will be a super way to spend the morning, she thought. I am so lucky!

The dock of the sailing club was empty; kids' sailing classes were already out on the water with their instructors and no one else was around. There was a light wind blowing off the shore. Allie put her phone and the iPad in a waterproof case and rowed the dinghy out to Calliope. The little wooden sailboat bobbed at its mooring, shipshape and gleaming from the work David Brewster had put into it that spring and early summer. The varnish on the wooden mast and boom shone in the sun. Allie admired the boot stripe and waterline her father had painted a sea blue, while the rest of the hull was a light gray.

The interior of the cockpit was freshly painted white, and the teak combing around the cockpit matched the mast and boom in gleaming varnish. Bench seats extended along each side of the cockpit and a box in the center held the centerboard when it was raised. Two large nylon bags containing the mainsail and the jib sail—the big main sail that ran up the mast and was attached to the boom and the smaller forward sail that was attached at the bow and ran up the forestay—were stashed under the cuddy, the small covered area under the foredeck. At eighteen feet long, Calliope was a comfortable vessel for a few hours of sailing if the weather cooperated.

Allie noticed her father hadn't reattached the small outboard electric motor to the transom. I guess I'll have to rely on the wind today, she thought. Just in case the wind died, she transferred the oars from the rowboat to the sailboat. She got busy attaching the sails, and in about ten minutes, she was ready to let go of the mooring line and sail down the bay.

The wind was behind her, and the sea was calm. Two ospreys flew above, chasing a bald eagle. The distant sound of a lawn mower at a summer cottage on shore could be heard, as well as the shouts of the sailing class, but the only sounds nearby were the gentle splashes of the water on Calliope's bow and the occasional flap of the sails. Allie checked the time and tide on her phone, knowing that it would take much longer to return to shore against the wind. She set the timer for half an hour, after which she'd turn around and head back. Luckily, she thought, the tide will also be running back toward the shore and will help push Calliope toward the mooring.

Twenty-Two

Allie returned to the office around two o'clock that afternoon, her cheeks pink from her time on the water. She had dictated into her phone many details about the work she'd done those weeks in May and early June, and she found the variety and number of tasks surprising. Sitting at her desk, she opened her calendar on her laptop to see if she'd missed or misremembered anything.

"How'd it go?" rasped George. "Was it helpful to get away?"

"I had the most idyllic sail," Allie said. "The wind was perfect, I hardly had to trim the sails, no one bothered me, and I could really concentrate. Thanks for the idea."

"I always find I do my best thinking that way," said George. "Not sailing, of course," he said with a look of horror, "I instantly get seasick—but going someplace peaceful and distant from everyday pressures and distractions."

"So I'm just going to check my calendar to make sure this information is accurate. Then I'll type it up to give to the board." Allie turned to her laptop.

"Oh, I spoke with your dad and also Ken Hanson and Esther. Ken Hanson has volunteered to chair the committee to consider next steps..."

Allie raised her eyebrows, knowing that Ken Hanson was no supporter. "And...?"

"And I made sure he selected board members who would be fair and open to considering you as the interim replacement. So, Esther Swift, Robin Hall, Peter Drumlin, and Arnold Schimmler will also be on the committee. I think it's a good group. Your document will go to them and they will disseminate it to the rest of the board."

"Ok, I guess that's alright. I'd better get to work then and finish it up." Allie put in her earbuds but didn't turn on any music this time; she wanted nothing but quiet with no distractions.

"Allie, you're here!" Thomas burst through the office door.

"I'm really busy..."

"I need to talk to you. It's about the Family Concert I'm conducting on Sunday."

Allie regarded Thomas's earnest expression, a lock of his wavy hair tumbling over his forehead. He seems like such a good guy, she thought. Still, Allie didn't trust him. His attempt at a hook-up in the spring made her wary.

She sighed. "What about Sunday?"

"Well, I had an idea for publicity. You know, to appeal to people more our age. And not so many families with young kids."

"Thomas, you know we've pitched the concert as a family event. Families include kids. That's why so many family tickets have been sold. It's too late to change things now—the concert is sold out. I told you that."

"Oh, well, right. But what about the idea of seating some people on the deck? I heard that was a possibility."

"I haven't heard yet whether the board approved that idea. But anyway, it will just be more families."

"Here's an idea!" Thomas interjected. "What if we encourage families to sit outside on the deck, and invite our generation to sit inside?"

"No way." Allie was definite. "What's your problem with kids? And who our age is going to want to come to that concert?"

"Kids make so much noise. And they don't pay attention. I don't know... it feels demeaning to me. To have to conduct in front of little kids."

"Ok, a couple of thoughts." Allie was terse. "One. This concert has been on the schedule for months. You've known about it ever since you took the job of assistant conductor. Two. This type of concert can change a kid's life. They might hear something that inspires them to pursue a career in music. Three. There is a time-honored tradition of famous conductors doing concerts for children. Think of Leopold Stokowski and "Fantasia" and Leonard Bernstein and his Young People's Concerts. Four. Now get out of here and let me work!"

"Ok, ok. You don't have to get mad. I just thought..."

"You didn't think. Now, leave!"

George stepped out of his office. "What was that all about?"

"Oh, Thomas is being a prima dona," Allie answered. "If you can call a conductor a *prima dona*..."

"They can definitely be the equivalent. What would that be, *primo maestro*?" They both laughed.

"Listen, Allegra," said George. "How are you coming on the paper describing your work this spring? The committee wants to meet tomorrow at nine o'clock to consider my proposal installing you as my temporary replacement. Can you send something out this evening?"

"Well, I'd like you to look at it first, George, to make sure it's as clear and complete as possible." She motioned to her laptop. "It's pretty well done. How 'bout if I finish up and send it to you in an hour?"

"Sounds good. I'll be sure to turn it around quickly for you."

"Ok, thanks."

Twenty-Three

Allie waved at inn owner RuthEllen Cox, who was in her garden picking lettuce, as she drove by the Kennimac Inn's kitchen garden on her way to Anne's cottage. The low sun sparkled on the water through the trees as she drove down the dirt road and parked next to the cottage. Stepping out of the car, Allie took a deep breath of the salt-tinged air. It hadn't rained in a while, so the dirt road's dust stirred up by her arrival lingered in the air for a moment. A couple of gulls wheeled and screeched overhead as she retrieved the plate of brownies she'd brought to add to dinner.

"Allie! Here you are. Come on in." Anne held the door of the cottage open so Allie could enter with her cello. Allie was startled to see Tony Bainbridge standing in the middle of the main room of the cottage. A large circle of pizza dough was spread on the counter, with various chopped vegetables waiting to be scattered on the dough. A crumpled paper bag was off to the side.

Allie looked questioningly at Anne. "Hi, Tony, I didn't know you would be here. I would have brought more brownies..."

"Oh, Tony's not staying. Are you, Tony," Anne said pointedly.

"That pizza looks good," Tony said longingly. "I could grab a bottle of wine..."

"No. Actually, Allie and I have some serious cello work to do here. So, Tony, you need to scoot next door."

"Oh, alright." Tony reluctantly walked toward the door. "But Anne, how about after, when you and Allegra finish with whatever it is you're doing?"

"Tony. Absolutely not." Anne followed him to the door and shut it firmly behind him. Turning around, she said, "Sorry about that, Allie. I can't convince him I don't want to have the kind of relationship he seems after." She shook her head. "I'm under enough pressure as it is, with Ruben's concerto coming up. That," she pointed toward Tony's cottage, "I don't need."

Allie nodded in agreement. "I think I know what you mean."

"How so?"

"Oh, nothing that important. It's just that everyone—including my mother—thinks Luke and I are practically married. Or should be. It doesn't feel right to me." Allie shook her head. "Don't get me wrong; Luke's a great guy."

"You two have been friends forever," said Anne.

"Right. But I don't want to 'settle down' and if I did, I'm not sure it would be with Luke. Wow, this looks like an epic pizza—artichoke hearts, pine nuts, fresh tomatoes, fresh mozzarella," she said, changing the subject. "Hey, what's in this bag?" Allie peeked inside. "Mushrooms? They're covered in dirt. Wait, I thought you hated mushrooms."

"Damn right I do. That bag was on my doorstep when I got back this afternoon. I assume they came from RuthEllen. It was with these gorgeous heirloom tomatoes from her garden." Anne held up a tomato that looked like a sculpture. "Looks like a fleshy Rubens nude, doesn't it?" She laughed.

"Actually, sort of looks like RuthEllen," said Allie, smiling.

While they arranged the ingredients across the pizza dough's surface, the two women talked about the festival. Anne wondered how Allie was coming with getting the board to agree to have Allie act as interim manager, and Allie filled her in on the latest.

"The committee that's making the decision is meeting tomorrow morning," Allie said.

"Jeez, they got right on it. Did that give you enough time...?"

"Yep. I finished up my narrative of the spring and George is checking it over as we speak."

"I'm sure it's impressive. You'll have to let me know how the meeting goes."

"I'll send you a text right after, if you like."

"That would be great. Wine with the pizza? Or beer? I do have iced tea, too."

"I'll go with a beer, thanks."

Anne poured herself a glass of red wine and beer for Allie. She took the pizza out of the oven and set it out to cool for a few minutes.

"Tell me about the concerto," said Allie.

"It's a beast." Anne sighed. "I do really enjoy playing parts of it, but some of it..." She shook her head. "I'm hoping you'll have some ideas about it. I mean, from a cellist's perspective, but also from a listener's perspective. I want people to be able to make sense out of it."

"What's the orchestra's part like?"

"Chaotic. Really wild. Some of it is aleatoric, with players making their own decision about how fast to play, what to play, when to come in, and when to drop out. So that's different every time they play it."

"Wow. Is the solo cello part like that, too?"

"Not really. There are a few places where Ruben gives the soloist some latitude, but most of the time the part's written out. Here, let's eat."

"So, what's the deal with Tony?" asked Allie, between pizza bites.

Anne rolled her eyes. "You tell me. For some reason, he seems to have developed an interest in me that, I don't know, feels weird. I mean, most summers he's had a dalliance with some young, impressionable orchestra member. That's not me!" She stopped to chew for a moment, thinking. "Maybe he's worried about the concerto? Trying to bolster me? Make me feel more secure? I don't know—whatever the reason, he's driving me crazy. He's gone all romantic."

"Ugh. That's gross. Not what you need."

"Yeah, right. For one thing, I'm ten years older than he is. And I'm not interested in him—not more than as a colleague and a friend." She took a sip of wine and shook her silvered curls. "It's driving me crazy. He hangs around... And he's right next door... Any advice for your old teacher?"

"Guys," Allie responded with derision. "Ugh. Can't live with 'em, can't live without 'em." They laughed.

"Actually, I *can* live without them just fine," Anne said. "Except for Andrew, of course." She cleared the empty dinner plates and brought out the plate of brownies. "Now here's something I can't live without—chocolate." They each took a brownie and munched contentedly.

"Ok, time to get to work. Allie, would you mind clearing the rest of the dishes while I get out my cello?"

Twenty-Four

Anne carried her cello over to her chair while Allie picked up the glasses and silverware and carried them to the sink. She put on a pair of rubber gloves she found under the sink and turned on the hot water to rinse the dishes. The cottage had an old electric hot water heater that took forever to heat the water, and Allie knew she'd have to wait. Since they hadn't used the forks or knives, she opened the silverware drawer to put them back. As she did, she stepped back in shock: a lethal-looking black pistol sat in among the knives. "Anne?" she said. The sound of water pouring from the faucet covered her voice, and Anne continued to set up her cello.

"Anne," Allie said a little louder. Anne turned to her with a questioning look.

"Yes?"

Allie turned off the water and quickly set the dishes in the soapy water. "What's with this gun in with the silverware? Did you know it was there?" Anne nodded. "Where did it come from?" asked Allie.

Anne set the cello back down and walked over to where Allie was standing by the open drawer. "I've had it for eons. My dad gave it to me when Mark died. He didn't think a single mother living in Chicago should be without 'protection.'" She used air quotes as she said 'protection.' "I forgot I had it with me. It popped up a few days ago when I was going through my large duffle bag. Since I came by car, I didn't have to think about it, I guess." She shrugged. "But I sure don't need it here."

Allie looked at it warily. "But why is it in with your silverware?"

"Oh, I was trying to figure out what to do with it and somebody knocked on my door, so I quickly shoved it in there. Meant to put it in a better hiding place but haven't gotten around to it." She sat down and began to tune her cello.

"Is it loaded?" Allie continued looking at the small firearm with trepidation. Standing over the open drawer, she could smell the distinctive odor of oil and metal. She shook her head as if to clear it. Anne and a gun—they just didn't go together.

"Oh, jeez. Probably loaded. I don't know. If it is, it's locked. Don't worry about it, Allie. My father was a cop, remember. He thought I needed it. I'll take care of it later. I came across it when I was looking for my cottage key. Still haven't found that... Just move the gun to the counter if it's in your way." Anne motioned to Allie to come sit down. "Hey, let's get started on this. Get your cello out."

Allie gingerly set the gun on the Formica counter, put the clean silverware in the drawer, and slid the drawer shut. Still somewhat spooked, she took out her cello and bow and pulled a chair close enough to see the music on Anne's music stand.

Anne was oblivious to Allie's discomfort. "I'm debating whether to use my iPad in the concert," Anne said. "There are so many pages and the music goes by so fast in some places. I don't know..."

"Have you played from an iPad in a concert before?"

"Not as the soloist. And it probably doesn't make sense here—we will no doubt be making changes right up to the last minute. Ruben seems really stuck about the fourth movement."

"I want to hear it. Play some of it for me."

Anne played through the opening measures, which forcefully introduced the cello's voice. Allie nodded in appreciation. "That's so powerful," she said. "Great beginning."

"You try it." Anne turned the music stand to face Allie, who quickly checked the tuning of her strings. Then, in an attempt to mimic her teacher's resolve, she laid into the opening bars.

"Not bad for a first reading," said Anne.

"Really feeble," said Allie. "A pale imitation of your version."

Anne laughed. "Don't be too hard on yourself. I've been practicing that for weeks, no, months!"

She skipped to a lyrical passage in the second movement. Slower, meditative, plaintive, it showed off the cello's ability to sing in a soulful way. "I'm pretty happy with this part," Anne said. "I think I almost have it where I want it."

"It's like a folk ballad or something," said Allie. "I can almost hear it sung by, I don't know, maybe Carrie Newcomer, like in her song "Sanctuary."[18]

"You'll have to play that for me sometime. I don't know her." Anne turned over many pages of music manuscript. "Now here's the third movement. Very playful and fun." She launched into a jangly jazzy tune with tricky rhythms and big jumps. "It's wicked to play, but I really like it," she said as she played. "What do you think?"

"Wow! It's pretty wild. But fun. It sounds great. I don't know how you played this," Allie pointed to a place in the music, "but you pulled it off." She tried to play the first few bars, but soon gave up.

"Practice, practice, practice," said Anne, laughing. She turned many more pages of manuscript. "Here's the part that's a real bugger. It's in the fourth movement." She played a series of loud disjointed phrases, dissonant, growling leaps around the cello's strings, her bow working furiously. After a couple of minutes, she set down the bow. "Christ, I'm never going to get that."

"The beauty is, no one will know if you play the right or wrong notes," Allie said, smiling.

"I will know."

"Where is all this angst of Ruben's coming from?" Allie said. "He seems so laid back. I wouldn't have thought this was his composition."

"I know," Anne agreed. "It is another side of him. This fourth movement sounds more like some other composer, but I can't put my finger on who. Someone I've played in the past..." she mused. "Just don't quite know..."

"I do think it's a bummer that you aren't premiering a work by a woman composer," Allie said. "I wonder if any women composers applied for the gig. I only heard about Ruben when it was already a done deal with Tony."

"I agree, yeah. There are some wonderful young women coming up. I don't know, I think Tony made the decision all by himself. You know, Tony thinks he so 'evolved' and such a supporter of women. And I have nothing against Ruben—he's certainly talented." She sighed. "But I hope he makes a final decision on this last movement soon. It's driving me crazy, not being able to practice the final version. There are only two weeks to go!" She sighed. "You know, between the two of them, Ruben and Tony, I'm going a little bit crazy. Ruben is just young and feckless, but Tony—I don't know... He's having a midlife crisis or something. He seems to want something that I'm not about to give him, that's for sure." She shrugged her shoulders and turned back to the music.

For the next few minutes, Anne played through bits and phrases of the fourth movement, and she and Allie discussed ways to attack them. Then, as a break from the hard stuff, Anne pulled out a duet book they had used when Allie was her student. They ran through a couple of their favorite duets, laughing and teasing each other. Anne would change the tempo in the middle of a measure and Allie would try to follow. Or Allie would change the dynamics, playing a section fortissimo that was supposed to be soft, and Anne would echo. Finally, it was getting late, and the two friends decided to call it a night. Just as Allie was leaving, Anne had a brainstorm.

"You know who I was thinking of?"

"The composer, you mean?" asked Allie.

"Yes. It was Janice MacKenzie. I studied with her in college. Her compositions often had a similar crazy angry feel to them."

"Don't know her. I'll have to look her up," said Allie. "Thanks for dinner, Anne. This was fun."

"Oh, wait," said Anne. "Take this leftover piece of pizza—I'll never eat it." She wrapped the pizza in the waxed fabric that she used instead of plastic and handed it to Allie. "Let's do it again, soon." Anne waved from the porch as Allie got in her car. "And good luck tomorrow!"

Twenty-Five

Romance blooms during summer music festivals. Sometimes inappropriately, temporarily, superficially. Sometimes deeply and sincerely. Allie knew this well after her years connected with the Kennimac SummerFest—first as an observant child, then teen, and now adult. She'd seen how orchestra members, living in vacation-like proximity perhaps without the constraints of normal daily life, would couple. Often it followed the music. After a sensuous pairing of oboe and flute in Ravel's 3rd movement, Menuet, of "Le tombeau de Couperin,"[19] for example, the two woodwind players followed the music's lead and continued their amorous pairing outside rehearsal. Or the conductor became infatuated with the comely concertmaster after working closely for hours on bowings. (Bowings tell a string player whether to push the bow to the left over the strings or pull it to the right and when to change direction.) Sometimes it was a serendipitous pairing, a bass player who caught the eye of a trombonist, shared a reaction to a ridiculous statement by the conductor, and discovered a mutual sense of humor. Occasionally, an orchestra member would fall for a local; several them had married and stayed in Maine as a result. In a way, romance was a common hazard of the job. Musicians, like actors, are bound to be expressive. To succeed, they must interpret compositions' emotional content in a way that is clear to not only the audience but to their co-creators, fellow musicians. Most musical dalliances are expressed through music alone, but some become physical.

Allie thought about Anne in that context. When she first started studying cello, Anne was married, though Anne's husband was ill with cancer. He died soon after, and Allie knew her teacher was sad, though she tried not to let her grief intrude on their lessons. But after a few years, Anne's demeanor lightened. One summer, she seemed particularly giddy; Allie saw her holding hands with one of the violists. But by the next summer, that relationship appeared to have ended. Allie didn't know of any other romances of Anne's, but that didn't mean there had been none. Anne was private and discreet.

Anne was also protective of her two children, Cara and Andrew. The summer of Anne's affair with the viola player, Cara and Andrew had both been away at camp during the festival. But most summers they had been around. Allie guessed their presence inhibited Anne's chances of finding romantic companionship.

Her thoughts of the romantic implications of music led her to remember the close call she'd had with Thomas that April. Engaged to perform a cello duet together at the SummerFest's spring fundraising concert, they'd quickly become more than just collaborating musicians during rehearsals. Even now, Allie's heart quickened thinking of those times. Thomas was so handsome, his dark wavy hair falling over his forehead as he played, his gray eyes serious, his expression intense. He would shoot a glance at her as they played, his cello answering hers, and their eye contact stirred something in Allie. It was a fizzy feeling she didn't experience with Luke, though they, too, were close. But there was something about communicating wordlessly through music that seemed to evoke a different level of desire. Her passion and longing poured out through the notes. It was as if they were coupling in the music, melding the two voices into one.

How false that had been, though, Allie reflected. Soon enough, it had become clear that Thomas was only interested in a brief fling, a hook-up with no deeper meaning. It was lust, not the beginning of love, that was for sure. And Allie wasn't comfortable with that. Thomas had shown vulnerability in other ways. His relationship with the murdered Sylvia Abbott turned out to be complicated. Though not her killer, he had been a viable suspect for a while.

Allie thought back to that time with a shudder. Her mentor and substitute maternal figure, Kate Zeller, was now awaiting trial for the vengeful murder of Dr. Abbott, whom Kate blamed for the drowning of her young son. Allie's discovery that Kate was the murderer profoundly affected her. She had loved and trusted Kate and had relied on her. More than that, she held Kate up as a role model as she, Allie, traversed the wilderness of maturing into womanhood without the guidance of a mother (at least, not one nearby). Kate's crime and loss of sanity threw into question Allie's belief in her own ability to make judgements about the people around her. If Kate had been able to hide the monstrous part of her personality from Allie, what were others hiding? Indeed, what tendencies were hiding within Allie herself? Her world had truly been shaken.

Perhaps distance was the answer. Don't let others get too close. Don't count on anyone else. It felt painfully lonely, but maybe it was the only sure way.

Allie's dark thoughts called out for musical accompaniment: something tragic and foreboding. She recalled studying Benjamin Britten's *War Requiem*, written after World War II. That first movement, "Requiem aeternam,"[20] with its growling basses and sorrowful voices, including an ethereal children's chorus, was hair-raising. Perfect. She played it on her portable speaker, the music melding with the night sounds of the dark woods surrounding the cottage.

Twenty-Six

As the second movement of the requiem began, Allie looked at the clock—eleven o'clock. Bedtime, she thought, stopping the recording. The night quiet filled the cottage, moonlight seeping through the trees. Big day tomorrow, Allie thought. She had looked through George's comments on her report covering the work she'd done that spring, and she'd added some details that he had suggested. He was very complimentary, and his faith in her was a morale booster. Still, she wondered what would happen tomorrow morning at the meeting. Esther Swift would be on her side, Allie knew that, but Ken Hanson would need to be convinced. The others—Peter Drumlin and Robin Hall—were two big question marks. I just have to wow them, Allie said to herself. But how? She thought of Anne's advice to her before any important performance: "Be yourself. You're well prepared. Just let it flow." That advice made sense here, too, she decided. And then she thought of her mother, always the self-assured warrior. I'll channel Melissa, she thought.

The sound of car tires crunching on the gravel driveway came in through the open windows, followed by the beams of car headlights. Allie looked out; it was Thomas getting out of his car. What was he doing here? She met him at the screen doors with a questioning look.

"Allie, oh, good, you're up. Can I come in for a few minutes?"

Reluctantly, she opened the door and motioned with an ironically elaborate gesture that he could enter.

"Look, I know this is late." Thomas paused as if unsure how to continue.

"Late? Yeah, I'd say so. I was about to go to bed."

"Well, I need to talk to you about the family concert. It's, well,..."

"What about it? It's coming up on Sunday, Thomas. We can't change anything now."

"No, no, I realize that. It's just that I wondered if you might help with something. You have such a way with people."

"What are you talking about? What do you want me to do?" Allie had no patience for his reticence.

"Ok. Here's what I was thinking. What if you address the audience before I come out? You could ask that the parents keep their kids quiet. In their seats. You know, so they learn how to act at a symphony concert."

Allie felt her ire rising. How could Thomas be so dense? He really didn't understand the point of the family concert at all.

"Listen, Thomas, you've got it all wrong. This concert might be the very first live orchestra concert these young kids have been to. The last thing we want to do is to make them think it's a stuffy occasion where they have to sit still and 'behave'." She put air quotes around the last word. "Remember when we talked about Leonard Bernstein's Young People's Concerts? I suggest you try to pull up a video of one of them. Watch the kids. They are wriggling around, laughing, copying his conducting motions. They are totally into it."

"Yes, but..."

"Your job on Sunday is just what Tony Bainbridge said: to make the kids fall in love with orchestral music. Think about it, Thomas. You could actually change a child's life. When we play for adults, it's not like someone in the audience says, 'I'm going to become a world class conductor.' But when we play for kids, we might inspire the next Bernstein. Right?"

"Well, if you put it that way..." Thomas ran his hand through his hair. "So, sure, if you want, I can talk to the audience beforehand. This is what I'll say: 'Have a wonderful time, everyone. Let the music seep into your bones. If you feel like wiggling to it, or pretending to be the conductor, go for it. If you need to dance to it, go right ahead. Music is about feeling, so we want you to feel all the feels.' Or something along those lines. Do you want me to do that?"

Thomas grimaced. "Hmmm, ok. I get your point. Yes, I do want you to say something. But, maybe also..."

"If I'm going to stand up there and talk, I'm going to say what *I* want to say. You will not get to approve it." Allie was adamant.

Thomas smiled. "You're pretty damn convincing when you get riled up. Your cheeks get deliciously pink." He stepped closer.

Allie closed her eyes and exhaled impatiently. At the sound of another approaching vehicle, her eyes flew open and Thomas stepped back. A car door slammed and feet could be heard on the steps.

"What the hell?" Luke scowled through the screen door.

"What are you doing here?" Allie was surprised to see him. They hadn't made any plans to get together tonight. "Come in, Luke; don't just stand on the porch."

"I thought you might want some extra support to calm your nerves before the big meeting tomorrow. But I guess I was wrong about that," he said as he entered the cottage.

"Hi, Luke," said Thomas. "What big meeting?"

Allie put her hands to her head. These two were so clueless. "To see if the board will hire me to be interim managing director when George leaves."

"Oh, right," said Thomas. "I'd better be going. I'll leave you two to it." Thomas left the cottage. "You'll need to move your car, Luke," he shouted from the driveway. "You're blocking me."

"Oh, for fuck's sake," muttered Luke as he jingled his car keys on the way to the door.

"Luke," said Allie. "Just go home. I really need to get some sleep and you don't seem to be in a calming mood. I'll see you tomorrow."

"You sure, Al?"

"Totally. And Luke?" She gave him a stern look. "Please don't just drop in here unannounced again."

"If that's what you want, fine!" Luke slammed the screen door as he left.

Not cool, thought Allie, as the sounds of the quiet night finally returned—the rustling of small animals in the underbrush, the hooting of an owl, the wavelets rhythmically caressing the rocky shore. Now it was quarter to midnight. Time for bed, for real.

Twenty-Seven

Fortified with a double espresso from the Barnloft Bakery, Allie unlocked the door and hurried into the office. She had planned to be early and she was, but she still felt rushed and out of breath. Though the morning was young, the day promised to be a scorcher. The sun had risen a fuzzy glowing peach and already at eight o'clock the air was thick and muggy. The sky was hazy, a combination of high humidity and smoke from distant Canadian fires.

Allie had used double her usual antiperspirant, anticipating an attack of nerves during the meeting. She plunked her coffee cup down on her desk and ran into the bathroom. After peeing for the third time that morning, she checked her hair in the mirror and sniffed her armpits. I already look bedraggled, she thought. And smell like I ran a mile. She hurriedly coaxed the escaping strands of her hair back into its professional-appearing bun.

Her phone beeped with a text from her dad.

Knock 'em dead. You'll be great!

Hope so, she thought as she answered with a thumbs up emoji. Allie raised her arms in a victorious stance. I've got this, she thought. "I've got this!" she said out loud as she left the bathroom.

George had just arrived and caught her self-affirmation. "Of course you do, Allegra. This will go well, I know it. You deserve this, and the festival deserves to have your leadership. It will all work out."

Allie grimaced. "I hope I seem more confident than I feel," she said.

"Hey, 'fake it 'til you make it,' right? That's always been my motto." George chuckled. "Ok, let's get ready. Your report was great. I assume you made the minor changes I suggested last night? Good. So we'll print a copy for each member of the committee. Let's see, it's Ken, Esther, Peter, and Robin—that's four."

Allie sat down at her laptop and called up the report. As the printer spit out the copies, she busied herself by setting a pad and pen at each place on the conference table, as well as a glass. She grabbed a glass pitcher from the kitchenette and filled it with ice cubes and water. She also started a fresh pot of coffee. When the printer finished, Allie clipped each set of pages together and placed them at five seats at the table.

George looked in and rearranged the seating. "Let's not put anyone at the head of the table," he said. "That will give the other members of the committee a chance to get a word in edgewise with Ken." He winked at Allie. "Ah, the tricks you learn as a managing director..."

Oh, yeah, Allie thought, Ken Hanson. She'd been trying not to dwell on him, probably the least enthusiastic member of the committee but also the chair. He would undoubtedly wear a sports jacket, navy blue, no doubt, and a button-down shirt. Maybe white or maybe pale yellow. Or if he was feeling really wild, a blue and white tattersall. She smiled ruefully—she would soon know which. She heaved a sigh. Well, she could count on his khaki slacks, that was for sure. And loafers.

The door to the office rattled and Allie looked to see who had arrived. Hooray, it was Esther.

"Are you ready for this, dear?" Esther clasped Allie's hands and looked into her eyes with a smile. "I am so excited to think that you might be running the show here! There have been too many gray men in suits."

George cleared his throat to let Esther know he was right behind her.

"Oh, George, I think you've done an excellent job, don't get me wrong. It's just that it will be refreshing to have a woman in charge for a change. No offense meant."

"None taken." George smiled.

"And I'm so happy for you. Imagine, you're getting married! You couldn't have chosen a nicer fellow."

"I certainly agree," said George. "And I never would have thought I'd have the chance for marital bliss, until Obergefell in 2015."

"Hey, we passed same-sex marriage in Maine earlier than that," said Allie.

"Yes," said Esther, "It was 2012, I believe."

"But I didn't live in Maine then," explained George. "Anyway, it's wonderful and I'm very excited."

The office door opened, and Robin Hall and Peter Drumlin entered. They greeted Esther and Allie.

"And what are you excited about, George?" asked Robin. She was a local piano teacher. Tall and thin with a patrician air, she used to seem daunting to Allie. That is, until she caught Robin giggling helplessly over a Victor Borge video that Esther had shared with her. Allie had always loved those comic videos, especially the one where Victor Borge turned a rendition of Beethoven's 'Moonlight Sonata' into 'Happy Birthday.'[21]

"He's excited about his upcoming nuptials," said Esther.

"Oh, yes, of course. Will it be a big wedding, George?"

"No, very small. Just immediate family. Thank goodness." George wiped his brow in mock relief.

"So we're waiting for Ken?" asked Peter. "Why don't we head into the conference room. I'd love a cup of coffee, if there's any available."

As Allie turned to get the coffee, George waylaid her. "Coming right up, Peter," he said. "Anyone else?"

Both Esther and Robin raised their hands, and George headed to the office kitchenette just as Ken Hanson strode through the door.

"Ready to get started, all?" he boomed. He and the other three headed into the conference room. "I'll take a cup of coffee, too," he said to George as George passed out the three cups he'd poured.

"Of course," George said, smiling. "Cream and sugar are on the table," he added.

Esther, Robin, and Peter took seats on one side of the table, and Ken sat across from them.

Ken spread both hands on the table before him. "Now that we're all here, let's begin," he said. "George, I think you and Allegra should wait outside the room. We'll call you in when and if we need you."

George gave Allie a quick look and headed out of the room. Allie followed behind.

After she closed the door, she turned to George. "You know, we'll be able to hear every word they say." She gestured toward the air vent in the wall.

"I know," George whispered. "Let's go in my office so we can't hear them."

Allie brought her laptop and answered some emails from audience members about ticket availability, while George busied himself at his computer. After about 20 minutes, Ken opened the door to the conference room and beckoned to Allie.

"Allegra, please join us," he said. "We have some questions for you."

Allie took in a big breath and walked into the room. Ken motioned for her to sit at the head of the table. All four faces turned toward her. They looked serious. Allie wished she'd set a glass of water at her seat. Her mouth felt like Death Valley.

"I should say that I was rather doubtful about this idea," said Ken. "I mean, putting a 24-year-old in charge of a large arts organization..."

"25. I believe Allegra had a birthday recently," Esther said.

"Alright, 25, then. Anyway, as I was saying, with the personnel issues and the fiduciary responsibilities and the audience pressures and, well, everything it takes to run an organization like this, I just didn't think any *25*-year-old," he said, looking at Esther, "would be up to the task."

Ken paused. Allie braced herself to hear the bad news.

Ken looked at the other four members of the committee. "However, you have some powerful advocates here. I believe they came prepared to plead your case, even before reading your report about the work you did this spring."

Robin took advantage of a slight pause in Ken's speech to break in. "We've known you for a long time, Allegra. We've watched you grow into a capable, hardworking, trustworthy young woman."

Allie smiled weakly. Room to hope?

"That said, I was concerned about the ongoing health of the Kennimac SummerFest Music Festival," Ken said, taking control of the conversation again. "I still am."

Allie's heart sank.

"But your report, and the advocacy of your supporters, has led me to think that for the next couple of months, having you at the helm wouldn't be a terrible idea. And in the meantime, we can initiate a serious search for George's permanent replacement. So, Allegra, the interim managing director's position is yours if you want it."

Allie blinked. Wait. What did he say? "I... yes... I definitely would like it. To be the interim director. Yes, I would."

Esther, Peter, and Robin smiled as Ken shuffled the papers in front of him. "Your report was comprehensive and detailed, Allegra. I think that none of us realized how much extra work you did this spring to keep things going while George was in the hospital and then recuperating. That, more than the glowing recommendations of your longtime acquaintances, gave me the faith in your abilities to offer you the position. I would like your report to accompany my email recommending your promotion to the entire board."

"Wow," said Allie. "Thank you. I appreciate your support." Allie looked around the table. "I appreciate all of your support."

"And you'll need it as we go through this transition, Allegra," said Esther. "Be sure to call on us for help as various things arise."

"I'm sure she will," said Ken.

"And your father," said Peter. "I'm sure you'll have him as backup if needed."

Ken looked like he had bitten into a sour grape. "That will hardly be necessary," he said. "Let's bring George in to discuss some of the details. Allegra, would you tell him we're ready?"

Allie got up from her chair and opened the door. She wasn't surprised to see that George was sitting in her desk chair, positioned right by the vent. He'd heard the entire discussion. He flashed Allie two thumbs up and followed her back into the conference room, where he congratulated the committee on reaching the right decision.

As the six of them discussed what needed to happen for the transition, there was a commotion in the outer office. Luke burst into the conference room, stopping short when he saw who was there.

"Uh, Allie," he said. "Umm, I just heard that there's been a death... I thought you should know..."

She sucked in a quick breath, memories of the spring tragedies flooding her brain.

"Where and who?" asked Ken.

"I don't know who, but it happened out at the Kennimac Inn, according to the police department text. They said the road is blocked because they're investigating a death."

Twenty-Eight

There were seven cottages and ten rooms at the inn. Allie did a mental count of the SummerFest musicians who were staying there. Anne, of course, in her cottage, and Tony Bainbridge in his. And Ruben and Thomas in the cottage they shared. She hurried to her desk and looked at the festival housing list on her laptop: two members of the SummerFest Woodwind Quintet had rooms in the inn, Krissy Kanafax, oboist, and Carol McCreary, clarinetist. Oh, and Steve Kennison, the quintet's bassoonist, was also staying at the inn. So, of the seventeen accommodations, seven SummerFest musicians were occupants. Allie crossed her fingers, desperate for good luck. Surely none of them were liable to be mixed up in a shooting. In fact, they all must be in rehearsal right now. Allie sprinted out the office door, bashing into Luke as she ran by, on her way to the barn.

As she got close, she could hear the orchestra warming up. Suddenly, a thought struck her. The gun, Anne's gun. It had been so weird to find that in her kitchen. She shook her head as if to clear the memory. It was simply a coincidence, wasn't it, she thought. Of course it was.

She wrenched the barn's main door open. There, just inside, were Thomas and Ruben, laughing together about something.

She grabbed Thomas's sleeve. "What happened at the cottages?"

Both men stared at Allie. "What?" "What do you mean?"

Thomas started again. "Allie, what are you talking about? We left pretty early this morning. It was totally quiet then."

"Yeah," added Ruben. "We had no coffee in the house, so we decided to get here early after a stop at Dunkin'."

"At 7:00 am," said Thomas.

Allie looked around. "Is Tony here? Or Anne?"

"I haven't seen them yet," said Ruben, as Thomas shook his head. Just then, Thomas's phone buzzed. "Oh, here's a text from Tony. He says he's going to be late, and he wants me to start the rehearsal."

Allie looked around. The orchestra members were now mostly in their seats, and Thomas was walking up to the podium. Where was Anne? Her seat at the front of the cello section was empty. Maybe the two of them were stuck at the inn because of the shooting, she thought. After all, Tony hadn't alluded to any catastrophe in his text to Thomas. She stood still for a moment, trying to figure out what she should do. Her phone vibrated, and she quickly pulled it out of her pocket, hoping that it was a message from Anne.

And...?

It was from her father. She realized she hadn't told him about the result of the meeting. For a moment, she relived that feeling of euphoria that came when she realized she was going to get the job.

Dad! I'm in — fill you in later

Maybe I should send Anne a text, too, she thought. Then, if she answers, I'll know everything is ok.

Hey, I got the job. Woot! Woot!

Allie's phone immediately pinged, but it was her father, saying, "Great!" She waited for a reply from Anne, but there was nothing. Silence. Anne's probably in the bathroom or something, Allie reasoned. Or in the car on her way to the rehearsal. She knew how much Anne hated being late. Allie could envision Anne driving as fast as possible without catching the attention of the police. She expected her teacher to come bursting through the door to the barn, hauling her cello behind her, waving and saying, "Sorry, sorry. I got stuck because of a problem at the inn."

A problem at the inn. In reality, it was a *death* at the inn. Allie felt a thrumming in her ears. Thomas picked up his baton and gave the upbeat for the orchestra to start.

Suddenly, the barn door did burst open, but it was Anthony Bainbridge who rushed through. Thomas heard him enter and turned to look. Seeing the wild expression on his face, Thomas cut the musicians off and waited for Tony, who set his portfolio of music on a chair and jumped up on the stage.

"Sorry I'm late, but I think we should all take a break now," he said in a breathless voice.

"But...?" Thomas said.

"Take twenty minutes, everyone," Tony said to the orchestra. "Please be back in your seats, ready to play in twenty minutes." He turned to Thomas. "I need to go to the office," he said in a lowered voice. "Have you seen George or Allegra?"

Thomas motioned to the back of the hall. "Allie's right there."

She came forward as Tony rushed to meet her. "We need to go to the office and find George," he said. He grabbed Allie's hand and pulled her out of the barn and up the hill toward the office.

"Why? What's going on?" asked Allie, her head spinning as she tried to keep up with the conductor.

"Wait until I have you both together," he said.

George, organizing some papers in the main office, met the two of them with a look of confusion.

"Allegra, George, I think you should sit down," said Tony. They backed into chairs and waited for what he was going to say.

"Something unimaginable..." he started. "Something bloody awful. ..."

"What?" asked George, bewildered.

"There's been a gun accident. A shooting. With a gun." Tony stopped for a breath. "Anne Kirschner is dead."

"No!" cried Allie. "It can't be!" Her face crumpled, and she bent over into a ball. A moment later, she jumped up and ran to the bathroom. The two men could hear her retching. George went to the door. "Allie, are you alright? Allie?"

She wiped her face and came out of the bathroom, motioning wordlessly at Tony.

"I don't know what happened," he said. "Just as I was leaving for rehearsal, a parade of emergency vehicles came barreling down the road to the cottages, sirens blaring, and stopped at Anne's cottage. They blocked the road, and when I asked them what was up, they said someone was hurt. Then RuthEllen Cox came out of the cottage and walked to my car and said that Anne had been shot."

"But if they said someone was hurt, how do you know she was dead?" asked Allie.

"RuthEllen said she was. She saw her. Then the police told RuthEllen to stop talking to bystanders and come back toward them. They interviewed me for a few minutes before they let me go. Asked if I'd heard any gunshots. Of course I had not. Bloody hell. Even if she's alive, she probably isn't going to be able to... I can't believe it..."

George had turned a pasty white. He returned to his chair after helping Allie to hers. A siren sounded outside as a police car turned into the festival parking lot. A minute later, Chief Chester Knowles entered the office.

"There's been a death," he said. "It appears to be a suicide. But until we know for sure, I'm going to have to ask you to make sure that you and the rest of the festival personnel stick around while we investigate."

II: Largo Lacrimoso

“Music is my life, and my life is music. Anyone who does not understand this is not worthy of being called a human being.” —*Clara Wieck Schumann (German pianist and composer, 1819-1896)*

Twenty-Nine

Anne? Dead? Allie couldn't wrap her head around that thought. Her mind felt as though it had grayed out and a great yawning hole filled with mist had opened up. Allie closed her eyes and pictured Anne's smiling face, her short curly hair a mixture of silver and blond, her sharply perceptive hazel eyes. How could she now be dead? Gone from this world? It was incomprehensible that Anne was gone forever.

No longer in Allie's life.

All the color drained from Allie's sight. The sounds of the office receded. She felt numb. Empty. She sat at her desk, motionless, staring ahead, sightless. Then, slowly, she became aware of someone whispering her name.

"Allegra... Allegra." George's raspy voice broke through Allie's blank thoughts. "I'm so sorry. I know she was a close friend of yours. But... her passing means we have a lot of extra work to do. *You* have a lot of extra work. The concert..."

Allie met George's kind expression with a blaze of anger. "How can you think about that right now?" she asked, her voice catching. "It's horrible. I can't... It can't be right. Not Anne." She blinked, her eyes tearless. "It must be a mistake. It's got to be!"

"I'm sorry, Allie. It seems there's no question." George's voice was soft.

"But how? Why? The police don't know anything about it. They are clueless. She was perfectly happy. Suicide makes no sense!"

Allie noticed pings of messages coming into her phone as it lay on her desk. Her father. Luke, orchestra members. She quickly fumbled for it; did she have a voice message from Anne? Yes! There was one from a week ago. Allie played the recording, shocked at how vibrant and lively Anne's voice was. There was some mistake. This couldn't be true. She put the phone back down.

"Maybe you want to go home and take some time?" George was hesitant. "I mean, take the rest of the morning?"

Allie covered her face in her hands.

"Look, Allie. This is awful, I understand that. And it will take time for you to get over it..."

"Get over it!" Allie said from between her fingers. "George, you don't get it! This is... this is... I..." Her voice trailed away.

George lightly patted the top of her head, then turned and went back into his office.

"Allie. Allegra." David Brewster shook his daughter's shoulder. "Allie, I'm going to take you home."

Allie looked up at her father, solemnly standing next to her, his eyes full of tears.

"Oh, Dad," she said, standing and burying her face in his chest. He gently gathered up her long hair and encircled her in a powerful hug. "I just can't believe it," she said, her voice muffled by his shirt.

"I know, I know." Together, father and daughter rocked, both heavy with sorrow.

"I love her so much. She is such a good person. Was..." Allie's voice broke.

"Let's go, honey. I'll bring you home. Archie is waiting for us."

At the thought of Archie, Allie was hit with a new spasm of pain. Anne loved that little Westie. When Allie was younger, sometimes during lessons at the house, Anne would play a funny tune for Archie and he would gambol like a baby lamb as if dancing to the music.

"Nothing will ever be the same," Allie said.

"I know, I know," her father whispered, as he led his daughter out to his waiting truck.

"What about Pablo?" Allie asked.

"We'll get the Volvo later today or tomorrow. Let's just go home."

Thirty

The weather put a lie to the tragedy: the sun was fiercely bright. Vacationers clogged Main Street, enjoying treats from the Barnloft Bakery at sidewalk cafe tables, traipsing in and out of art galleries and gift shops, and crossing the street anywhere but at the crosswalks. Decked out in bright summer colors, the tourists wore a rainbow of coral pink and cerulean blue, with a dab of grass green, summer white, and strawberry red thrown in. Allie felt the colors as an affront and turned away from the car window. How could people be happy? How would she ever be happy again? Anne's death tore a huge void in the fabric of Allie's life.

"Oh, come on, hurry up," said her father to himself, as he was forced to stop the car while a passel of oblivious tourists jaywalked across the street. He sighed impatiently.

"Don't, Dad," Allie said, worried that he might beep the horn. "We'll get there."

There was no rush. There was no time. It was standing still, much slower than those tourists. Ahead of Allie was an open pit of time. A black hole. Allie shut her eyes. How could Anne have done this? Allie couldn't make sense of it. Not Anne. She had too much to live for. At that thought, Allie's eyes flew open. "Cara and Andrew," she said to her father. "Who will tell them? Oh my god." The tears welled up once again as she thought of Anne's two kids, teenagers on the cusp of adulthood.

"I think Esther is calling them," said David. "They've known her since they started coming to the festival with their mom."

"Esther is the right person to do it. I couldn't, without breaking down. Oh, Dad, what's going to happen? To Anne?" Allie couldn't bring herself to say 'to Anne's body.'

"Let's not worry about that now, sweetheart. I thing the best thing for you is to take a few hours to..."

"To what? Get over it? I'm never going to be able to get over it!"

"No, no. To let it sink in, I suppose. Your life is going to have to continue, your work, the people who are counting on you. You'll have to figure out a way... You just took on a huge responsibility."

"But now George will have to stay, right?" Allie sat up straighter. She didn't see any way she would be able to take on the responsibilities of the festival management. Not now.

"No, Allie. George will still be leaving. Anne's death won't stop him from marrying Grant and moving to Minnesota. Life goes on, sweetheart."

"How can you say that? Life for Anne is NOT going on." Allie covered her eyes. "How could this happen? I just don't get it."

When Allie and her father got home, she retreated to her old bedroom. It was still filled with her things, the stuffies she had lined up along the side of her bed against the wall, her posters of favorite musicians and musical groups, her awards from various competitions. She closed the curtains and threw herself on the bed, burying her face into the quilt her late grandmother had made years ago. She thought she'd cry, but no tears came. Instead, there was an ache in her chest and a lump in her throat that seemed to block her breath. How could it be, that someone could be so alive one day and gone forever the next? Gone forever, *forever*—what did that mean? Never to hear Anne's laugh again, her calm words of advice. Never to feel her warm hug—the hug she had given Allie just last night as they said goodbye. Allie pounded the quilt with her fists. How could this be? How could Anne have done this? To her, to Cara and Andrew, to Anne herself? How?

Allie felt something soft nudging her side. "Archie," she said, "Archie, you came to console me." And as her tears flowed, Allie buried her face in the little dog's fur.

"Allie?" There was a light tapping at her bedroom door. "Allie, your mother is on the phone. Do you want to talk with her?" David Brewster had brought Allie's phone upstairs.

Allie cleared her throat. "I guess so." She sat up and took the phone as her dad handed it to her. "Hi, Mom," she muttered.

"Allie!" Her mother's voice was crystal clear, as if coming from the next room instead of her office in Switzerland. "I worried when I hadn't heard anything..."

"Didn't Dad tell you just now?"

"So, everything went well?"

"What?"

"Your new job. Taking over as interim festival manager. I thought you were going to text me after the board meeting. What did you think I was talking about?"

Allie groaned. She didn't want to say it. "Didn't Dad tell you? The meeting was fine. But..." She choked up.

"What is it? What's the matter, Allegra?"

"It's Anne, Mom."

"Anne Kirschner?"

"Yes."

"What about Anne?"

"She... she's dead."

"Oh, honey. I'm so sorry. Was she sick? Or was there an accident? What happened?"

"I don't know, Mom. The police say she killed herself. She had a gun. But I can't believe it. It makes no sense."

"Had you seen her recently? How did she seem?"

"I saw her just last night! She was fine. The same as always. She didn't seem depressed or sad or anything." Allie started crying.

"Oh, hon, I wish I could give you a hug. Anne means so much to you, I know. Take a deep breath..."

"Maybe we should talk later, Mom," Allie said between sniffles. "I can't really..."

"That's fine, Allegra. I know you'll need to pull yourself together so you can take on your new responsibilities."

"Oh, Mom, I don't think I can, not now."

"Of course you can. Think of it this way: you'll be doing it for Anne. For the SummerFest that she loved. For her kids, who will need all the support they can get. Somehow, you'll get through it. You can do it, Allegra. Right?"

Allie took a ragged breath. "I don't know. I'll have to try. I will. I gotta go, Mom."

"Love you, hon. I'm so sorry. Take care of yourself. You can handle this. Don't let yourself down."

Thirty-One

Allie woke in the afternoon light slanting through her window. She had dreamt of Anne. In the spring, Allie and her father had played a duet during the memorial service for Sylvia Abbott, the woman who had been murdered. In her dream, Anne was telling Allie that she wanted Allie to play at her, Anne's, funeral, and she wanted Allie to play an arrangement of "Ring Around the Rosy." Allie kept insisting that there wasn't a good arrangement of that tune. Finally she had said to Anne, "You don't get to choose, since you killed yourself. That's against the rules." At those words, Anne had crumbled into a pile of ashes that flew away in the wind. Allie was overcome with grief as she tried to catch the ashes as they scattered. She woke up with tears streaming down her cheeks; the hair around her face was wet, and her pillow was soaked.

Allie looked at her watch. Three o'clock—she'd been asleep for a couple of hours. She sat up and took stock of herself. She'd have to keep going. Her mother was right: people needed her. She had an important job now. It made her feel a little better to think that she was doing it in Anne's honor.

"Dad," Allie called from the top of the stairs, "Can you give me a ride back to the office?" Her voice was oddly strained.

"You ready? Want something to eat before you go?"

"No, I just need to get there and figure out what comes next." She washed her face and brushed her hair, noticing how colorless her face looked in the mirror. As she walked down the stairs, she noticed that she had several texts, including one from Luke.

Al, I can't believe this. I know you must be wrecked. its like a bad dream happening all over again. Deja vu. I can come to the cottage tonite and cook you a good dinner and wrap you in my arms and rock you to sleep. would you like that? Oh Al, I am so sad Anne did this. I love you.

But *did* Anne do this? wondered Allie. She still couldn't believe it. Clearly Luke believed it, but that didn't make it true. If anything, this must have been an accident. Maybe the gun went off when Anne was moving it to a safer place. She did say she thought it was loaded.

"Thanks, Dad," Allie said, as she buckled her seatbelt.

"You doing ok?" David Bewster understood what a shock this was to his daughter. In the past, Allie had experienced loss. People she loved had died—her grandparents on her mom's side, for example. And she'd endured the end of her parents' marriage and her mother's move far away. That was real loss for sure, but not a permanent, gone-forever loss. And her grandparents, though beloved, were in their late eighties and had both been sick for awhile. So it wasn't a shock. Not a punch to the gut like Anne's death. He rubbed Allie's left shoulder as he drove along.

"I have to be," Allie said. "People are counting on me and I'm not going to let them down." She clenched her jaw. "Like Mom always says, 'Sometimes you have to do what you didn't think you could.'"

"Yes, that's right," said her dad. "Yup..."

They rode in silence the rest of the way to the festival office. When they arrived, Allie leaned over and gave her father a kiss on the cheek. "Thanks, Dad. Don't worry about me. I'll be ok—maybe hurting a lot—but ok in the long run." She gave him a lopsided smile and got out of the car.

"Want to come to the house for dinner?" he asked.

"No, thanks, I think I just want to go home to the cottage and be by myself."

"Well, let me know if you change your mind."

Allie shut the car door and turned toward the office. The place looked different to her, not as friendly and cheery. Allie sighed as she opened the office door.

Thirty-Two

"Ah, Allie, you're back. Good." George brought her a soda, something she didn't usually drink, but the fizzy cold liquid tasted good. It was hot in the office. Clearly the air conditioner was too feeble to keep up with the heat and humidity . Allie held the chilled can to her cheek. Focus on the work, she told herself. Focus on the work.

George was watching her. "I know there's a lot to do," Allie said between sips. "Where do you want to start?"

"To my mind, the biggest emergency is the concert in three weeks. Without Anne to play the new concerto, I don't see how we can keep that on the schedule."

Allie squeezed her eyes shut, trying to block the memory of listening to Anne work on the solo part just last night. "Ruben's piece is really hard," she said. "I doubt another cellist could pick it up and play it well enough in such a short amount of time."

"That's what I guessed," said George. "I think that will be a blow to Ruben."

"Yeah, we already had some decent interest from reviewers. Wasn't the guy from *The New Yorker* going to come? And someone from *The New York Times*, right?"

"Oh, they're always happy to come to the Maine coast in the summer," George said. "Here comes Bainbridge," he added, glancing out the window. "I'm sure he'll have an idea of what we should do."

"Allegra, George," Tony nodded to the two and took a chair. "So, here we are." He looked defeated, Allie thought. Older. Grayer. Extremely sad.

"We were just talking about Ruben's concerto, Tony," said Allie. "Have you thought about what we should do, since Anne..." Allie choked up, then took a big breath. "I don't think anyone else could pick it up in such a short time."

"I'm in total agreement. So we'll need to find another piece to fill in. It'll have to be fairly major—that concerto was at least forty minutes long," said Tony.

"Do we want to program another cello concerto instead? I'm fairly sure we could get someone decent to play the Elgar or the Dvorak..." said George.

"What about the Errolyn Wallen cello concerto?" asked Allie. "That's a terrific, and not too long, concerto. Though I don't know how many cellists have it in their repertoire yet..."

"That's a thought," said Tony. "I wonder if we could find someone. Probably could..." He looked up at the ceiling, as if mentally cataloguing the list of cellists he knew.

"There are the two Philip Glass cello concertos. Perhaps one of them would do," said Tony.

The door to the office opened again. This time, Ruben walked in. "Just the people I was hoping to find," he said. "Look, I've been thinking..."

"As have we," said Tony. "We're considering substituting one of the Glass concertos. I was about to ring some folks I know to see who might be available."

"Well, the Glass... they are good. But, hang on," said Ruben. "I had a different thought." He sat in the one remaining chair. "I have a piece for orchestra that shares some of the same characteristics of the concerto. Not nearly as hard, though. I was thinking of Bartok's Concerto for Orchestra[22] when I wrote it. It follows the same form, roughly, and lasts about the same. I have the score here in Maine with me." He smiled ruefully. "It hasn't been performed in its entirety in a concert yet."

George, Allie, and Tony looked at each other. Finally Tony spoke, "Can I take a look at it? What kind of shape is it in? Has anyone gone over it with you?"

Ruben cleared his throat. "Clayton Sharpe didn't love it, to be honest. He thought it was 'derivative.' But that was three years ago—I've worked on it since and I'd say it's much improved. I have the score back at the cottage."

"Well, then, let's go to your digs and have a look. No promises, now. What's the instrumentation like?"

"Nothing outrageous. Same as what you've already got here, pretty much. You might need to hire another percussionist."

"No doubt." Tony said, raising an eyebrow. "We might as well take a look at it." The two quickly left the office, Tony saying over his shoulder, "I'll let you know what I think as soon as I can. No promises," he added to Ruben as they disappeared.

"If that works, it would be a good solution," said George, "don't you think?"

"I suppose so," said Allie. "Though I was really looking forward to the cello being the main attraction. I guess this plan might be more realistic. It's easier than trying to find a soloist at the last moment." She looked at George. "It could have been a big break for someone," she said, shrugging.

"True," said George. "But at this point, you know, with all that's happened, I don't think we want to take any chances." George yawned. "I'm beat. This has been one hell of a day. I'm going to head home—we have started packing. You ok here?"

"Guess so," said Allie. "Go ahead. I'll close the office at 5:00."

Allie spent the next hour or so responding to emails, texts, and voicemail messages. Orchestra members were distraught at the news of Anne's death. Everyone really loved and respected her, thought Allie. She wondered if Anne knew that she'd been so beloved. Almost every message contained the phrase, "What a loss."

An email from Esther Swift explained she hadn't yet reached Anne's children, and was also trying to connect with their aunt, who lived in Chicago. Allie's heart sank at the thought of them hearing about their mother's death. She and Esther agreed to meet tomorrow to talk about the next steps regarding a service for Anne.

At about four-fifty-five, Chief Knowles stuck his head in the door of the office. "We'll be around interviewing people tomorrow, Allegra. Just so you know."

"That's fine, Chief Knowles. We'll all be here." With that, Allie closed her laptop, turned off the printer and the lights, and locked the door. It would be a relief to get to the cottage and have some solitude. Then she remembered Luke's text.

She responded:

Not tonight need time by myself

Thirty-Two

Allie took a big breath of the balsam-laden air as she drove Pablo down the dirt driveway to her cottage. The old Volvo's air conditioning had died the summer before and Allie hadn't bothered to get it fixed, driving instead with the windows wide open. In Maine summers, air conditioning used to be a superfluous luxury used for only a few days. Though, to be truthful, Allie thought, these days it was necessary more and more.

Global climate change. She felt her stomach sink with a feeling of dread. Yet another depressing subject. She remembered Anne talking about the ways the SummerFest could be more responsible in combatting the environmental challenges. She had encouraged players to carpool to rehearsals. She and Allie had discussed ways to save paper on the printed programs, though Anne's idea of making the programs available online by QR code didn't fly with George, who thought older audience members wouldn't be able to manage the online access. "And besides," he had added, "Our advertisers want their program ads to be visible for more than the night of the concert. People like to refer to their programs for days afterward." Allie had to agree that online programs might be a stretch for the SummerFest crowd.

Anne was always trying to make things better, to fight for equality and fairness. Tears filled Allie's eyes as she parked and headed toward the cottage. She stopped on the deck and sat in one of the rickety slatted rocking chairs, letting the sorrow crash down once again. The world was now much poorer without Anne Kirschner in it. "We are the change we seek," she once said to Allie, "That's a quote from Barack that I try to follow." A Chicago native, Anne had been a huge supporter of Obama, inspired by his calls for activism. She was the conscience of the festival in so many ways, thought Allie. How could she have deserted her friends, the festival she loved? How could she leave her cello? Cara and Andrew? Especially Cara and Andrew! How could Anne leave her kids behind? It didn't make sense, it just didn't. She hadn't seemed at all depressed or upset. Was there no note explaining her suicide?

The light was fading with a rosy glow out on the water, glimpsed through the trees. Humidity still lay heavy in the air, and Allie wondered if she'd find it too hot to sleep. Would she ever really sleep again? There was no breeze. Through her tears, the air looked thick and milky. Soon it would be dark. Allie heaved herself out of the rocker and entered the kitchen. She wasn't hungry, but she knew she should eat something. The leftover piece of pizza from the night before at Anne's cottage caught her eye when she opened the fridge. She felt sick at the thought of eating it.

Allie was sitting at the small round table, picking at a peanut butter and jelly sandwich made from two stale ends of bread, when she heard a car's wheels crunch down the driveway. It better not be Luke, she thought, I can't deal with him tonight. But it didn't sound like Luke's car.

Thomas knocked on the screen door. He saw Allie at the table, chin in hand, looking down, a circle of light from the hanging lamp above her head the only light in the cottage. Maybe he shouldn't have come, he briefly thought. But... "Allie?"

"Thomas, is that you?" Allie looked at the door but couldn't make out who was standing on the other side in the dark. "What are you doing here? It's late."

"Can I come in for a second?" Without waiting for an answer, he opened the screen and came in and sat in the other kitchen chair. "I need to talk to you. It's kind of an emergency."

Allie closed her eyes and sighed. "What," she said.

"I know you're upset and I'm sorry to bother you. But this came up."

"And..." The word trailed off.

Thomas was not sure how to proceed; Allie seemed so dejected, so unlike herself. "Ok, well, I had a talk with Tony about a half hour ago..." He grimaced. "I guess I didn't know how much he cared about Anne Kirschner. I mean, her death has really hit him hard. And, well, he wants me to cover for him on Friday night."

Allie opened her eyes wide. "Are you serious?"

"Yes. I think he's going to talk with George and you tomorrow morning. Or send you an email tonight, or something. He wasn't really that clear." Thomas pushed his hair back on his forehead. "Jesus, it's hot. Could I get a drink of water?"

Allie motioned to the cabinet by the sink. "I guess you are the assistant conductor," she said. "I'm surprised that Tony is dropping out, but he must think you can cover." What's Tony's problem, she thought to herself, the rest of us are carrying on. A small flicker of anger showed in her expression.

"I hope so," said Thomas, filling a glass. "I know the program pretty well. It's a lot, Friday night *and* Sunday afternoon—two different concerts in one weekend." He nodded. "But that's what I'm here for, right?"

"Sure." Somehow, Allie wasn't that interested in Thomas's news.

He took a long gulp and wiped his mouth sheepishly. "You know, Allie, what you said the other night about how I should approach the family concert on Sunday, that was really helpful. I wanted you to know that."

"Good, glad it helped."

Thomas looked around the cottage. It looked mysterious in the shadows, the wood even darker than in daylight. He noticed a faint odor of camphor as if mothballs were somewhere nearby. The surface of the kitchen table was sticky in the heat and the glass of water was slippery in his hand. He set it down and put his hands in his lap. He cleared his throat. "I know you're hurting," he said. "This was a shock for everyone, but I know you were close with Anne."

"For many, many years." Allie's voice was strained.

"I know. Look, I should go," he said, without moving to leave. "I dread going back to the Kennimac."

Allie shot him a look.

"Not because of that," he said. "Though that's so sad. It's because of Ruben—he's like a madman tonight. He's so excited that Tony might choose to use his Concerto for Orchestra instead of the cello concerto. He's madly doing revisions and singing the parts. God, I'll never be able to sleep. And it seems so wrong, somehow. Like he's taking advantage of Anne's, you know..."

"I thought you two got along," Allie said.

"Oh, we do. Pretty much. It's just, now, I could use a little quiet." He smiled. "I guess that's what ear pods are for."

"Right." Allie stood up to encourage Thomas to leave, and he took the hint.

"I'll head out. Thanks, Allie, for everything." He reached out to give Allie a hug, but she evaded him. In the awkward silence, he patted her arm and said, "I just want you to know that I'm here for you," as he walked out the door.

Silence blanketed the cottage after the screen door's spring-loaded slam. Allie picked up the water glass and her plate, set them in the sink, turned off the light, and drifted to the dark bedroom, shedding her clothes as she went.

Thirty-Four

A thin gray light greeted Allie in the morning, sun hiding behind high clouds. She had slept, a little. And restlessly. But she was ready to face her work at the office; it would be better than moping around the cottage. She made herself a cup of coffee and picked out her clothes for the day. It was cooler, though not by much. A sleeveless shift of light cotton would do. She slid it over her bra and underwear, applied deodorant, brushed her teeth, splashed water on her face, caught her hair up in a messy bun, sipped the coffee, and picked up her phone to check email.

From Anthony Bainbridge 11:30 PM
To gpark@summerfest.org
abrewster@summerfest.org

George and Allegra,

I'm writing to warn you of a topic I wish to discuss in the morning: my decision to have Thomas conduct the Friday evening concert. I know that your attitude to Anne's death is to, as they say, keep calm and carry on, but I find I cannot face the public as soon as two days from now. I cared deeply for Anne, more deeply than you know, and I am, in a word, bereft. I just can't summon up the necessary joyful attitude to conduct the bloody happy tunes on Friday's program. I'm sorry if this is an added burden on you, but it's one I'm sure you can handle with aplomb. I will—I promise—be back in form for next week's rehearsals and concerts.

Tony

Just as Thomas had said last night, Tony was ducking out of conducting the concert on Friday. She thought it was no big deal. In fact, in contrast to the changed shape of her life and what she thought she had known to be true, this was a minor wrinkle. Tony was right about one thing, though. She hadn't known that he was so devoted to Anne. She didn't think that Anne knew it, either.

"So I assume you read Tony's email from last night?" George was already in the office. He'd opened all the windows to catch whatever morning cool air was available, and a lethargic bumblebee buzzed around the room in a random pattern. George waved a sheaf of papers at it, trying to shoo it to an open window.

"I saw it this morning," said Allie. "And Thomas had already let me know it was coming." George noted that she spoke the words flatly, with a lack of enthusiasm. She didn't even flinch when the bee rambled by her head. He hoped she would be able to recover her usual energy; she'd need it when he left.

The sound of another car entering the parking area by the office took them by surprise. It was early yet, and orchestra members weren't due to arrive for another couple of hours. After the sound of a car door closing, Tony Bainbridge appeared in the door. His normally frenetic appearance, short spiked silver hair and frosty sapphire eyes beneath bushy silver eyebrows, seemed somehow deflated.

"I assume you got my email message," he said.

"We did, Tony," said George as Allie nodded.

"I'm sorry to be such a bloody wanker about this, but I just can't stand the thought of standing on a podium and conducting gleeful happy music. I mean, Copland's 'Hoe Down,'[1] the Overture to Glinka's 'Russlan and Ludmilla,'[2] , the bloody Grieg piano concerto, more sparkling froth—ugh—can't do it." He wagged his head from side to side with a fake smile, pantomiming a foolish false joy.

"We get it, Tony," said George. "And I'm sure Thomas is happy to step in. Do you think he'll have any trouble?"

"No, no, I've already gone over the most challenging parts with him last night. He's quite game for it." He turned to go. "I'll leave it in your hands. I'm sure it will be fine. I appreciate your understanding." With that, he exited. His car threw up loose pebbles as he drove off.

"How shall we announce the substitution?" asked Allie. "Should I prepare an insert for the programs?"

George rubbed his forehead. "Yes, I think that's necessary. Why don't you take a look at Thomas's bio in our files. See if it needs to be updated or gussied up. You can run it by him before we print them." George clapped his hands. "Well, this is certainly a nice opportunity for Thomas. Let's hope he's up for it." He shook his head. "That's a surprise about Tony. No accounting for love, I guess."

"I guess," said Allie.

Tony Bainbridge's exit was followed a few minutes later by his assistant conductor's entrance. Thomas looked even more sharply handsome than usual, his dark wavy hair rolling back from his wide forehead except for a single escaped strand artfully arrayed above his left eye. He wore a black long-sleeve tee-shirt, fitted tightly enough to display his wide shoulders and slim torso. The shirt was tucked into a pair of jeans belted with a black and white beaded belt, ostensibly of a Native American design.

"So, you must be up to date on the change for Friday," Thomas said. "I'm here to conduct the rehearsal this morning."

"You'll die of the heat in that long-sleeve shirt, Thomas," said George.

"Oh, no worries," he replied. "I'm a Texas native, remember? And anyway," he gestured to his portfolio bag, "I brought another shirt if this one gets too sweaty."

"Ah, the man is prepared..." George murmured.

"Thomas," said Allie, "I was just about to start putting together an insert for Friday's program announcing you as the substitute for Tony. Is there anything in particular you want me to say?"

Thomas leaned over to Allie's desk, and together they looked at his official biography on the festival's website. Leery of the still circling bee, he dodged it several times, before backing away.

"Afraid of the bee?" asked Allie. "It won't hurt you. It's just an annoyance."

"I know. I just couldn't see..."

Together they worked on the language of the insert. Allie wanted it to be fairly short, and Thomas wanted to include some details she thought were unnecessary, but they eventually came to an agreement.

"Well, I'd better be off to prepare for rehearsal." He pulled his baton out of his bag. "Two different concerts in one weekend—I feel like I won the lottery." His excitement was in sharp contrast to Allie's downcast expression. "You feeling ok, Allie?"

"Uh, not really." She concentrated on formatting the insert. Soon the printer would be spitting out hundreds of copies.

Thirty-Five

"Oh, you again," Chief Chester Knowles said to Thomas. The police chief had walked into the office with Officer Ouelette. He had briefly suspected Thomas of murdering Sylvia Abbott in the spring and didn't hold the young man in high regard. For one thing, Knowles didn't like having to admit to being wrong.

Thomas looked at Officer Ouelette. "Hey, you're the policewoman who came to Boston to question me about the murder," he said.

"Correct," she answered.

"Well, I need to be on my way." He waved his conductor's baton as if to show what he intended to do. "If you want to talk with me this time around, we'll have to find another time. Though, I don't have anything to add. I mean, it was a suicide, right?"

Chief Knowles grunted in assent. "Ouelette," he said, "you talk with Mr. Park in his office and I'll talk with Miss Brewster here."

Allie got up and retrieved a chair for the chief to sit on. "Do you really think it was suicide?" she asked, once they both were seated.

"Look. It's pretty cut-and-dried. The victim was shot with a gun that she owned and the gun was found by her hand, with no other fingerprints on it. The cabin was locked and there was no sign of a forced entry." He folded his arms on his chest. "It all points to suicide."

"I just can't believe it. She seemed fine. Happy."

"I understand you were the last person to see her. The night before. Is that right?"

"Yes. As far as I know."

"So are you sure there were no clues that she was about to, to do what she did?"

"If you think it was suicide, then why are you talking to me?" Allie took a breath. "I'll tell you, I *don't* think she killed herself. I just don't. I can't tell you what happened, but I know she would never have done that."

Knowles shrugged his massive shoulders, straining the seams of his uniform. "Do you know how many people commit suicide in this country? Especially with guns. You hear all the talk about gun deaths—the vast majority of those are suicides. But, since she didn't leave a note, I'm trying to do my job and conduct a thorough investigation. It's best to be sure."

"Well I'm not sure. At all." Allie pointed to a poster on the wall. "See that poster? Anne was supposed to play the solo in a premiere in a couple of weeks. It is a big deal. She wouldn't have wanted to miss doing that."

"That so?" said Knowles. "Maybe it was nerves. Maybe she didn't feel up to it. I've been in this job long enough to learn that we can't read people's minds."

Allie shook her head. "Not Anne. She was a professional." She looked down for a moment. "Who else are you going to talk to?"

"Oh, maybe your head music guy, what's his name, Brainbird?"

"Anthony Bainbridge."

"May not be necessary, though. This is basically a closed case already. And with all the tourists around, we have plenty of other things to keep us busy." He turned to Officer Ouelette, who had just emerged from George's office. "Right, Ouelette?"

"Yes, sir."

"Anything of interest in there?" Knowles indicated George's office with his head.

"No, sir. Nothing out of the ordinary. No warning signs but no problems, either."

"You called this a 'closed case,'" said Allie. "What happens if something turns up to prove that Anne didn't kill herself?" She swallowed. "That someone else was involved?"

"In that unlikely case, we'll open it up again. But for now, I think our work is done here." He stood and turned to go, twisting back toward Allie at the last second. "We are sorry for your loss," he added.

"Ok," she said after a second, training her unwavering gaze on his face.

Ruben came through the office door just after the police officers' departure. "What are the police doing here?" he asked, out of breath as though he had been running.

"Oh, they're questioning people, just to be sure," answered George.

"But it was a suicide, right? I mean, why bother questioning people? Did they say there's something suspicious?"

Allie shot him a look. "I sure think there's something suspicious. Anne gave no sign that she was contemplating..." Allie paused.

"Offing herself. Right. But that's often the case with suicide." Ruben shrugged. "It's sad, but no one really knows what makes another person tick. On another topic, I want to give you the orchestra parts for my piece so you can get enough copies to go around." He placed a sheaf of papers on Allie's desk.

"Hang on there, Ruben," said George. "I'm not sure that Tony has given his final ok on the program switch. Let's let it rest for a few hours at least."

"Yeah, well, just wanted you to be prepared." Ruben turned and walked out of the office.

Thirty-Six

After Ruben left, George went back to his office. Allie sat at her desk for a while, staring blankly at the screen of her laptop. When a pile of pages from the printer started cascading onto to the floor helter-skelter, she jumped up and gathered them up. Allie noted with satisfaction that each page had two copies of the announcement of Thomas's substitution for Anthony Bainbridge, as well as a short biography; she would have to use the paper cutter to halve the pages—nice repetitive, fussy, mindless work. Then she'd have the pleasure of stuffing them in all the programs. More time-consuming but not very challenging labor. Just what she needed right now. She dragged out the paper cutter from under the work table and began to slice the pages.

"Allegra," said Esther Swift, as she walked in the office door. "Would you like some help with that? It looks like a good job for a witless volunteer." Allie shook her head but didn't say anything. Esther came closer and looked at Allie with concern. "How are you faring, dear?" she asked. "I know this must be so hard for you, and on top of George's leaving..." She gestured to the office as if he had already vacated it.

"I'll be alright," Allie said. She continued to take a few sheets of paper, straighten them, and position them on the paper cutter's surface, then quickly guillotining the pages with a powerful slice of the blade.

"Heavens," muttered Esther.

"If I don't use enough force, the papers bind and the edges are ragged," Allie explained. She stopped for a moment and looked at Esther. "You talked to Cara and Andrew, didn't you."

"I didn't actually reach them yet. I'm not sure I will." Esther grimaced. "I decided to speak first with Anne's sister in New York. Oh, that was a hard conversation. They obviously were very close."

Allie nodded. She had met Jennifer a couple of years ago, when Jennifer had stayed at the festival with Anne for a few days. She was nice enough, but like Allie's mother, she was a Type A businesswoman. According to Anne, her sister had once been an excellent bassoonist but had decided the professional musician's life was not for her. Too much uncertainty, too little pay, Anne had told Allie. And Allie could certainly understand. Although Anne made a decent living as a performing cellist and music teacher, she didn't make enough money to live in Manhattan, wear expensive clothes, and take glamorous vacations. Not that she seemed to mind, thought Allie. Anne fully enjoyed her life as she had made it. A pang struck Allie—her life, Anne's life, that was now gone, stolen. By Anne! It just didn't make sense. Allie shook her head.

"Jennifer was quite broken up on the phone," continued Esther. "Obviously, it was a total shock to her."

"What will she do?" asked Allie. "I mean, with Anne's ..."

"She's planning to fly here tomorrow. She'll land in Portland and rent a car, though I offered to pick her up. She plans to go directly to Henderson's funeral home to view her sister, then perhaps talk with the police." Esther picked up a program insert from the pile and fanned herself. "My word, it is stifling in here. That air conditioner obviously can't keep up."

"What about Andrew and Cara?"

"She said she would talk with them and see what they wanted to do. I'm sure she didn't relish that job. Such heartbreak..." Esther looked at the paper she was using as a fan. "Is Tony indisposed now? Why is young Thomas conducting the Friday concert?"

Allie wasn't sure how much of his story Tony wanted to be told. "He... I guess Anne's death has hit him hard, and he's worried about finding a replacement for the concerto premiere concert..."

"Oh, well, yes, that is an issue," Esther said. "And it's good practice for Thomas. He'll do well, I think. That, at least, is a bright spot to look forward to. Well, I'll let you carry on with your work. Are you sure you don't want some help?"

"All under control."

"As per usual, my dear." Esther gave Allie a light one-armed hug around the shoulders. "I'll let you know if I hear anything else from Jennifer," she said as she went out the door. "Be sure to drink plenty of liquids in this heat, Allegra." Her voice grew softer as she walked away from the building.

Allie returned to her straightening and slicing work, wielding the blade with a vengeance. In a few minutes, though, her concentration was interrupted by another visitor.

"Oh, Allie, sweet child," said RuthEllen Cox, as she barreled through the door holding an open box of blueberry muffins. "Look, honey, I just made these 'cause I thought y'all could use a little bucking up. After, you know..."

"Thanks, RuthEllen," said Allie, taking the box. "Not sure I feel much like eating anything, but I'm sure these will be appreciated."

"I just don't get it," said RuthEllen, seating herself in a chair. "I would never thought of Anne Kirschner as being a suicide risk. It's got me some tied up in knots, it does."

Allie nodded. What was there to add?

'I guess you were the one who saw her last—is that right?" asked the Kennimac Inn owner. "How did she seem to you, honey? Was she depressed? Sad? What did you see?"

"No! She was her normal, cheerful self. We made pizza—your heirloom tomatoes were fantastic, by the way. Then we worked on her solo, you know, the piece that Ruben Perrotta composed. She seemed really excited about playing it."

"Nothing seemed off?"

"Not at all. We laughed about the mushrooms you dropped off with the tomatoes, by the way. I didn't know you grew them. Or maybe you picked them in the woods? They looked like it, pretty rough. We were laughing because neither of us can stand mushrooms—no offense."

"Mushrooms? I didn't drop off any mushrooms. I do like them but when I need them I buy them at the grocery store. I'd be scared I might pick hallucinogenic or poisonous ones." RuthEllen looked puzzled. "Where in God's name do you suppose they came from?"

"Ann said she found them on her doorstep in a paper bag, in with your tomatoes."

"Hmmm. Now that's a mystery. Must have been a friend from the orchestra," said RuthEllen, "but I didn't see any other cars besides my renters' and yours come down the drive. Oh, well, maybe they were dropped off while I was in washing the vegetables."

"I guess so," said Allie, "But whoever it was must not have known that mushrooms are one of Anne's most despised foods. Were one of..."

"Look, honey, the whole thing's a mystery to me. Why that lovely lady would have... People are mysteries, I guess. Who knows what lurks in the deep recesses of their minds." RuthEllen sighed. "I'd best be off—got a hundred errands to run and my day's been all shot to heck. That brilliant conductor of yours wouldn't let my girl in to his cottage to do her usual cleaning today. My lord, everything is gone plumb crazy. Pass those muffins around. Nothing like a little sugar and flour to lighten up people's feelings." With that pronouncement, the inn owner lumbered to her feet and left.

Allie watched her leave. What a varied group of people I come in contact with, she thought. RuthEllen was one of the nicest ones, she added to herself.

The day wore on. Allie found a forgotten Skyr yogurt in the office minifridge and ate that at around 2:00. Various people, mostly orchestra players, stopped in to share their shock at the death of Anne and eat a blueberry muffin. Every last one of them said they had no idea Anne was struggling; everyone was heartbroken. To Allie, it felt like a physical wound was being flayed open again and again. As soon as she managed to get her mind off Anne's death, someone would call, email, or come through the door and remind her. They all needed solace, they all needed to share their grief. And none of them seemed to realize that Allie was grieving more than most.

As her workday came to a close, Allie thought about the night that lay ahead. She still didn't feel like eating—maybe a peanut butter and jelly sandwich would do. And a cup of tea? No, a can of beer, she thought, or three. And she was going to put the earbuds in and blast music into her brain, in hopes that would erase the pain of grief and remembering.

"Contrary to what you might think, you should listen to something sad," said George, on his way out the door. "Believe me, when you're feeling down, that's exactly what you need," he added, noticing Allie surprised expression. "Something happy and light will not help. For example, try the Fauré Requiem[1]. Oh my god, that "Pie Jesu" gets me right here," he said, placing his hand over his heart. "Three and a half minutes of glorious sorrow. Somehow it helps, maybe knowing that a composer was feeling the same as you? Whatever it is, it works. Try it."

Allie had heard the Requiem in concert years ago but never played it, so she didn't really remember it well. She decided to take George's advice and downloaded the piece onto her phone. She would go to the cottage, eat a P.B.&J., drink beer, and listen to some "glorious" music. Then hopefully sleep until morning.

"Al, glad I caught you." Luke breezed into the office, passing George on his way out. "How about I get us some takeout and come down to the cottage. I can keep you company for the night. Cheer you up if you're feeling down. You know." He wiggled his eyebrows.

"I know *what*?" Allie was reminded of how he had minimized her pain when young Toby Zeller had died in the sailing accident. It caused a rift in their relationship that had only recently been patched. "No, Luke, I think I'd rather be by myself tonight. I'm still just beginning to process all this."

Luke looked down, twisting his old baseball cap in his hands. Allie had to restrain herself from brushing the sawdust out of his tousled hair. "Luke," she said. "It's just, well, it's going to take time."

"But Al," he said. "You have to eat. Life goes on." The minute he said those words, he regretted it.

"Oh, thanks for that wisdom, asshole."

Luke sighed, put his hat on, and turned. "Al, when you're ready, you know where to find me." His shoulders slumping, he left the office.

Allie watched him go. He didn't get it, she thought. Would he ever?

Thirty-Seven

Allie made it into the office at seven-thirty the next morning, though she felt hungover. She'd only had two beers, but for some reason—empty stomach?—they'd hit her hard. She decided that something contrapuntal was called for, and put Bach's Two and Three Part Inventions[26] on the office system. Hearing the second Invention, she remembered how her father had been so proud of mastering the first one and then had given up in frustration on the second. His piano playing never matched his violin and fiddle playing, much to his dismay, though how hard he tried to improve.

Today, many of Bach's short pieces sounded as if they were wandering in the wilderness, each hand playing a line seemingly unrelated to the other, only to resolve by joining at the end. But their precise rhythms helped Allie focus, and the astringent harmonies seemed to put a stopper in any sentimentality. With Glenn Gould's interpretation ticking away in the background, she set to work. Ugh, she thought, I hope this isn't a Gould recording where he moans and grunts along with the music.

Allie began by checking her email. There was a stack of unread emails from the evening before; she had turned off her phone's email when she got home. First she read that Anne's sister Jennifer was arriving at 11:00 and coming to the office after stopping first at the funeral home to view her sister. Esther planned to bring in some lunch for Jennifer and anyone else in the office, though Esther said (and Allie agreed) it might be best to keep the office cleared of extra people during that time. "I know she wants to discuss a memorial service of some sort," Esther wrote. "I don't think she's thought out any of the details—still in shock."

Allie remembered with a pang the memorial service in April for Sylvia Abbott she and her father had performed at. That had been hard enough, and she hadn't even liked Sylvia very much. (Though what she had learned about the late SummerFest board chair after her death had revised Allie's opinion somewhat.) She turned her thoughts away from memorial services and read the next emails. Her mother had written from Switzerland hoping that Allie was coping and, to Allie's surprise, saying she planned a trip to Maine at the end of the summer. Hopefully when the festival is over, Allie thought, imagining the disruption her mother's visit would likely cause.

An email from Thomas let her know he wanted to make an addition to his bio that was included in the concert program insert for Friday. Too late, thought Allie, I've already printed and stuffed 600 of them into the programs. He also proposed adding a short somber piece at the beginning of Friday's concert in Anne's memory. Allie wrote him a short email back saying she was sorry, but it was too late to change the insert, but the addition of a short piece for Anne might be possible.

An email from Tony Bainbridge to her and George said that he had studied Ruben's "Concerto for Orchestra" as a substitute for the cello concerto, and he was convinced it would work. Since it wasn't published yet, Ruben had agreed to let the orchestra play it without paying any royalties, provided that the story of the substitution was given wide distribution. "I think that means he wants you to publicize it," added Tony. Tony said that Ruben was finishing up the parts and would print out a master set that could then be photocopied. Hmmm, thought Allie, Ruben had dropped off the parts yesterday for photocopying. Tony also said that it was a good thing he didn't have to conduct on Friday, as this new piece was going to take a bit of "heavy lifting."

Allie quickly read through the rest of the emails: Karin Anders, first horn in the orchestra and head of the musicians' union, said that the union wanted to do something to honor Anne; some friends of the festival wrote asking if the rumors of Anne's death were true; Ken Hanson wrote to say that the board was ready to help in whatever way necessary (that's uncharacteristically considerate of him, thought Allie); and several other orchestra members had written, wondering what music would take the place of the cello concerto, because they wanted to get a jump on practicing.

Allie stared at the last email in the string. It had arrived from Kate Zeller, long past midnight last night. Kate had been held in a mental hospital in Massachusetts since being discovered as Sylvia Abbott's killer. "Allie," her email said, "I'm so sorry that you're having to deal with yet another death. I remember how broken up you were when your grandparents died. I guess that was your first exposure to the finality of it. Then there was Toby's accident… I know you and Anne were super close. My heart aches for you, and I feel terrible beyond description for the pain I caused you as well. I don't ask you to forgive me. But know that my love for you is still as strong as ever; I will always consider you almost a daughter." Allie closed her laptop and sat still. She didn't know what she thought about that. It was true, Kate had been like a surrogate mother to her. But after what she had done… Allie closed her eyes. She couldn't write back. Not now. What would she say? The thoughts and conflicted feelings whirled around her head, and she tried to breathe.

"Allie, I didn't expect to see you in so early." George peered at her. As she reopened her laptop and gave a little shake to her head, he could tell she was coming back from someplace dark and confusing. The dark circles under her eyes belied her attempt at a perky response.

"Oh, George! I thought I'd get an early start on all the work we have to do. It's much cooler this morning, isn't it?"

"Right," he said. "Did you see Tony's email from last night? Looks like he's all set to use Ruben's composition as a substitute."

"I did. Nice that we can use it for free, isn't it."

"Sure is, though all that photocopying is going to be a pain. Oh, well. And I guess Perrotta wants some publicity in return." He turned to head into his office. "That shouldn't be too difficult," he said.

"Wait, George," Allie said. "One more thing: Anne's sister Jennifer is arriving today and she wants to meet with us. It'll be around noon, and Esther is bringing lunch by."

George turned around. "Ok, that should be fine. Let me know when she arrives."

Allie's phone beeped. Her dad texted:

Doing ok?

Allie responded:

Guess so feel a little weird

She noticed a text from last night sent by Luke. All it said was

Al?

What was there to say? she wondered.

Thirty-Eight

Noon came around and Esther appeared at the office with a basket filled with chicken salad sandwiches, Cape Cod chips, apples, chocolate chip cookies, and cans of Polar seltzer. "Jennifer is just finishing up at the funeral home," she said, placing the basket on the conference table. "I thought if we met in here, we could keep the masses at bay and give Jennifer some privacy."

"Sounds good," said Allie. She got up to help Esther unpack the basket and realized that she still didn't feel like eating much of anything. As she knocked on George's office door to let him know that Jennifer was on her way, a car drove into the parking lot and a tall dark haired woman got out. Allie recognized Jennifer Kirschner, even though she looked older than when she had visited Anne about five years ago. Jennifer shut the car door and walked toward the office. Allie walked out to meet her.

"Jennifer? I don't know if you remember me from your last visit—I'm Allegra Brewster. I work here at the festival now." She reached out a hand, but Jennifer enfolded her in a sudden hug.

"Allie Brewster, of course I remember you. And how could I forget, when Anne spoke of you so often." Jennifer released Allie and they both entered the office. Allie placed a little-used OFFICE CLOSED sign on the door and ushered their guest into the conference room. Esther and George solemnly shook Jennifer's hand, and the four sat down around the table.

"We are so sorry for your loss," started George.

"It's your loss, too," said Jennifer. "I know that." She looked at the framed festival posters that lined the walls. "This was such a special place for Anne." She shook her head. "I just can't understand it. I spoke with Anne just a few days ago and she was brimming with excitement about the cello concerto and the other stuff going on." She passed a hand over her forehead as if to clear her thinking. "Anne wasn't inclined to depression or... It was surreal seeing her lying there... I felt like I should be able to wake her up."

"I feel the same way," said Allie. "I saw her the night before and she was her usual self. No sign of any problems."

"Here," said Esther, passing out the sandwiches and chips. "Now, how can we help you, Jennifer? What would you like us to do?"

Jennifer exhaled. "I just don't know. First of all, I'm picking up Cara and Andrew this afternoon and evening. They want to see their mother..." Jennifer's voice had a hitch in it for a moment, and she cleared her throat. "So I'll drive them up to Henderson's Funeral Home tomorrow morning. And then we've decided that she will be cremated. That's what she would want." She looked down. "That's as far as we've gotten."

"How are they doing?" asked Esther.

"Oh, it's awful," said Jennifer, "They are completely torn up. They feel as shocked as I do. I mean... " She paused for a moment. "So, I've decided that I will move to Chicago, at least for the next year. I hate to make them move in the middle of high school. I'll work from their home there. It'll be fine, and I think they will need the continuity. But they'll be ok eventually—they're young and strong."

"Yes, so young," said Esther.

"The entire orchestra is in mourning," said George. "You probably know that Anne was a beloved colleague. They are looking for ways to... ah... commemorate her relationship with them and the festival."

Allie remembered Thomas's suggestion about playing a short piece in Anne's honor at the start of Friday's concert. She explained what he had said. "Do you know of a piece that would be meaningful to Anne?" she asked Anne's sister.

Jennifer thought for a few seconds. "She loved Ravel's "Pavane pour une infante défunte"[27] when she was a kid. That seems morbid, though. I don't know—you folks would be better answering that question." She paused again. "I think you should decide what would be appropriate."

"The concert is tomorrow night," said Allie. "Is there any chance you and Andrew and Cara will still be here?"

"No, they're arriving tonight and we'll be leaving in the morning, after they see... their mother. But if you do play a special piece for Anne, perhaps you could record it and send it to us?"

"We record every concert for rebroadcast on public radio," said George. "We would be happy to send you a link, and perhaps a CD?"

"A link is fine," said Jennifer. The room was quiet while the sandwiches were eaten. Each of the four people around the table was thinking of Anne, remembering her musical laugh and some considerate thing she had done. Allie had known her longest, except for her sister. And over the years, Esther, as a longtime board member, remembered many occasions where Anne had done something to help out an orchestra member. George had known Anne least of all, but even in the four years he'd been at the helm of the Kennimac SummerFest, he'd recognized her as one of the key orchestra members: always positive, always constructive. Grace personified. He shook his head.

After a few minutes, Jennifer took an apple and stood up. "I'm off to my sister's cottage to collect her belongings. Then back to Portland late this afternoon to meet the kids. We'll stay in Portland tonight and make a short trip here tomorrow morning. Then I'm bringing them to New York with me while we figure out what comes next."

"Please give them our love," said Allie, and the other two nodded in agreement.

"I will. And thank you for lunch. Sorry I ate so little. Perhaps one of you could tell me how to get to the Kennimac Inn from here. Or I guess I could just use GPS..."

"GPS is notoriously fallible around here. Let me give you directions," said Esther.

Allie jumped in. "I'll do it, Esther. Let me walk you to your car, Jennifer."

The older woman, elegant in her navy pantsuit and precisely trimmed dark hair, and the younger woman, dressed in a black tee shirt with a sketch of a cello and white lettering that read "I try to stay out of treble" and a pair of faded jeans, her streaked taffy-and-fawn-colored hair escaping from a loose bun, walked side by side out to the parking lot.

After giving Jennifer directions to the inn and cottages, Allie hesitated. "I want to ask you something," she finally said. "I saw the gun that your dad had given Anne."

Jennifer nodded. "He gave me one, too."

"But I can't figure out why Anne would have..."

"...I know. It's totally incomprehensible." Jennifer shook her head.

"Could it have been an accident?"

"It doesn't sound like it. Chief Knowles called me before Esther did, maybe you didn't know that. He said it looked planned, organized." A tear trickled down her cheek.

"Oh." Allie stared at the pavement.

"Look, honey, we can't know what people are thinking, really. Even so, I find it so hard..." Jennifer gave Allie's arm a squeeze. "Thanks for being her friend. She cared about you, a lot."

Allie nodded, unable to speak. Jennifer got in the car and waved as she backed out. Allie gave a small wave in return.

Thirty-Nine

The day continued. Allie focused on small tasks in the office, trying to keep her mind focused on what was directly in front of her. Outside, the temperature was more merciful than the day before; the sun moved in and out of the clouds, and a light breeze ruffled the leaves on the trees.

Allie noticed that the orchestra members came back after lunch for a second rehearsal. They walked slowly in clumps, some with their arms around each other, their heads down, shoulders slumped. She assumed Thomas had asked them for additional time to get the Friday night concert in good shape, and they were willing but also mourning Anne. Then, at four o'clock, Thomas stopped by the office.

"Hi, Allie," he said as he walked through the door. "I want to check on something with you and George."

Allie took out her ear buds. "Oh? George is out. What is it?"

"I'm thinking of adding a short piece to play in memory of Anne at tomorrow night's concert. Several orchestra members mentioned they wanted to do something to mark her passing."

Allie nodded. "Yes, I heard that, too."

"Ok, well, I went through all the short, sad pieces I could think of. Barber's *Adagio for Strings*[28], for example. But that's so well known, I don't know—it almost seems trite. Or at least, overused."

"I agree."

"Then other pieces I thought of call for a solo voice or instruments we don't normally have. Or, frankly, they are too hard for me to learn by tomorrow night." He shrugged. "I didn't want to make too big a deal out of this, you know. But I want it to be respectful of Anne's memory. So I'm stuck. I was hoping you might have some ideas."

"Let me think," Allie said. Memory, she thought. In Anne's memory. "Ok, here's an idea."

"What's that?"

"On Tuesday night, the night before Anne... died, when I was at her place for dinner, we were playing around on the cello while working on Ruben's concerto, the second 'phase' (that's what he calls the movements, you know), which is slow, and at one point she started playing this haunting tune that wasn't from the concerto. Just for fun, I think. She said it reminded her of Ruben's piece. It went like something like this: D, C#, B, D.., C#... A, B, C#, E..., D.... and so on." Allie hummed a few bars.

"I know that. It's the horn solo in the second movement of Tchaikovsky's fifth symphony[29]."

"Right. And Anne said that she would be forever furious at Tchaikovsky for giving that solo to the principal horn instead of the principal cello." Allie smiled at the bittersweet memory. "When she played just a few bars, I could see exactly what she meant. I don't know, maybe that movement? Or part of it? Is it too long?"

Thomas fiddled with his phone. "It's about ten minutes, according to ChatGPT. But I think we could cut it off somewhere. The cellos do get to wail on the tune later on, by the way. So I would run it until after that point, at least." He gave Allie a triumphant look. "I know the piece fairly well, and I'm sure we have it in the library. What do you think?"

"It's entirely your decision, 'maestro'," she said, with an ironic bow. "But I think it would be perfect. If Karin is up for playing the horn solo, that is."

"Are you kidding? She probably plays it every day to warm up." Thomas smiled. "And it's not technically difficult. I think she'll be thrilled. It's a brilliant solution. So, I'd better get the score out and figure out the cut. And could you email the musicians to let them know we'll be rehearsing it tomorrow morning? They all probably know that symphony by heart—almost, anyway."

"Ok, I'll get on it. Do you want me to check with Beth to warn her to get the parts out for tomorrow's rehearsal?"

"That would be great. Allie, thank you so much. This is going to be fantastic, thanks to your genius." He reached out and gave her a quick hug, as someone came through the office door.

"What genius are you talking about?" Luke raised an eyebrow, noting the fact that Thomas had just hugged Allie.

"She had the perfect suggestion for a piece to add to tomorrow's concert. It will be fabulous and I never would have thought of it."

"Of course not," Luke said.

"I've got to run. Thanks again, Allie. You're a life-saver!" Thomas picked up his music case and rushed out the door, whistling the theme.

"Life-saver," muttered Allie to herself. "Hardly..." She inserted the ear buds and returned to the spreadsheet she was working on.

"Al." Luke snapped his fingers in front of her face. "Al, what was all that about? Seems like you and Thomas are getting pretty chummy again. I thought you said he was a worthless P.O.S."

"Did I say that? No, he's alright." Allie opened up the email program to send the message to the orchestra members.

Luke placed himself in line with Allie's laptop. "So, Al, what about tonight? Shall I bring some takeout over? What do you think?"

Allie sighed. "I don't think so, Luke. I've got a lot to do. And I'm not feeling very sociable."

"You don't have to be 'sociable.' It's just me, Al."

"I know, I get it. But not tonight. I still want to be by myself. If you don't mind..."

"I don't mind. Just let me know when your mood changes."

"It's not a mood, Luke. It's not some stupid, temporary, minor ***mood***. My world has changed—there's a huge fucking gaping hole in it. Now go away. I have to finish this work."

The office door slammed behind him.

Forty

Friday morning was even cooler than the day before. The humidity had dried up and a light breeze made the balsam boughs dance outside the cottage. Allie brought her coffee cup out on the deck and took in a deep breath. She had slept, though she'd had some strange shadowy dreams that she couldn't really remember now. The coffee was strong and bitter. As she sipped, Allie noticed faint stirrings of hunger. Maybe some toast, she thought. Then she remembered that Cara and Andrew were probably on their way to Kennimac with their aunt. She couldn't imagine how they must feel. She wondered what Anne's body looked like. Luckily, Anne hadn't shot herself in the head. A blanket or something would cover up the wound in her chest. Allie felt sick. She tried to block the thoughts of how some people killed themselves with guns.

Guns + suicide. Allie remembered her research back in high school: Why was it so easy to get a gun in this country? How many lives could be saved if people didn't have a gun at the moment they felt despair? Senator Crank McGregor was attending tonight's concert. He had always been such a gun rights advocate. Maybe she could talk to him for a minute before the concert? Allie searched on her phone for the most recent data on suicides by firearm in the U.S. as reported by the Centers for Disease Control and Prevention. She was horrified to learn that almost 75 people died every day, adding up to close to 30,000 people every year. Combine that with the statistic that more than 50 homicides occurred daily (approximately another 20,000 gun deaths per year). Allie felt outrage and anger fill the space that sorrow had taken just seconds ago. She was going to make sure she spoke to the senator. Damn right. It was the least she could do in Anne's honor.

Between Anne's death and the mass shooting in Lewiston—two examples of the extreme danger of firearms in the wrong hands—Allie felt she could make a strong case for gun safety reform. He had been impervious to the entreaties of Allie and her fellow students years ago, but maybe now he was ready to rethink his opposition. It was worth a try, anyway.

As she quickly dressed and got ready to head to the SummerFest office, Allie rehearsed the short speech she planned to make to the senator. "A valued member of our orchestra killed herself without warning on Tuesday. She had a gun handy. We all feel that if she hadn't had such easy access to a deadly weapon, she'd still be alive and playing in tonight's concert. The number of people who kill themselves with guns each year in our country is more than the population of our county here on the coast..." What else should she say? How could she reach him? Were statistics the answer? Should she give him a letter or just speak to him? She remembered his condescending reply all those years ago, and she worried that a similar response would cause her to lose her temper.

Whatever. She had to do it and she would. Let the chips fall where they may.

The day went smoothly. Thomas stopped in at lunchtime and reported that Beth, the music librarian, had managed to put the music for the Tchaikovsky on the music stands, awaiting the musicians' arrival at rehearsal. Karin had outdone herself with her soulful interpretation, and many of the orchestra members had played with tears in their eyes. Thomas himself was vibrating with nerves and anticipation; it was a challenge for him to step in and conduct a full concert on two days' notice.

"I texted with Tony about the Tchaik," he told Allie. "He agreed with me about where to stop, so that was good. And he said something funny. He said not to make it maudlin. He said, 'Even though it's marked *con alcuna licenza* (that's 'without license' in Italian), don't let Karin bog it down.' I guess he meant don't let it be sappy." So I plan to keep it moving along."

Allie nodded. She was glad that Thomas was feeling confident and excited, but she didn't have time to listen to every detail. "I'll see you tonight, Thomas," she said. "Now go rest up for your big debut." Jeez, she thought, it's not like he's Leonard Bernstein stepping in to conduct the New York Philharmonic at the last minute. She wished some people could have perspective instead of thinking the world revolved around them.

Later in the afternoon, she and Beth spent some time printing out and looking at the parts for Ruben's Concerto for Orchestra. The parts were computer generated and quite clean; that was a relief. The piece was long and the parts had many pages. The photocopying would take ages.

When Ruben stopped by, he was strangely subdued. "Thomas is beside himself with joy at filling in for Tony tonight," Ruben said about his cottage-mate. "But he didn't explain why Tony was dropping out tonight. Is he sick? Should I be worried?"

"About what?

"If he'll be able to conduct my concerto. In three weeks. It's not a straightforward piece for a conductor, I think."

"Tony will be fine by then," said Allie. "To be frank, Anne's death really shook him up. I think he just needed a couple of days off to pull himself together."

"I wonder why he was so upset? I mean..." Ruben gestured.

"He's known her for many years. And he cared about her." Allie straightened the pile of orchestra parts on her desk. "It's private. Besides, we all feel bad."

"Yes, well, the show must go on!" Ruben didn't register the look that Allie blazed at him.

"You should get going, Ruben," she said. "I have work to do."

Allie ducked into the office bathroom to straighten up her hair and apply some mascara and lipstick. She wasn't speaking at the concert but as the soon-to-be festival manager, she needed to look professional. She walked down to the concert barn to make sure that everything was ready, joining the clumps of people already arriving. As she returned up the hill to the office, she noticed a black SUV with tinted windows arriving in the parking lot. As soon as it parked, three people got out: a thin, slightly stooped, gray-haired older man, a tall solid younger man wearing aviator-style sunglasses who had been driving, and a small well dressed older woman. The senator has aged, Allie thought. She membered him as being much taller and more formidable looking. She walked over to the trio.

"Senator McGregor and Mrs. McGregor," she said, putting her hand out. "So glad you could come. I'm Allegra Brewster of the SummerFest management." After a few pleasantries back and forth, Allie turned to the senator. "I wonder if I could have a minute of your time, sir."

McGregor motioned the other two to head down to the concert barn. "What can I help you with, Allegra?"

"I don't know if you recall, Senator, but when I was at Kennimac High School..."

"... So you're a local girl. Glad to hear that. Isn't that nice."

"Yes, well, when I was in high school, a group of us visited your office to talk about a gun control bill that was in the senate. We were urging you to vote in favor, but you didn't."

"Look, Allegra, a lot goes into these votes. I'm sorry you were disappointed, but I have to do what I think is right. Maine has a grand tradition of gun ownership and hunting." He turned as if to join his wife, while waving to some arriving ticket holders who recognized him.

"But senator," said Allie, "The situation of gun deaths has gotten even worse. Not just with homicides but even more with suicides.

Why, just on Tuesday night, a beloved member of the orchestra killed herself..."

"...I'm sorry to hear that, Allegra. Tragic. But you know, suicide now, that's a mental health problem, not a gun problem."

"I disagree, Senator. Studies show that if the lethal weapon isn't readily available, often the suicidal impulse passes."

"Look, Allegra. I can't stay here and talk and then cause a commotion with a late arrival. Believe me, I've looked into this. I just don't hold with the idea of going against the 2nd Amendment of the Constitution. Write me a letter if you have more information you want to convey, but I assure you I have heard it all before." With that, he strode down the hill, joining a group of concert-goers who were thrilled to find themselves accompanied by a U.S. senator.

Shit, thought Allie. That was a waste. He didn't pay any attention to what I was saying. She slowly headed down the hill to the concert barn. Clearly, a letter would be a waste of time.

Once inside, she stood in the back next to George, waiting as the last arrivals were seated. The orchestra musicians were making their usual warming-up cacophony. Allie watched as George gave a nod to Luke, who left his spot in the wings and turned. In a moment, out from the green room walked the concertmaster with her violin. She bowed to the applauding audience and signaled to the first oboe to play a concert A, the note to which the all the musicians calibrated their instruments so they'd play in tune with each other. Once the tuning finished, Thomas walked quickly and confidently to the podium, nodded to the musicians, then turned to address the audience.

"We experienced a tragedy this week," he said in a firm voice. "A talented and beloved member of the orchestra died unexpectedly. We all wanted to mark her passing in some way, to share the meaning her life had for us. Music is the best way, I think, especially in her case. So this first piece—not listed in your program, a short excerpt from Tchaikovsky's Fifth Symphony—is dedicated to the memory of cellist Anne Kirschner." He turned and immediately took up his conductor's baton. The quiet chords of the second movement of Tchaikovsky's fifth symphony[1] filled the barn. When Karin entered with the horn solo, Allie felt shivers up and down her spine, and tears flooded her eyes.

Forty-One

The Friday night concert was a triumph for Thomas. The audience clapped and clapped, requiring multiple bows. He singled out the players who'd had lengthy solos. The pianist who soloed in the Grieg had three curtain calls. Finally, at the very end of the concert, when the audience started chanting, "Encore! Encore!", Thomas turned to the orchestra once again and told them to put up Shostakovich's Waltz No. 2[1]—the piece that was dropped to make room for the Tchaikovsky piece in Anne's memory. The audience was entranced by the waltz, swaying together to the music and laughing and clapping at the end. As they filed out, Ruben stopped by Allie, whispering, "Movie music from a Communist Soviet composer, and they love it." He shrugged as if to say, "How ignorant!"

"I disagree," Allie replied. "I'm not sure Shostakovich was a willing collaborator. Lighten up, you music snob." Ruben had smiled in response and had walked on.

Allie replayed her memory of the audience's enthusiasm as she ate her Saturday breakfast on the deck. Granola, yogurt, banana, coffee—yes, she felt like eating again. It was a typical normal sunny Saturday morning on the shore. Allie caught glimpses through the trees of weekend boaters heading out on the water. The flapping of sails was audible as a dinghy race got started. She basked in the warm, dry air. Birds were flitting among the branches, black-capped chickadees singing their summer song, B-G#, B-G#. Allie felt herself unwinding.

She checked her messages and found several that had come in the night. Thomas, obviously savoring the glow from his conducting success, wrote:

great concert! hope Sunday is as good

too excited to sleep!

This came from her father:

Wonderful concert – good job, honey. The Tchaik mov't for Anne was brilliant. Bet it was your idea.

Yup, thought Allie, you got that right, Dad.

And from Luke:

good concert shall i stop by?

didn't hear an answer so guess not

miss you Al

Allie shook her head. She was glad she hadn't seen Luke's text—she would have been forced to fend him off. She didn't feel like going back to their old ways, not just yet anyway. The pain of Anne's death was too raw. And Luke didn't seem to recognize its magnitude. Would he ever, she wondered? Thomas, for instance, perhaps because of their shared musical language, seemed more aware of her feelings right now than Luke did. Of course, it was true Thomas was no one she could count on. She had been burnt once already by his cavalier attitude to romance.

Allie reflected that George was right about the therapeutic value of listening to sad music; the Fauré and the Tchaikovsky and other melancholy pieces had helped her work through the top layer of her feelings. Now she was left with more anger than sorrow—not anger at Anne, because she still didn't believe that Anne would have killed herself. Anger at Senator McGregor. What a pompous idiot he was. And anger at everyone's assumption that Anne had killed herself.

Allie decided to try to distance herself emotionally from Anne's death to examine at the situation more dispassionately. Were there in fact any signs that Anne was suffering? Allie opened the Notes on her phone and typed:

> Possible signs pointing toward: 1) worried about concerto. 2) Something about Tony? Was he bothering her? Pressuring her? 3) had taken the gun out.

> Reponse: 1) not actually worried. seemed excited to play concerto 2) she never said anything bad about Tony, didn't really complain. 3) having the gun was hard to figure.

> Possible signs pointing against: 1) appeared happy. 2) Cara and Andrew!!! 3) no one saw signs of depression.

> Response: 1) hard to fake being happy. 2) would she have deserted her two kids? she brought them up as a single mom. why now? 3) maybe she masked her depression? If so, she did it really well.

It didn't make sense. The gun was the only unknowable factor. But Anne's sister Jennifer had been fairly blasé about the fact that Anne had the pistol. In fact, Jennifer admitted she had one as well. Did Jennifer find Anne's suicide unbelievable? Allie tried to remember their conversation of Thursday. How had Jennifer seemed? Yes, she had acted as shocked as Allie felt. She said that the last time she talked with Anne, Anne had been "brimming with excitement" about the concerto, that was how she put it.

A tone on her phone alerted her that an email from her mother had arrived. Allie opened it.

> Allegra, how are you doing? Do you want to talk? I'm free this afternoon—no plans. Shall we FaceTime or Zoom? In a half hour or so?

Allie didn't want to have a video call with her mother., especially not this morning. She wanted to take it easy this morning, sit in the sun, think about her next steps with the orchestra, and whether there was anything she could or should do about Anne's death. She wrote back.

> Don't need to talk. I'm trying to decide what I can do to convince the police that Anne didn't kill herself. I just know she didn't. And I may go out for a sail in Calliope this afternoon. Beautiful day here.

Melissa quickly wrote back.

> Sure, ok. But if you think Anne didn't kill herself, then you must think there is a killer at large. Is that what you think?

> I hadn't really focused that. But yeah, maybe.

> Allegra, if you believe that, then you need to convince Chet Knowles and his crew to do an investigation. For one thing, this may be someone you know. You yourself may be in danger. You'll need to come up with some information that proves Anne didn't shoot the gun herself. See if you can figure out what the police know and don't know. Maybe they are overlooking some important details. Be persistent. Chet will probably brush you off, but stick to it. Your own safety may depend on it!

Good point, Mom. I'm going to try to talk to Knowles today then. I'll let you know what he says. Love you.

Love you, too, honey. Be careful, please!

Allie sat on the other side of Chief Knowles's desk in the small combined police and volunteer fire department station. He had brought Officer Ouelette into the room to be there while talking with Allie.

"Look, Allegra, I know you're pretty torn up about your friend's suicide, but..." the chief said.

"... I just want to go over the facts to make sure there are no lingering questions." Allie pressed her lips together and locked eyes with the chief, who sighed.

"Alright. What do you want to know?" he said.

"First of all, what made you so sure that it was a suicide?"

Knowles motioned to Officer Ouelette. "Theresa, you tell her."

Officer Ouelette nodded. "Ok. Well, first of all, Allie, she was laying on the couch. She had arranged herself like she planned to be found. And the gun was right beside her."

"In her hand?"

"No, not exactly, it was kind of under her hand, like she had let go of it. And no one had been seen coming or going down the road to Cormorant Cottage after you left that evening."

"Right," said Knowles. "And RuthEllen keeps a close eye on her place. She'd have noticed a car, we think. Actually," he winked at Allie, "If we thought this was a murder, you'd be our main suspect."

Allie didn't smile in return. "So what did the room look like? Was it neat? Was her cello put away?"

Ouelette looked at the chief before answering. "It was fairly neat. I mean, her instrument was lying on the floor and there was sheet music on the music stand. She was still dressed. Let's see..." Ouelette closed her eyes, trying to remember the scene. "...There was a book lying open—that was a little weird. And there was music playing, the same piece over and over like a broken record."

Allie frowned. "There was music? Do you know what it was?"

"Nah, some classical piece with a lot of violins, I guess. RuthEllen had thought there was a group practicing in the cottage before she realized something wasn't right."

"Oh, a chamber piece then," Allie said to herself. "Do you know what the book was?"

"Something about music performance. Playing contemporary music. Right, Chief?" Knowles grunted in assent.

"Well," said Allie after a pause to think, "Did you check the gun for fingerprints?"

Officer Ouelette looked at the chief, who decided to answer. "There were no other fingerprints. It was a little odd—usually we find others, too. These were very clear and there weren't any others, not even smudged ones. But we didn't worry about it too much, especially because..." He gave Officer Ouelette a significant look.

"Because," Ouelette took up the thread, "the door was locked. And there was no sign of forced entry." The two police officers looked at each other and nodded, as if that was the final determining factor.

Something pinged in Allie's memory. "Wait, Anne told me she had lost her keys."

"Yes, but the door was locked from the inside."

"But how do you know that?" Allie asked.

"It's plain common sense, Allegra. Now, it's a gorgeous Saturday afternoon. I suggest," Chief Knowles lumbered to his feet, "that you leave us to our work. I know you're still upset—suicide is very hard to understand—I can't say I do. Best thing to do is try to find some relief, maybe go to the beach or something."

Allie could tell it was a dismissal. "I might go for a sail," she said.

"Great idea," said the chief. "Clear your head."

Forty-Two

The sky was its brightest blue, with only a couple of fluffy clouds sauntering across. Allie wasn't sure there would be enough wind for a sail, but she decided to go down to the harbor to see. There might be just enough breeze for a gentle glide downwind. If she ran out of wind on the way back, she could always row (though handling those big heavy oars was a challenge). Or perhaps she could hail a passing powerboat to give her a tow. Anyway, a gentle drift was a great way to spend some time thinking over what she had heard.

When she got to the harbor, she saw Calliope tied up at its mooring. She called her father to make sure he wasn't planning to go out for a sail himself. But he was busy in his garden this afternoon and had a gig with his Celtic band that evening in Brunswick. So the boat was all hers for the rest of the day.

There were kids jumping off the dock into the roped off swimming area, and the sailing dinghies were returning from their races out in the harbor, the skippers shouting insults in jest at each other. Families were finishing up their picnics in the grassy picnic area, and the usual phalanx of retired sailors was rocking in unison on the harbormaster's porch, trading tales of their exploits on the water in younger days. A usual idyllic summer Saturday, Allie thought. Except it felt anything but idyllic to her. She waved to various people on her way to the dock, but didn't stop to engage anyone in conversation.

A slight breeze created cat's paws on the bay's surface, probably just enough to push Calliope along at a knot or two. Fine for her purposes. Once Allie had the little wooden boat underway, she leaned back against the gunwales and felt a bit of her tension drain away.

Where to start, she wondered, thinking of her mother's advice. What were the "anomalies," as the chief had said? One, it was totally inconceivable that Anne killed herself. Begin with that, Allie told herself. Another: why weren't there any other fingerprints on the gun? That was really strange. And impossible—did the police screw up and wipe them off somehow? Anne's fingerprints were on the gun, at least. But,, realized Allie with a shock, hers should have been, too.

So, what if someone *did* kill Anne? Who? Why? And how could they have gotten in if the door was locked? Anne never locked the cottage, she even said so. But, wait. If Anne lost her keys, maybe it was because the murderer had picked them up. Was it premeditated, then?

Back to the question of who. According to the police and RuthEllen Cox, no one had driven down the road Tuesday night. But that didn't mean someone couldn't have walked. So, the killer was someone who was staying at the inn or the cottages, or someone who parked up on the road and walked down the driveway. Allie ran through the list of people staying on the Kennimac property.

Ok. There was Tony in his cottage, of course. And Ruben and Thomas in the cottage they shared. She didn't know who rented the other cottages; they weren't connected to the SummerFest. In the inn itself were Krissy Kanafax, Carol McCreary, and Steve Kennison, members of the festival's woodwind quintet. She couldn't imagine any of them as murderers. For one thing, most were old friends of Anne's. Tony, in a jealous rage? No, he seemed much too distraught at her death. Ruben wouldn't have wanted her to die and lose the opportunity to premiere his new concerto. Thomas? No, Thomas had no reason to murder Anne—he hardly knew her and had had little contact with her. And what little contact he'd had was positive.

It must have been someone from outside the SummerFest community, Allie reasoned. Someone from Anne's past? Or was it a burglary gone bad? But the fact that Anne's cello and bow—worth hundreds of thousands of dollars—were not taken made the burglary idea seem unlikely. All her thoughts seemed to collapse in dead ends.

Allie looked at the shore. She was opposite her cottage, its gray shingles and green trim barely visible through the trees. A glint of metal caught Allie's eye. Oh, damn, it looked like Luke was arriving at the cottage in his jeep. Glad I'm not there, Allie thought. I guess I need to talk with him sometime soon, though; it's only fair. She remembered how angry Luke had been when he'd seen Thomas that night at the cottage. And it had been completely innocent—Luke had been jealous for no reason. That night... wait... that was the night that Anne died. Thomas had driven to see her and it was fairly late, like ten or so. Yet, RuthEllen had said no cars came or went after Allie left Anne's.

Obviously, RuthEllen was mistaken. If she missed Thomas's car, she could have missed others. That blew the whole idea of who the culprit could be wide open.

Allie decided that her next step would have to be checking out what she now thought of as "the scene of the crime." She turned Calliope around—she 'came about,' in sailors' lingo—and started tacking up the bay toward the moorings. Judging by the light quality of the wind, it would take about twice as long to return as it had taken to sail down. Allie drank from her water bottle and impatiently willed the wind to rise. After about fifteen minutes, it did pick up strength. Allie pulled in on the lines controlling the sails, and Calliope steamed ahead, tilting—or 'heeling'—in the wind, Allie's hair streaming out behind.

"I thought I might find you here." Luke held the dinghy as Allie jumped out onto the dock. She had spotted him on the dock as she rowed in after securing Calliope to the mooring. She debated rowing back to the sailboat to avoid him, but decided that was ridiculous. Ugh, she'd have to deal with him sooner or later.

"Yeah. I just went for a little sail."

"I would have gone with you, you know. I stopped at the cottage, but you weren't there."

"I just wanted to get away by myself for awhile. And do some thinking." Allie gathered up her knapsack and water bottle and walked toward her car.

"Thinking about?" asked Luke, trailing behind her.

"You know, Luke. Anne's death. Who might have wanted to..."

Luke stopped. "Al. Come on. Anne killed herself. You know that."

Allie turned around to face him. "Actually, I don't know that. In fact, the more I think about it, the less likely I think it is."

Luke groaned. "Al, you're still wrapped up in Sylvia Abbott's murder. This is different. Face it."

Allie shook his hand off her arm. "You don't know the first thing about it. And, frankly, I'm insulted that you assume I'm so stupid. Let me go, Luke."

"Where are you going now?"

"It's none of your business. And I don't need your help. Bye." She spoke the last word sharply.

"Come on, Al ..."

"I said good-bye." Allie dumped her knapsack onto Pablo's back seat and, without looking at Luke, jumped in, started the engine, and sped out of the parking lot, tires squealing. Luke was left standing, speechless, a worried look on his face.

Forty-Three

Allie drove toward the Kennimac Inn with the windows rolled down and music tumbling out. Pablo, the ancient Volvo wagon, didn't have satellite radio, but luckily Maine Public Broadcasting had a classical station. As she passed through Kennimac's Main Street, Allie saw the SummerFest woodwind quintet set up on the sidewalk in front of the bookstore, getting ready to play for passersby. Allie remembered hearing that Ruben had whipped off several fun arrangements for them to play to publicize tomorrow's Family Concert. She stuck her arm out the window to wave, and Karin Anders saw her and waved back.

Seeing the quintet on the sidewalk reminded Allie of all the times she and Anne had done a similar sidewalk performance. Anne was great at turning popular music into cello duets, and she also "borrowed" music that was featured in videos like those of 2Cellos. Some of Allie's favorites had been informal arrangements of Taylor Swift songs, like "Me!" and "You Belong with Me." Had Anne kept those scribbled arrangements? Allie would love to have them to remember those times together. By now, though, they had probably been tossed out. Anne considered them temporary amusements—"ephemera" was the word she used to describe them. Allie thought about the word *ephemeral.* It seemed like Annc's life was now another type of ephemeral. Gone, torn to shreds, disintegrated, and scattered to the winds... no more.

Allie shook her head in hopes of banishing those thoughts. She couldn't afford to be weepy and morose. That sort of emotion clouded thinking and led to inaction. She was on a mission.

As she drove past the Kennimac Inn, she spied RuthEllen in the garden. I should stop on my way back and question her about whether she might have heard other cars, thought Allie. She continued down the dirt driveway and parked at Cormorant Cottage. The door was wide open and a basket of laundry sat on the steps.

"Hello?" called Allie, sticking her head through the doorway.

"Yes?" answered a woman's voice from inside the cottage. She walked out and squinted in the sun. "Can I help you?"

"Um, yes. I'm Allegra Brewster, a friend of Anne Kirschner, who..."

"Yeah, I know what she did. Tanya Frost. I'm the one who found her. Sort of." The woman put her hands on her hips. "What is it you want?"

"I thought I would look around. If that's ok."

"Well, not much to see. Her sister cleared out all her things the other day—Thursday, I think it was." She gestured with the toilet bowl brush in her hand. "I'm doing a final cleanup. New renters coming in tomorrow."

Allie sucked in her breath. "Tomorrow? So... soon?"

"RuthEllen's gotta make a living, you know. These cottages are in high demand."

"But someone *died* here, just a few days ago..."

"Can't help it if your friend decided to shuttle off the immoral coal, as they say. Oh, yeah, sorry for your loss," she added.

Allie stepped in far enough to look around. Just as the woman said, the place appeared to be devoid of Anne's belongings. Clearly, the police hadn't felt it was necessary to preserve the place as a crime scene. But maybe it was worth checking further.

"Would it be ok for me to have a look around?"

"If you make it quick. I'll be finished in about ten minutes. Just have a couple of things left to do, and then I'm locking her up. And don't you dare touch anything," she said.

Allie stepped inside and was immediately admonished, "Shoes off!" She left her sneakers on the doorstep and tiptoed in as Tanya returned to the bathroom. The cottage smelled of cleaning solutions. The counters were bare and a new couch had been installed. All Anne's stuff, her "personal effects," as Allie remembered they were called, were gone.

No piles of music, no music stand, no cello or cello case. No half-full wine bottles by the refrigerator, no sweater slung over the back of a chair. No bowl of apples in the center of the table. The place was empty, lifeless, anonymous. A scream of gulls hit Allie's ears, and she realized no music playing—live or recorded—that's what made it seem especially Anne-less.

Allie peered into the bedroom. She hadn't been in there before but had caught glimpses from the main living area: concert outfits hung on hangers festooning the door; a book-laden bedside table; jewelry strewn across the bureau. Now the bed was perfectly smooth, and the surfaces were clear. The closet door was open and empty hangers lined the rod. Anne had disappeared, gone without a trace.

"I'm done, dear. Did you see what you came to see?" Tanya came out of the bathroom carrying a bucket of cleaning supplies. "There wasn't a note, you know."

"Oh, I know," Allie said. "I guess I'm done, too." Tanya locked the cottage door while Allie sat on the steps to put on her shoes. "I might look around outside a little more," she said.

"Suit yourself. I'm off."

Allie walked around outside the cottage, looking for clues. There was no sign of anything untoward. No sign of violence, no sign of trouble. It was a sunny Saturday afternoon, and she was looking at a typical Maine cottage rental. That was all.

I'll see if I can catch up with RuthEllen, Allie thought. She drove Pablo up to the inn. RuthEllen was on her way into the kitchen with a basket of vegetables—tomatoes and cucumbers, basil and lettuce—as well as nasturtiums, zinnias, and marigolds.

"Looks like quite a haul," said Allie, nodding at the basket.

"It's been a great summer for gardens so far," said the innkeeper. "Except for a few hot days that made me think of Alabama, that is." She looked at Allie. "How're you doing, sweet girl?"

Allie blinked back the rush of tears that RuthEllen's kind voice engendered. "Uh," she said, "Ok, I guess. I was just thinking that it makes no sense..."

"That's for sure. But you know, we think we know and understand each other, but there is a lot of dark mystery in all of us." They entered the kitchen and RuthEllen set the basket on the big work island in the room's center. "I know you're broken up about it," she said, wrapping her arms around Allie's shoulders. "Losing someone you love is the hardest thing that can happen to a person, isn't it."

Allie nodded mutely. Then she sniffed, and remembered her reason for dropping by. "RuthEllen, did you know that Thomas drove to my cottage the night Anne died? Just to ask me something," she added quickly. "For a few minutes."

"Can't say I knew that."

"Well, then, you must not have heard every car driving down to the cottages, because you would have heard his, both leaving and returning. I mean, it was pretty late. Past ten."

"Hmmm," said the woman, tying her apron around her ample waist. "I guess you're right. You sure he left and came back from here?"

"I think so..." Allie hadn't considered that maybe he hadn't. But where could he have been, if not here at his and Ruben's cottage? She would have to ask him. "That's a good question."

RuthEllen bustled around the kitchen, rinsing off the vegetables and putting the flowers into pitchers and vases. "Well, honey," she said, turning to Allie. "My advice is to try not to dwell on it. On that night, I mean. Keep your mind on your fond memories of your friend. Let grief do its work." She adjusted the straps of her apron. "Now if you'll excuse me, dear, I've got to get to work," she said.

Allie took the hint. "Thanks, RuthEllen. See you later." Lacking any reason to stay, she got in the car, pondering her next steps. There must be something more at the cottage. She decided to drive back one last time before the renters took over. Maybe she would just sit in the driveway and let something come to her.

Forty-Four

Allie jumped as Ruben knocked on her car window.

"Whoa, didn't mean to startle you," he said as she rolled the window down. "What brings you to Anne's cottage, anyway?"

"I just can't believe that she killed herself."

"Really? I know, it's hard to get that to jive with your sense of her. Guess people can hold mysteries, eh?"

Allie shook her head. "I don't know. That's more than just a mystery. It throws everything I thought I knew into doubt." She shook her head again. "I just don't get it. At all."

"Hey, Allie. I don't mean to upset you. Shit, first I scare you, then I get you crying. Not cool." He reached in and patted her shoulder. "What makes you so sure she didn't shoot herself?"

"I was with her just a few hours before she died. She was fine, happy, talkative. Maybe a little tired, that's all." Allie cleared her throat. "You know, I found the gun."

"You did? How?"

"It was in the kitchen drawer. I left it on the counter. Anne said she'd find a better place to store it. I didn't think another thing about it."

Ruben gently took Allie's chin and turned her face so she was facing him. "They say that suicide is often a spur-of-the-moment, opportunity action," he said, with a serious expression. "Like, maybe seeing the gun on the kitchen counter brought something up in Anne..."

Allie turned her face away. "Oh, great, maybe it was my fault for leaving the gun there."

"I wouldn't say that. We don't know what the trigger was."

"Trigger," said Allie. "Interesting word in this situation..." She wiped her eyes. "I can't seem to get this out of my mind."

"Ok, let's think about something else."

"Like what?"

"Well, how about we make a plan for you to take me sailing? You have a boat, right?"

"My dad and I share a little wooden sailboat, yeah. Calliope. We keep it at the sailing club on a mooring."

"So, maybe there some time coming up where we could go for a sail? You think?"

"Um, sure. I am pretty busy. With this new position and all. Maybe, I don't know... how about next week sometime?"

"Oh, sure, I can hang loose. My schedule is much more open than yours." Ruben stepped back from the window.

"Ok, well, I'll try to find a time. It would be fun."

Ruben laughed. "Knowing how tough you are, I bet you would try to scare the crap out of me."

"What? Who, me? I wouldn't do something like that." Allie laughed, too, then rolled up the window. Ruben raised a hand in goodbye as she drove up the dirt road.

As she headed toward the cottage, she found herself humming a little tune. Trying to figure out where it came from, she realized it was that old song with the words, "You made me love you, I didn't want to do it, I didn't want to do it." Her grandfather had liked that record, and when she was a kid, she thought it was funny, she thought, smiling.

But her mood shifted as the words continued to run through her head, "you made me... I didn't want to do it..." What Ruben has said about opportunity... Was she partly responsible for Anne's death. by leaving the gun on the counter? That would be the worst.

Forty-Five

When she got home, Allie opened up the doors to the cottage to get some air moving. It felt stuffy inside, and the air outdoors was warm and clear. The sun was getting lower in the sky, shining on the shore on the other side of the bay like a stage light. The low light picked up the painted lobster buoys that littered the water's surface, dropped like so many baubles discarded by the boats that set and hauled their traps early each morning. Allie knew many of the boats by sound. As she settled in a porch chair with a can of seltzer, she heard the unmistakable roar of Harvey Hancock's engine. His was one of the last fishing boats out on a Saturday, as well as one of the first boats around in the morning. Allie wondered why he hadn't fixed his engine's muffler in all the years he'd been out lobstering; he put in enough hours, she thought, to have made money for the repair. Harvey tended to drive his boat forward at extremely high speed or, with a gnashing of gears, quickly in reverse. Annoying boat noise aside, Allie admitted, Harvey was a decent guy. He certainly was a hard worker, even now at an age somewhere north of 70.

Allie tapped her fingers on the little metal table next to her chair as she contemplated the situation. Her visit to Cormorant Cottage had yielded nothing in the way of enlightenment—neither why Anne might have ended her life nor whether someone else ended it for her. In fact, it had made her more confused than ever. Allie mentally listed the array of facts that she knew so far:

1. Anne had shown no sign of depression or anxiety or any sort of mental or emotional distress.

2. The gun, however, belonged to Anne.

3. Strangely, though, the gun didn't have Anne's fingerprints on it, nor anyone else's.

4. There was no note left at the scene.

5. Anne's sister discovered nothing strange or suspicious when she cleaned out Anne's belongings. Or at least she hadn't mentioned it to anyone, if she had.

That last thought made Allie sit up. What if Jennifer *had* found something, but Allie just hadn't heard about it? Or maybe Jennifer didn't know the significance of something she had discovered. Allie realized that she needed to talk to Jennifer but she didn't know how to reach her. Then she recalled the roster of SummerFest musicians included next of kin in case of emergency. Allie grabbed her laptop off the kitchen table. Sure enough, after Anne Kirschner, Cara and Andrew Kirschner were listed but also Jennifer Kirschner. Allie grabbed her phone. She started to dial Jennifer's number, then remembered that Cara and Andrew were there; a phone call might be unwelcome. She decided to send a text instead:

Jennifer, Allegra Brewster here. could we talk sometime? I have a few questions about what you saw at Anne's cottage, if anything. let me know when you might be available

After only a few minutes' wait, Allie's phone pinged with a reply:

How about around 9? In the middle of arranging our trip to Chicago. A & C are here.

Allie quickly responded:

Great, thnx 207-555-1234

Allie looked at the time. It was only seven o'clock—why was she so hungry? Oh, right. No lunch. She decided to make a peanut butter and banana sandwich. She brought it out on the deck, along with a glass of beer. The minute she sat down, her phone—left on the kitchen table—pinged again. Thinking it was Jennifer texting a change of time or something, Allie set her sandwich down and dashed in to the kitchen. The text was still visible on the iPhone screen:

dinner Al?

Luke had written. She answered:

no – phone call @ 9

you want me to call u?

responded Luke.

NO someone else is calling me

well EXCUSE ME!

Allie shook her head. Now Luke probably thought it was a call with Thomas or something like that. She didn't feel like putting him straight. Her phone pinged again and she looked at it with impatience.

Getting ready for tomorrow. You're introducing me, right?

It was Thomas, not Luke. Did she tell him she would introduce him at the family concert? She didn't remember that. Ugh, she really didn't feel up to it.

did I agree to that?

Damn right and I'm counting on it

ok let's discuss tmro

thnx alley

Allie chuckled in spite of her annoyance. Thomas's phone had autocorrected her name to "alley." Her phone pinged yet again.

Allie I mean Sorry!

The texts stopped, and Allie ate the rest of her sandwich, swishing it down with sips of beer. The sun was now quite low, and even Harvey had gone back to his mooring in the harbor. Allie moved inside and put on a light sweatshirt over her tee. If Jennifer called as planned, it would be in about 45 minutes.

Maybe she could practice her cello for a short while. She opened the case, releasing the imprisoned air. As if her body knew exactly what to do when encountering the astringent, piney smell of rosin, the musty, woody odor of the aged cello, the tang of steel from the cello's strings, and the texture of the bow's scratchy horsehair, she felt her arm muscles tense and her breath quicken. Yes, she still loved to play—the cello between her knees felt solid and comforting. She hadn't picked it up since Wednesday at Anne's... She tried not to think about that night. Instead, she concentrated on how Anne had taught her to approach the Bach cello suites[32]. She would start with No. 1 and see how far she got before Jennifer called. For the Prelude, Anne had always said to play with a feeling of urgency. "You're going somewhere, but you don't know where. Until suddenly you do," she had suggested. Allie played the three-minute piece, occasionally bending the rhythm but working to keep driving the music forward in a crescendo. It was a lot of notes. Halfway through, there was a false resolution. But, no, it wasn't a conclusion; the music continued. Toward the end, there was a set of impetuously repeating figures that grow in intensity and move higher and higher. Then, at the pinnacle, it all slowed down, finally resting on the foundational note of the key—G.

After a few minutes of playing, Allie realized she had become immersed in the act of playing; other thoughts had melted away, leaving only the notes of the Bach. It felt good to play. She swayed to the rhythm and let her face show the emotion in the music.

Hmm, Allie thought. The musical progression in Bach's Prelude mirrored her feelings about Anne's death. But would she reach that final note?

Forty-Six

Allie played through the Prelude again. In the middle of the fourth movement of the Bach, the Sarabande—the slow, stately, sorrowful dance—Allie's iPhone rang. Jennifer's name flashed on the screen, and Allie answered as quickly as she could, first carefully setting down her bow. "Jennifer," she said, "thanks so much for calling me back. I know this is a hard time."

"Not to worry," Jennifer replied. "Anyone else, I wouldn't have bothered. But I knew you weren't calling for some trivial reason."

"Right."

"So, what's up?" asked Anne's sister.

Allie paused. How much should she say? Would Jennifer think she was meddling? "I still feel that there has to be more to what happened with Anne. It was so unexpected. I mean, I saw her just hours before... before she died, and there was no hint. Nothing."

"I know." Jennifer's voice was soft.

"I can't get it out of my head—Anne, you know, it doesn't seem..." Allie heard a sniffle. "So, anyway, I decided to look at the cottage. Cormorant Cottage, where Anne was living."

"Right."

"But there was nothing there. You had cleared out all her stuff, and they were already getting ready to rent it out again. Really, there was just no sign she had ever been there. It was eerie." Allie gulped. "So I wondered if you had seen anything when you were there. Anything at all."

"It was hard, collecting her things." Jennifer took a ragged breath. "And I wondered, too, like you. How did this happen? There was no warning, no note explaining, nothing! I kept thinking, Anne wouldn't do this to us, to Cara and Andrew and me. Or you, Allie. It's not the Anne I know." There was a small moment of silence. "Knew."

"Yeah... You have her laptop, right? Did you find anything there?"

"It took me a long time to figure out her password," Jennifer said. "Actually, Cara told me. So I've only just opened it. But it feels like I'm prying. Jesus Christ! I think I'm living in some nightmare, some horror movie. In what life would I be looking for clues to Anne's suicide in her damn laptop?" Jennifer's voice was strained.

"It totally sucks. Well, maybe when you have a chance to see more of what's on the laptop, there will be some answers?"

"I don't know, Allie. Maybe. Oh, and then to make things a little worse, I had food poisoning when I got back to New York. I was sick as a dog for about 24 hours. That hasn't helped my mental acuity. I've just been trying to hold everything together for Cara and Andrew. They need me. I have to be the strong one."

"That's a bummer, about being sick. What did you eat, do you know? Something here in Maine?"

Jennifer laughed dryly. "Actually, I think it was something from Anne's. I threw out all the food I found, except for some apples. But there was a paper bag of mushrooms on the counter, which surprised me. I know how Anne despises mushrooms. But they looked good, and I happen to love mushrooms. So I brought them back with me and added them to an omelet I cooked that night. I don't know for sure if that's what got me, but if it was, they were really potent; I only used a couple. Ugh." Jennifer groaned at the memory.

"Wow." Allie was thinking. "I remember those mushrooms. I'm not a fan, either, and we couldn't figure out where they came from. Someone dropped them off. I thought it had been RuthEllen—she's constantly dropping off baked goodies and things from her garden. But she said it wasn't. So, who?"

"Clearly, someone who didn't know that Anne hated them, that's for sure. Hang on." Jennifer muffled her phone, but Allie could hear her speaking to someone. In a minute she returned. "Allie, I need to go.

Cara just told me that she can hear Andrew crying... I think I'd better check on him."

"Before you go," Allie said. "If you find anything strange on the laptop, will you let me know? Like, what was Anne searching in the days before she died? Or did she have any weird emails from people, or did she send any?"

"Allie, don't get your hopes up. This may be a mystery to us forever. But, yes, I will let you know if I find anything. *If*," Jennifer said. "Now I'd better go. Take care of yourself, Allie. I know you're a strong person. We all need to try to act the way Anne would want us to."

"Ok, yeah, right, Jennifer." Allie cleared her throat. "Give my love to Cara and Andrew."

As Allie hung up, she wondered if she had any idea of what Anne would want her to do. Or who Anne even was.

Forty-Seven

The summer weather continued to taunt Allie as she woke up the next morning. It was already warm. There was a slight breeze. The shadows of birds hopping from branch to branch outside her window played against the far wall of the bedroom. It was the sort of morning that tourists flock to Maine for: warm but not humid, bright blue clear skies. Allie could hear the buzz of outboard motors as families got an early start on the water.

It didn't seem right. The world was oblivious to the dark hole Anne's death had ripped open. It didn't feel healing at all. No, it felt callous, oblivious, aggressively unconcerned. Allie shook her head as she poured her cup of coffee and walked out onto the deck, squinting in the sunshine, her bare feet treading on the already warm rough boards.

"Oh, well," she muttered to herself, settling into a rocking chair. At least it was the perfect weather for the Family Concert that afternoon. That should make Thomas happy.

She remembered she had promised Thomas to introduce the concert to the audience. It was possibly the last thing in the world she felt like doing. I should probably write down a few notes, she thought, and she rose to get a pen and some paper from inside. The crunch of car wheels on gravel got her attention. Now who could that be at this hour? She moved a little faster, first heading to the bedroom for her bathrobe. Who drops by at seven o'clock on a Sunday morning?

The car door slammed as Allie emerged onto the deck, her tee shirt and underpants now decently covered. Ruben waved as he walked up the path to the deck. "Allie!" he shouted too loudly. "Glad to see you're up." He caught his breath after climbing the deck stairs. Allie looked at him, eyebrows raised.

"Look," he said. "Sorry to interrupt your peaceful morning. But I'm just so excited. I had to talk to you. I've been up for hours. Actually, Thomas woke me up, studying for his silly concert this afternoon."

Using the word "silly" to describe the concert didn't enhance Allie's welcome. "I suppose you want coffee," she said. When Ruben rapidly nodded yes, she got up and went into the cottage, letting the screen door slam loudly behind her. She poured a cup for Ruben but didn't heat it up. "Black ok?" she shouted to the deck.

"Fine," Ruben responded, settling himself in the other rocking chair.

Allie brought the cup out and handed it to Ruben. "So?"

"I was thinking about my Concerto for Orchestra." Ruben took a sip of the coffee and then set it down on the wicker side table. "Actually, you know, I think it's better that the orchestra is premiering that piece, instead of the cello concerto. It will make a bigger splash. So I wanted to talk with you about the publicity for it."

Allie looked down at her mug. She forced herself to keep sitting in the chair, instead of stalking off into the cottage as she wanted to do. This was the last thing she wanted to talk about, especially this morning. "Couldn't this wait until tomorrow?" she asked.

"Oh, yeah, I suppose so." Ruben looked abashed. "But I didn't want to lose the ideas that were floating around in my head."

Allie rolled her eyes. "Ok, let's hear them."

"I was thinking about some of the teachers I've had and friends, or I should say, colleagues. I would like them to know about this premiere. And I wondered if we could send out a sort of announcement."

"Isn't that something you could do on your own? I mean, I don't know who you want it sent to or how to contact them." Allie batted away a fly that was circling her now empty coffee mug.

"I just think it will mean more coming from the festival administration. I can give you a list of names and addresses."

"Ruben, you know that we're really busy right now, don't you? George will be gone in less than two weeks. And Anne's death..." Allie's voice dwindled.

"Ok, yeah. I get it." He thought for a moment. "If I get you a bunch of email addresses, could you at least send out an email announcement? As the orchestra's interim manager?" He paused. "I want it to be official—not just me blowing my own horn."

"I suppose I could do that. The concert's coming up soon. So get them to me as soon as you can."

"How do you want them? I mean, written on paper?"

"Hell, no! Best way would be an electronic spreadsheet, with first name, last name, email address. That way I can load them int our database as a separate list."

"You won't send them fundraising emails and other spam, will you?"

Allie rolled her eyes. "No, I'll delete the list after I send the email. That work for you?"

"That would be perfect." Ruben smiled. "Now, if only I can find those email addresses. I'd like to send to my old teachers and composers I admire. It would be so cool if some of them could come to the concert. I suppose Philip Glass will be in Cape Breton, Nova Scotia. He spends his summers there."

"Oh."

"It sounds idyllic. It's beautiful, quiet, he can indulge his foraging habit."

"Foraging habit?"

"Yeah, he likes to search for native things to eat." Ruben seemed ready to launch into a long discussion of Philip Glass's summer activities.

"Ok, well, I've got to get moving—busy day today." Allie stood up. "Coming to the concert this afternoon?"

"Nah, got other stuff to do. Like collecting a bunch of email addresses for you." Ruben took the hint and stood up, too. "Thanks, Allie. I'll be in touch when the list is ready."

"Just email it to me," she said. She picked up Ruben's almost full coffee cup—another mark against him, she thought wryly—and entered the cottage. The sound of the screen door slamming echoed Ruben's car door, and soon his car was spewing gravel as drove up the driveway.

He might be an up-and-coming composer, but he is one clueless guy, she thought.

Forty-Eight

"Wow, look at how many of you are here!" Allie's sunny voice belied the gray feeling she held inside. She stood on the stage in her yellow sundress and sandals and looked out onto the audience filled with squirming children and smiling parents. "We are so glad you came," she continued. "And you know who's especially glad? Conductor Thomas Ramirez, who will soon be standing right here." She gestured to the podium. "Believe it or not, Conductor Ramirez was once your age. And once upon a time, he discovered he liked listening to music and going to concerts. In fact," she lowered her voice and leaned toward the audience, "he told me he liked to pretend he was the conductor and would wave his arms just like the conductor did!" She straightened back up. "So, while you're listening to the music, maybe you'd like to imagine you are the conductor? If you do, listen carefully and let the music tell you how to move. Now, there's one important thing to remember. The conductor doesn't make any noise!" She put her finger to her lips. "The musicians playing their instruments make all the music; the conductor tries to be as silent as a mouse. So, what is the conductor doing?" She looked around the audience as if looking for an answer. "Well, I'll tell you. The conductor is helping the musicians stay together. But if he or she is an excellent conductor, they are doing something more. They are silently helping the musicians understand what the composer—that's the person who wrote the music—is trying to say. The music might be happy, or sad, or scary, or peaceful..." With each adjective, Allie's face showed the corresponding emotion. "This afternoon, while you are listening, you can decide how the music makes you feel inside. It tells you something, without using any words. That's the magic of music. And the conductor's job is to make sure that magic happens." Allie gestured toward the edge of the stage. "So, it's time for us to welcome Conductor Thomas Ramirez. Can you all give him a big welcome?"

The audience erupted into cheers as Thomas walked confidently onstage. He stopped and gave Allie an enthusiastic hug before stepping onto the podium. A little voice piped up from the crowd, "Is he your boyfriend?" and everyone laughed, while Allie shook her head and laughed, too, as she walked offstage.

Luke was standing in the wings. He didn't notice how Allie's face lost its cheerful expression as soon as she was offstage. "Well, Al, that was certainly totally effusive," he said softly.

"What?" Allie hadn't noticed that he was standing there until he spoke.

"Effusive. Overenthusiastic. Over the top." He looked her in the eye. "Yeah, the kids obviously noticed it. 'Is he your boyfriend?'" He mimicked the child's voice.

"Oh, stop it, Luke," Allie whispered, brushing past him. "Get over yourself."

Luke turned to follow her, but she put her hand out, palm facing him, and he got the message. Allie took a deep breath and headed outside around the concert barn to come in through the main door, the sound of music following her. As she opened the door, music flooded her ears. Thomas was obviously totally engaged, and the orchestra was responding. Almost in spite of herself, Allie found herself smiling. Many little hands were waving, some carefully following Thomas's lead and keeping time to the beat, and others dancing in the air, interpreting the music's emotional content.

As usual, George was standing at the back, watching the concert as well. "Great intro," he whispered, leaning toward Allie, giving her a thumbs up. She smiled in return and let herself relax.

Forty-Nine

As the hourlong concert continued, even though the audience was enthusiastic, Allie found her emotions returning to their gray state. Anne had loved playing family concerts, and her absence left a vast hole. Allie departed just as the concert ended with the last movement of Prokofiev's 1st symphony[33]. By then, the kids were dancing with abandon in their seats. She needed to escape before the audience began streaming out of the barn. She didn't want to have to talk to anyone (she knew many of the attendees), and she especially didn't want to hear people tell her how good her introduction was.

The late afternoon sky had clouded over. Allie looked at the clock on the cottage stove when she got home: almost five o'clock. She didn't feel hungry or motivated to do anything but sit on the deck with a beer. She picked up her phone and started going through her photos randomly. Eventually, she realized she was actually searching for photos of Anne. She and Anne playing duets in front of the bookshop. Anne laughing as she played a funny piece with the SummerFest String Quartet. Anne demonstrating the correct way to hold the bow. A video of Anne playing a medley of Adele songs on her cello. The last made tears well up in Allie's eyes. The sound of Anne's cello in "Set Fire to the Rain,"[34] passionate and a little rough, scrounging the sound out of the strings, Anne's intense expression and the sound of her breathing—Allie had forgotten this performance. It brought back the memory of Anne's commitment to music, how she would use it to express deep emotions. Even without the words to the song, Allie could feel the sense of urgency and longing. She looked at the video's date: not too long after Anne's husband died. Allie had been much younger then; she probably missed the depth of feeling in this performance, she thought. Late afternoon had turned to evening. Allie was suddenly exhausted. She barely had enough energy to wash up. It was only eight o'clock, but she couldn't wait to crawl under the covers.

Allie's phone pinged as she was crawling into bed. She hesitated to look at it, hoping it wasn't something from Luke or Thomas. But when she finally checked, she saw it was a text from Karin Anders.

Allie, can we meet for coffee tomorrow morning? Say, at 7:30?

Allie texted back.

ok where?

Your place? Mine is overrun with fucking musicians.

ok look for the sign that says brewster cottage off bayside road and follow the arrows

Great! See you at 7:30 – I'll bring donuts.

Allie responded with a thumbs up emoji. Beneath her outrageous language and bluster, Karin was actually a thoughtful, caring person much beloved by her fellow musicians. Allie wondered what Karin was up to that would bring her out before rehearsal on Monday morning. She turned her phone off and buried her head in her pillow. Another day done. The rasping sounds of Anne's version of Adele's song was stuck in her head.

Fifty

Allie was up and washed, brushed (teeth and hair), and dressed by seven o'clock. Monday, another day. Yawning, she tried to energize herself by deeply inhaling the aroma of brewing coffee as she straightened up the kitchen. How odd, she thought, rubbing her eyes, that Karin wanted to stop by so early in the morning. Rumor in the orchestra had it that Karin was a reluctant early riser. Once again, the sun was shining. It was an unusually warm summer—probably the effect of global warming, Allie reflected glumly.

The kitchen was still in shade, its two windows partially obscured by overgrown lilacs. Allie took her mug of coffee out to the deck to wait for Karin's arrival. At that time of the morning, the sun on the deck filtered through the evergreens, though its warmth was already evident. The sun's heat released the scents of earth and pitch and mulching vegetation, odors that were intensely familiar to Allie from all her summers at the cottage. She leaned back in the rocking chair and closed her eyes.

At the crunch of Karin's tires on the dirt road, Allie's eyes flew open. She stood up to greet her visitor. "Coffee?" she asked as Karin climbed the stairs to the deck. Karin nodded yes and held out a white paper bag. Grease spots were visible; Allie gave a thumbs up. Karin had made the trek to Old Fashioned Donuts, a shop that was ten minutes out of her way.

"Cream and/or sugar?" Allie asked.

"Neither," Karin said. "But bring some napkins. These are raspberry jelly donuts. I hope you like that kind."

"What? Who doesn't!" Allie said over her shoulder as she hustled back into the kitchen to get another mug of coffee.

After an appreciative smile as she sipped her coffee and the sound of contented chewing from Allie, Karin set her mug down. "I'm sure you wonder what the hell was so important that I would get up with the fucking sunrise," she said.

"Mm-hmm," said Allie, her mouth full of donut.

"Well, I've been watching you, girl. And I can tell that you are having a god-damn hard time with Anne's death." She stopped to take a bite of donut, and there was silence for a few seconds. "So, look, I know how you feel." Karin said after swallowing. "I mean, I really do know. And I thought maybe I can help."

Allie gave her a quizzical look but didn't deny that she was wrestling with a muddle of conflicted feelings.

"Here's why I say that," Karin continued. "When I was 23, my brother killed himself..."

"...Oh, my god, I'm so sorry to hear that." Allie sat up straighter in the rocker.

"Yeah, well, that was long ago, twenty years in fact. And I'll tell you, it still hurts. But in a different way, I guess. The thing is, for the longest time, I couldn't believe it. He, of all people, didn't seem like someone who would do such a... a... hurtful thing." As Karin stuttered a little, her mouth turned down at the corners and she stared at the scuffed wood of the deck.

Allie felt her eyes begin to sting. "Why? I mean, why don't you tell me about him?"

"Yes, that's why I wanted to talk to you." Karin sniffed and seemed to pull herself together. "You see, no one saw it coming. He was two years older than me, and I had idolized him all my life. He was good at everything he tried—sports, school, friendship. He was the best big brother, always ready to listen to me, always on my side when my parents got on my case. I wasn't an easy kid," she added. "But Josh was my protector and my model. The one difference between us was that he didn't have my musical ability. And he loved that. He was my biggest fan." Karin stopped for a moment, staring at the deck.

"It must have been so hard," Allie whispered.

"It was shitty!" Karin said. "One day he was Josh, a constant feature in my life. And the next minute, without any fucking warning, he was gone." She looked angry. "And he did it himself. To me." Karin sighed and paused. Allie sat motionless.

"And that's what I want to talk about," Karin said. "I mean, I *thought* he did it to me. I blamed him for deserting me. I was full of anger." Karin emphasized the word *anger*. "For being so selfish and not thinking about what his suicide would do to me. I was so so sad but even more, I was furious. And I didn't know what to do with that feeling. I felt mad at the world. There was no hope, no joy left." Allie looked away, recognizing that feeling.

"But then, a friend of my mother's visited me, Mrs. Tomkin. She was great; I'd known her all my life. She sat me down and she told me that Josh hadn't meant to hurt me. She told me that he must have been in tremendous pain. And because he loved me, he didn't want me to know that. He tried to protect me from that. But in the end, the pain was more than he could bear. Mrs. Tomkin asked me to think of all the ways that Josh had shown and told me that he loved me." Karin smiled to herself. "She actually made me say as many things as I could think of that demonstrated how he felt about me. Including that fact that he'd written me a note a few days before his death, saying that even if he couldn't always be by my side, he would always be with me in spirit." Karin waved her hand as if wiping away that memory. "I thought he was talking about the fact that he'd just gotten a job in London. Ha." Karin stopped to sip her coffee.

"But Anne didn't leave a note." Allie's voice wobbled.

"No, I know that," Karin said quickly. "But what I'm trying to say is we can't know how someone else is really feeling." She looked at Allie. "Can we? Deep down. It's unknowable, unless they try to tell us. And even then, they might not be able to express themselves. It may be too fucking painful."

Allie nodded.

"So," Karin said, "when you think about Anne, you might try to separate what she did from what your relationship was. Her death doesn't mean she didn't love you. That she didn't care about you. That she wanted to leave you. When someone kills themself, it's because they feel they have no choice."

"I know, but they do have a choice. They just need to ask for help or something..."

"Yeah, it seems like it should be easy to solve, doesn't it. For fuck sake, why don't they just reach out, right? In Josh's case and in Anne's case, they were surrounded by people who loved them and would do anything to help them." She shook her head. "To us, it makes no sense. And of course we feel angry and abandoned."

"Right." Allie nodded.

"But we need to remind ourselves that their death... We need to keep this in the front of our little pea brains that their decision to kill themselves wasn't about us. It was about being in pain. Being lost in a world of pain that is unbearable, or so they think."

"I guess...," Allie said. "I guess that makes some sense. But... I don't know."

"What don't you know?"

"I just can't believe that Anne would do that. I mean, not just to me or to her friends in the orchestra, but to her kids, Cara and Andrew. To her sister." Allie looked stricken. "I just can't believe that. I don't think I ever will." Her eyes were dry now.

"It takes time. A lot of crappy, cry-your-eyes-out time. Fucking years. You just have to go through it. But I have to tell you, Allie, that I am convinced Mrs. Tomkin was right." She looked at her watch. "Oh, shit, I'd better take off. I need to warm up before rehearsal." She stood and held out her arms to Allie, who let herself be enfolded.

"You'll get through this, kiddo," Karin said as she patted Allie's back. "You know what they say: 'If you're going through hell, keep going.'"

"Thanks, Karin," Allie said, as she pulled away. "I appreciate it. Thanks."

Karin headed down the stairs toward her car.

"And thanks for the donuts!" Allie shouted after her. Then she went into the kitchen and poured herself another coffee. Well, she thought, maybe Karin was right, but it sure didn't feel right to her. She looked at her phone; it was almost time to go into work. Might as well go now, she thought.

Fifty-One

In the festival office, the morning passed uneventfully. Allie felt rather zombie-like, though no one would have known she was operating on automatic pilot. She acted like her usual capable self, if subdued. She and George went over the budget and the bank accounts and a myriad of details that she would soon be in charge of. Publicity, accounting, stage management, donors, keeping the musicians happy—there were so many moving parts to the job of general manager. And I won't have the benefit of someone like me helping out, she thought to herself. She would have to think about how best to parcel out the support jobs that she did under George. Which of the volunteers could take on some of those responsibilities? No doubt, she thought, she would be doing both George's job and part of her old job. A wave of weariness engulfed her. Maybe this wasn't a good idea. Heck, she thought, I'd better liven up. She took a deep breath. Music! That's what she needed. But what? Something lively and fast. A dance of some sort.

"George, I need dance music to listen to. Have any suggestions?" Allie called to George who was now back in the inner office. "Something lively."

"Try Brahms's Hungarian Dances," he replied without a pause. [35]

"Good idea." Allie found the Hungarian Dances on her app, inserted her ear buds, and felt herself get swept away to another place and time. A time of grace and romance, tinged with a bit of sorrow, but mostly joyful and full of life. Allie relaxed as the music flooded her mind, and she returned to the task she was working on.

"Hey! Al!"

Allie realized that a hand was waving in front of her face. She took out an ear bud and looked up at Luke, who was leaning over her desk.

"Al, I've been trying to get your attention."

Allie raised her eyebrows. "How can I help you?"

Luke shot her an incredulous look and launched into a rendition of an old comedy routine. "HOW can I help you? How CAN I help you? How can I help YOU?"

Allie shot him an annoyed look and drew her hand across her throat in a sign for cut it out.

"Jeez, Al, what kind of question is that? You act as though I'm a stranger or something."

"Sorry, Luke. Guess I was preoccupied. What's up?" Allie still had one ear bud in, and the next Hungarian Dance started.

Luke narrowed his eyes. "Al, I was hoping that we could get together tonight. I thought maybe you'd like to get a burger? Watch a silly show? Hang out for a while?"

Allie pressed pause on her phone and took out the other ear bud. She really didn't feel like doing anything. But how to tell Luke that, tactfully? She scrunched up her nose.

"Hey, wait a minute before you say no." Luke read her expression correctly. "You need to do something fun. You need to get out of... I mean, you've been working too hard. And anyway, I need to talk to you about Ruben's idea for his concerto. Another backdrop..."

Allie sighed. "Ok, tell me what he wants."

Luke settled into the chair at the end of Allie's desk. "He has this idea of, like, some sort of slideshow of art—paintings, I think. He wants it to play while the orchestra is performing his piece. We do have the ceiling projector and all, so I guess it would be possible, but..."

Allie took up the thread of the conversation. "...But who is going to get the paintings and get permission to use them and figure out the coordination with the music and figure out the lighting so the audience can see the slides and the musicians can still see their music and Tony and, and, and — all in the next two weeks."

"Yeah, I thought it seemed a bit much."

George had overheard the conversation from the inner office. "Tell him absolutely not!" he said, trying to roar with his still-raspy voice.

Luke looked at Allie. "Ruben's pretty insistent. He'll probably bug you about it when I tell him no."

Allie shrugged. "He'll hear the same answer from me."

"And me," added George, who then got up and closed his door.

"So Al, what do you say? Burger? Crab cakes? Beer?" Luke shot her an encouraging glance.

He looked like a hopeful spaniel begging for a treat, Allie thought. "Thanks for the idea, Luke," she said. "It sounds fun, but..."

"But you're too tired or busy or something. Right?" Luke exhaled sharply in frustration. "It's always the same these days. You never want to get together." His face changed to a whistful expression. "I miss you, Allie. I miss our time together." He lowered his voice. "You know how I feel about you."

Allie closed her eyes. "Just not tonight, Luke. Ok?"

Without a word, Luke stood up and left the office. Allie wiped her hand over her face. He wanted something she couldn't give him.

Fifty-Two

A few minutes later, Allie was back listening to the Hungarian Dances and working on her laptop. She felt rather than saw someone standing beside her desk and looked up.

"Thomas," she said, removing her ear buds. "What brings you to the office?"

Thomas was wearing a fitted black tee shirt that showed off his trim physique. His wavy dark hair cascaded over his forehead, and he pushed it back. "At least it's somewhat cool in here," he said.

"Hot in the barn? Was the AC running?" Allie knew how important it was for both the musicians and their instruments to keep the concert barn at a comfortable temperature.

"No, no, it's fine. Just got hot walking from there to here. That sun feels more like Texas than Maine." Thomas had grown up in Texas and Southern California and enjoyed the cooler summer temperatures of the north. "But, hey, that's not why I'm here, to complain," he added. "First of all, I want to thank you again for the fantastic job you did introducing the family concert yesterday."

Allie smiled and nodded. "You did a super job yourself. The orchestra sounded amazing. And the audience was so into it!"

"Ok." Thomas sent her a dazzling smile. "We both are stars, then. May I?" He gestured toward the chair that Luke had earlier vacated. When Allie nodded, he folded himself elegantly into the cheap metal seat.

"But," he continued, "I also want to know how you are doing. This has been real hard for you, right?" He looked at her, a serious expression on his face.

"Um, uh, I guess so." Allie was flustered by his frank appraisal. "It still doesn't make any sense to me. I just can't..."

Thomas covered her hand with his. "Of course, it's horrible. We are all sad. But I didn't know Anne the way you did. You have suffered a loss, a great loss. It's changed your world."

Allie swallowed and blinked, trying to stem the tears that began to fill her eyes. She nodded mutely.

"Allie!" Ruben's abrupt arrival in the office transformed the atmosphere, and Thomas quickly withdrew his hand. "Come on, Allie, what is Lucas telling me? That you won't even consider my idea for an arts backdrop to the concerto. Why are you so dead set against it?"

Allie splayed her hands, an *are you kidding?* expression on her face.

"It's a great idea and perfectly easy to do. I know we have the equipment all set up in the concert barn. What's your problem with it?"

"It's not so easy, Ruben."

"Really? Come on! Just get a few images, make a slideshow..."

Just as Allie began to explain why it wasn't feasible, George barged through his office door.

"Ruben! You are out of line!" he barked in his scratchy voice. "What the hell do you think we are doing here? We barely can hold the festival together in light of the fact that SOMEONE HAS DIED. Not to mention that Allie is having to take over the management on very little notice. And you have gotten your wish to premiere your composition, in spite of the fact that there is a very short time to prepare it. So don't be giving Allegra or me any guff about some hair-brained idea of displaying slides during the performance. It is not happening!" George was pink from the effort of controlling his temper and increasing his damaged vocal chords' volume.

"Hey, ok, George. I thought maybe Lucas hadn't explained it very well. It's really not that complicated..."

Allie now found her voice. "Not that complicated? You haven't got a clue, Ruben. We are all stretched to the limit here. No one can spend the time getting permission to use the images you're suggesting, let alone collect them, create the slideshow, and test the lighting and all."

George nodded in agreement. "And anyway, Ruben, the concert is about the music. Your music. Why take away attention from that?"

"Yeah, buddy, you don't want to do that," said Thomas.

"You didn't think it was such a bad idea when I mentioned it to you before, roomie," Ruben said, casting an angry look his way.

"I wasn't enthusiastic," Thomas said with a grimace. "It seems like a gimmick to me."

Ruben seemed to falter. "Well, when you put it that way. About focusing the audience on the music. Maybe that does make sense." His shoulders sagged. "I was hoping it would expand their experience..."

"Do you understand why we can't do it, Ruben?" Allie asked.

"Yeah, I guess so."

"Be a bit more definitive, Ruben," said George. "Like, 'Thank you, Allegra, that makes perfect sense. Sorry to have disturbed you by coming in here and yelling at you.'" George glared at Ruben.

"Fine, fine. Everything George said. It's not like I was badgering her or something."

"Oh, really? It sounded like badgering to me." George was still annoyed.

Felt like it, too, thought Allie.

"But you are going to do the publicity I suggested, right?" Ruben perked up. "You got my email list, didn't you?"

"Yes, and I've been working on the press release." Allie looked at George. "I thought we could send it out tomorrow. It might even make Thursday's papers."

"And online stuff, too?" Ruben said.

"Yes," said George, exasperation in his voice. "We'll do all the usual media. And send out that email to your buddies..."

"Oh, I already did that," said Allie.

"Ok, we're done here." George turned around and headed back to the inner office. "I've got to leave in about fifteen minutes," he said to Allie over his shoulder. Ruben looked sheepish as he headed out the office door.

"Look, Thomas," Allie said to the man still sitting next to her desk. "I have a ton of stuff to do. Thanks for stopping by but..."

"...But hit the road. Right?" Thomas laughed. "That's fine, Allie. I'll leave you to finish your work. Anything I can do to help?"

"Uh, offer me peace and quiet?"

"Got it. I'm on my way."

In a minute, Allie was once more alone in the office. Looking for something calm, she typed "cello calm" in her app. In a second, a list of potential choices came up. Allie chose one, "Relaxing Cello" with cellist Tina Guo.[1] A collection of themes from mostly classical sources arranged for cello, it was indeed relaxing, thought Allie. She remembered she hadn't played her cello since Saturday. Maybe I should do that when I get home, she thought. Yes, that's what I need.

The afternoon wore on. Several orchestra members stopped by to say how morose they were feeling. It helped to play the tribute to Anne at Friday's concert, they agreed, and watching the children at Sunday's family concert had raised their spirits, they added—but it wasn't the same without Anne at the front of the cello section. Oh, they were so sad. Of course they were, thought Allie. But she doubted any orchestra members felt Anne's loss as deeply as she did.

"Allegra?" Tony Bainbridge stepped through the door. "Can I talk with you for a moment? Privately?"

He looked terrible—bags under his eyes, his silvery hair flattened and stringy, clothes that looked slept in. "Sure," said Allie. "No one else is here, and I doubt anyone will interrupt us. Most of the players have gone home. George left and isn't coming back today." She sent the disheveled conductor an inquiring glance.

"I have to talk with you about Anne," he said, his voice cracking. "I'm feeling so guilty. It's all my fault." He sat in the chair by her desk that Thomas had recently occupied.

"What do you mean?"

"I... well..." Tony looked down. "I think I was pushing her. Too hard. And maybe it was too much. She already had tons of pressure because of the concerto." He looked at Allie with a bleak expression. "Do you think I drove her to it?"

"What? Uh, no..."

"I can't believe it. After all these years, you know, I suddenly saw her in a different way. And *I* am different." He wiped his forehead. "Bloody hell. I thought..." He started again after clearing his throat. "I thought we could be happy together."

Allie inclined her head, then shook it.

"You saw her last, I believe," said Tony. "Did you sense her desperation? Did she seem... like Anne? Or lost, upset?"

"She was her usual funny, cheerful self."

"Did she say anything about me? Did she complain about my pressing her?"

Allie thought back to what Anne had said, and decided not to mention it. "She really was her normal self. That's why I can't believe she killed herself. There was just no warning. None whatsoever." It was absurd that Tony thought his romantic advances would have driven Anne to end her life.

"But the police..." he said

"I know what the police think. But they're missing something. There's a clue somewhere—I just have to find it."

Tony's face lighted up at the idea that Anne hadn't killed herself because of him. Then it darkened as the thought of her being murdered entered his thoughts. "But who would want to do that?" he said in an angry voice. "By God, if I find out..." He clenched his fists in his lap.

"I know," said Allie, softly. "It's hard to imagine anyone would want to do that. She was so kind to everyone."

"Perhaps too kind," mused Tony. "And such a lovely, generous spirit. I mean, she made you feel good, just being around her."

"True."

"So, some random killer stalks the festival? Do you have any idea who that might be?"

"I don't. Not yet. But I'm determined to find out. For Anne and for her family." Allie's voice broke on the last word.

"And for all of us," added Tony. "And for the festival. We have to figure it out, Allegra. We simply must do and pronto." He got up. "I'll be off, then. I feel a tad better after talking with you. Though, a murderer in our midst. Grim thought, that."

Allie nodded thoughtfully as he left.

Fifty-Three

Allie got out her cello after a dinner of toast and scrambled eggs. It surprised Allie that she felt like playing. She thought it might have felt too hard, too close to touching her feelings about Anne's death. After all, Anne was an integral part of her enjoyment of playing. I will play for Anne, wherever she is, Allie told herself. I will send my music out to her, to her spirit, to whatever she is now—a ray of light? A bundle of energy? I don't believe in heaven as some place in the sky where angels are playing on harps and God is a White man with a long white beard, but where has Anne's energy gone? Death might erase the body, but where does the soul go? Is there a soul? What is it if there is such a thing? Can someone who was so alive, who electrified those around her with her humor and her love...

Allie shook her head and wiped her eyes. *Play the cello.* she commanded herself. Without thinking, she launched into the second Bach cello suite, surprising herself tonight with her ability to play the beginning without the printed music. Her hands and arms knew what to do independently of any intellectual contribution from her brain. Allie closed her eyes and let the sound wash over her, her body swaying to the music. Tears began to stream down her cheeks, but it wasn't from sorrow; it was more like a tide of emotion washing through her. She wasn't even aware of the tears until she tasted salt. She laughed to herself ruefully—clearly there was something in the Prelude that pulled emotions out of people. For example, she thought, there's the heavy breathing you can hear on Emmanuelle Bertrand's recording of the second suite.[37]

After the Bach, Allie's playing morphed into variations on "Twinkle, Twinkle, Little Star." Anne had created a cello duet, somewhat like Mozart's variations, based on the childhood tune. Allie had played it enough times, first one part and then the other, that she knew both parts by heart, and they sang out of her cello without pause.

Suddenly, in the middle of her reverie, an incoming text beeped on Allie's phone. She opened her eyes, peeved that she'd been interrupted, and picked it up to look at the screen. Her annoyance vanished when she saw it was from Anne's sister, Jennifer.

Finally had a chance to look at Anne's laptop. Some strange searches.

??

She seems to have been obsessed with this one composer. I'll send you some links.

Allie set her cello down and waited for the next text from Jennifer. Soon it appeared. The websites all had to do with the music of Janice MacKenzie, the composer Anne had mentioned the night before she died. One was a Wikipedia site, another was a bio from the American Composers of the 20th Century site. Others were links from reviews of performances. MacKenzie had died more than a decade ago, and it seemed to Allie that her music was not being played very much these days. Allie didn't remember seeing MacKenzie listed on any programs for the festival since she'd been involved. It didn't seem so odd to Allie that Anne had been doing research on MacKenzie. Maybe it was an effort to get a better handle on how to play that wild fourth movement of Ruben's concerto. Maybe Anne had done the typical thing people do when they look something up on the internet, going down the rabbit hole.

Another text came in from Jennifer.

Should have mentioned that all those links came from the night she died.

Allie was startled. So, after Allie had left the cottage, Anne had gone on her computer and looked up that composer. What did that have to do with her decision to put an end to her life? It didn't make sense.

thanks, jennifer i wonder why

Allie amended her previous thought: it *still* didn't make sense. She decided to look up the MacKenzie links herself.

III: Andante Accelerando

"Music has a great potential to affect people differently in very strong ways; someone out there will love what you write, and someone out there will hate it." *—Angelique Poteat (American composer and musician, b. 1986)*

Fifty-Four

Tuesday morning brought the start of another hot and muggy day. Through the trees, Allie could see that there was a haze over the water. The air was thick and still. Allie sipped her coffee on the deck in her t-shirt and underwear, the buzz of cicadas ringing in her ears. Monday night had brought desultory sleep. She'd looked up the composer MacKenzie before going to bed, but couldn't see why Anne had been researching her. Allie knew Anne had studied with MacKenzie back in her conservatory days, but hadn't heard that they were friends or close in any way. And Anne was looking at MacKenzie on her computer just hours before shooting herself? What did she find there that led her to end her life? The conundrum was like a terrible toothache that is made worse by exploring it with your tongue.

Everyone assured her that Anne's death by her own hand was not that abnormal: RuthEllen, Karin, Chief Knowles... But it didn't seem right to Allie. There was some factor that she hadn't yet identified, some clue lurking in the dim background, that made it impossible for Allie to accept suicide as an answer.

But, like her mother had said, if Anne didn't cause her own death, that meant someone else did. But who could have wanted Anne to die? Her fellow orchestra members loved her. Her students here in Maine and in Chicago adored her. She didn't have any secret vices, like a gambling or drug addiction, that would cause her to come in contact with dangerous people. She wasn't dating anyone.

Or was she? Was Tony Bainbridge's reaction to Anne's death overblown? Allie thought back to what Anne had said about Tony's attentions. Typical for Anne, she had mentioned them in an understated way, like it was no big problem that he was interested in her in a romantic way. But maybe Tony had been more trouble than Anne let on. Was he jealous, insistent, disappointed, deranged? Allie shook her head. God, no, Tony was a good guy. She'd known him for years. He had always been charming, courtly even. He was always in control of himself, even in the throes of a frustrating rehearsal. Allie smiled to herself, remembering how a temporary percussionist kept hitting the cymbal cues early, then late, in a rehearsal of a new version of the "Star-Spangled Banner" they were rehearsing one year for the Fourth of July. Allie remembered how hard Tony had worked to keep his temper, though he was obviously frustrated. But he knew that a display of anger would only fluster the poor man even more. Allie had seen them talking after the rehearsal, and at the concert the cymbal had crashed at exactly the right time, earning a big smile from the podium. No, she knew Tony. He couldn't have killed Anne.

And, yet... He definitely had lost his professional demeanor over her death. Was it too much; was he overacting? It was unheard of that he would back out of a concert, especially on such short notice. Had there been more to their relationship than Anne had let on? Had he been stalking her, or pressuring her, or could he have shot her in a moment of rage, or... ? Allie shook her head to clear out the thought of Tony killing Anne. It just didn't seem plausible.

What about Ruben or Thomas, who were in the neighboring cottage? Why hadn't they heard a gunshot? Allie remembered Thomas had made a trip to her place the night of Anne's death to plead with Allie to let him get out of the family concert. She smiled to herself, remembering how well that concert had turned out for the ambitious assistant conductor. Turning back to the night of Anne's death, Allie wondered if it was possible that Thomas could have stopped in at Anne's cottage and shot her on his way back home? Why would he do that? She thought about Thomas's demeanor since Anne's death. He seemed appropriately saddened. Not weird in any way.

And why would Ruben kill the artist who was going to premiere his new cello concerto? Was he unhappy with her interpretation? Allie shook her head. That was crazy. No composer was that maniacal. No,

Anne was going to bring acclaim to Ruben. It would have been against his own interests to kill her. Though he did seem excited that the orchestra was now premiering his Concerto for Orchestra, instead of the cello concerto. He acted rather callous about Anne's death, but Allie ascribed that to his self-absorption. Yeah, he was an egotistical jerk sometimes, but that didn't make him a murderer.

But why would someone from outside want to kill Anne? She did have an extremely valuable cello, but the cello hadn't been touched. Maybe the thief was interrupted, first by Anne and then by the sound of Thomas's car returning. Maybe? That was possible! Allie's breath quickened as she thought of this potential solution to her conundrum.

Searching for more answers, Allie thought back to the fact she had uncovered: RuthEllen wouldn't have heard a car driving down the road to the cottages. After all, she hadn't heard Thomas's car. Maybe Thomas had seen a strange car parked in Anne's driveway? But wouldn't he have mentioned that?

Allie glanced at her phone. Eight o'clock! She jumped up and dashed to the bedroom. Surveying possible outfits for another day at the office, she chose a rather limp faded red linen blouse and baggy blue striped crops. She slipped into her sandals, ran her toothbrush over her teeth, splashed water on her face (and applied a bit of mascara), ran her fingers through her hair, grabbed her keys and phone and jumped into Pablo, rushing up the hill. A cloud of dust followed the protesting ancient Volvo wagon.

Fifty-Five

Allie was eager to ask Thomas if he saw another car near Anne's cottage. Of course, she thought to herself, if he didn't see one, it didn't really mean anything. The attack could have happened after he returned home and was in bed asleep. Or maybe it was too dark for him to see a car if it was somewhat hidden.

She stopped along the way to the office to get a cup of coffee at Barnloft Bakery, having run out of time to make coffee before she headed to work. Sitting alone at a table, head bent over his phone, was Luke. She saw him as she walked through the door, and her heart sank. She didn't have time to deal with him right now. He looked up a moment later, before she could decide to grab coffee elsewhere to avoid him.

"Al!" Luke greeted her with a wide smile. "I didn't expect..."

"I know," Allie said. "I'm in a hurry—just getting a cup of coffee before I start work."

"So no time to sit with me for a minute or two?" Luke looked crestfallen.

"Well..." Allie paused. Maybe she did owe it to Luke to spend some time with him. She should at least tell him how she was feeling about their relationship. Not that it would be an easy conversation...

"Luke, how about lunch? I am pretty busy this morning, but maybe you can stop by around 12:30? We can grab sandwiches and eat in the conference room, where it's cool."

"Yeah, fine. Do you want me to get you a drink? Iced tea? Lemonade? I know how you love pink lemonade." He looked at her expectantly.

"I'll stick with water, thanks."

It was Allie's turn to order. She got a "gigantic" dark coffee (Barnloft's extra large size). "See you, Luke," she said as she departed.

"12:30," Luke replied.

Allie's thoughts turned back to Thomas as she got to the office. Would he be at the festival this morning? She deposited her salad in the office refrigerator and took a slug of coffee. Oh, good, George wasn't in yet. Allie opened her laptop and looked at the day's schedule. Thomas wasn't listed in any of the festival activities, but maybe he'd be around. It was probably too early to find him, but she decided to take a walk down to the practice rooms and the concert barn, just in case.

It was already too hot to enjoy being in the sun. Allie didn't remember such hot weather from her childhood. The practice rooms, lodged in what was once a stable, had portable air conditioners much like the festival office, but with this heat in those uninsulated cubicles, the air conditioners couldn't keep up. Allie could hear various instruments as she got close. The musicians with the loudest instruments tended to be the ones using the practice rooms. Flutists, other woodwinds and string players could often practice in their summer living quarters, if their neighbors didn't mind. But brass players and percussionists generally put in their hours of practicing in the festival's practice rooms. Allie identified a hornist playing etudes, a trumpeter going over and over a difficult phrase, and a someone on a marimba playing a jazz lick. Since she didn't expect Thomas to be in a practice room, Allie trudged on to the concert barn, where she was rewarded with the sight of Thomas's car parked out front.

She pushed open the hall's double doors and cool air swirled past her. Closing the doors quickly behind her, she waited for a moment to let her eyes adjust to the dim light after the blazing sun. The air was cool but a bit stale, scented by the wood of the beams and some half empty wine glasses left on the bar counter off to the side. At first Allie didn't see anyone, but she could hear the sound of a cello emanating from somewhere on stage. For just a flash, she imagined—Anne?—then immediately quashed that thought. Eventually she could make out a figure sitting in the midst of the cello seats. Allie walked closer and saw that it was Thomas. He hadn't heard her come in and was frowning as he played a series of scales, his hair tumbling over his forehead as he moved his bow back and forth. Suddenly, he caught sight of her.

"Allie!" he said. "What brings you here?"

"I should ask you that, mister conductor, uh, *maestro*," she said with a smile.

Thomas gave a short laugh. "Maestro, I like that." He set his cello down and laid the bow across his music stand. "It calms me, to come here in the early morning and play the cello. You know, grounds me. Back to my roots or whatever you want to call it. And it makes me more comfortable in the hall when I'm alone on the podium instead of being one of many cellists in a section. It also helps me understand how the acoustics work in here."

Allie nodded. That made sense.

"So, Allie, why are you here? Who are you looking for?"

"You, actually."

"How did you know I'd be here?"

"I didn't. But I saw your car, so that tipped me off." Allie smiled.

"Oh, right. I love that it's so peaceful and quiet in here in the morning. I almost can hear some echoes of concerts and rehearsals resonating in the rafters, but my god, it's such a relief when my roommate is getting crazier and noisier by the day."

"Oh?"

"Yeah, Ruben is absolutely manic now that his Concerto for Orchestra is going to be performed. He's such an egotist. He constantly makes a racket, even with his headphones on. So this," Thomas gestured to the surrounding space, "is my refuge."

"In that case, I'm sorry I interrupted you."

"No, no, that's all right. No problem. You can interrupt me anytime, Allie." Thomas looked her up and down with a grin. "By the way, *chica*, you must have gotten dressed in a hurry this morning. You didn't button your blouse right."

Allie looked down and saw that she'd mismatched the buttons. She felt her cheeks turn pink. God, she'd been in such a hurry. Then that reminded her of the reason she had sought out Thomas. She looked up at Thomas, who still sat on the stage.

"Thomas, I've been thinking about the night Anne died," she said.

"Oh, I know."

"Well, I wondered. After you stopped by to visit me and then went home, did you pass any cars on the road to the cottages?"

"No, I think I was the only car the whole way home."

"What about when you drove past Anne's cottage? Could there have been an extra car in the driveway? Maybe hidden a little?"

"Well, it was quite dark. But I don't think so. No, I'm pretty sure hers was the only car there." He looked at her intently. "Why?"

"If someone from outside came to steal her cello or something, maybe that's how it happened. I mean, maybe someone killed her. But if you didn't see anything, then it would have happened after you got home and were in bed."

"True. But..."

"But what?"

Thomas stood up, hopped off the edge of the stage, and walked over to Allie. He put his hands on her shoulders and looked in her eyes. "Allie, what about the locked door? The gun?"

"So," she began in a shaky voice, "the gun was already in the cottage but could have been picked up by the killer. And the door, well, maybe he grabbed the key earlier..." She looked down. "I don't know. Does that sound lame?"

"No, I think you are right to question." He tightened his grip on her shoulders just a little and gave her a slight shake. "You solved the first murder, after all." He stopped talking and looked at her with a thoughtful expression. "But it's eating you up. You have changed since the spring. Too much death. I'm so sorry." Thomas enfolded her in his arms and she melted into his embrace. It didn't feel like a sexual advance. It was consoling.

They stood like that for a few seconds, and then Thomas withdrew his arms. "We both have work to get to."

"Right. But, Thomas, what do you think I should do about my theory of a stranger killing her?"

Thomas shrugged. "I guess I would start with that police chief, Knowles." He raised his eyebrows to indicate he didn't hold out much hope for help there.

"You're right. I'll start there." Allie took a deep breath. "I'll let you get back to your reverie and I'll get to work in the office. Thanks, Thomas."

"Talk to me anytime you want, Allie." He hopped back on the stage and settled in the chair to resume his practice.

Allie walked quickly down the aisle to the double doors. The bright light blinded her as she emerged from the hall. It was like walking into an oven.

Fifty-Six

As Allie trudged back to the festival office, she could feel herself wilt under the blazing sun. Once again, she thought, the small office air conditioner will never be able to keep up with this heat. She entered the office and turned on the small fan by her desk, hoping that its breeze would augment the air conditioning. With wisps of hair fluttering around her face, she bent over her laptop and checked today's work calendar.

"OMG!" she said out loud. There was a meeting with the executive committee of the board scheduled in half an hour, and Allegra Bewster was listed as the only topic on the agenda. Hearing her exclamation, George emerged from his office.

"You just saw the meeting, right?" he asked.

"Holy crap! Is there an agenda? How come I didn't know about it?"

"Not to worry, Allie. They just want to check in with you about the upcoming transition. I think maybe some of them worry that Anne's death has knocked you sideways. They just want reassurance that you are still up for the job of interim manager. You are, aren't you?" George looked her in the eye.

"Of course I am. 'Knocked me sideways'—hmmm—sounds like something Ken Henson would say. George, do you think they are having second thoughts? Are some of them trying to get rid of me?"

"Not at all, Allie. They are genuinely concerned and just want to make sure you are comfortable going forward. I suggest you prepare by explaining the work you've been doing. I already told them you've been very productive and that we are getting everything ready for my departure." George raised his arms in a silent cheer. "They just want to hear it from you, too."

"Ok, ok." Allie gestured toward her laptop. "I'll come up with some sort of report to fill them in on the latest progress. But I have other stuff to do..."

"Oh, I know," said George. "You'll find that sometimes the board asks for things that take up your time, when you wish you could spend it on something more important. But the truth is, Allie, the board is important. You want to keep them on your side. And the best way to do that is by keeping them filled in. Even though it's sometimes an added burden." He shrugged and turned to go back into his office.

"Will you be at the meeting, too?" Allie caught him as he walked away.

"You bet," he said, over his shoulder.

Allie quickly got to work assembling a list of activities, decisions, and communications she'd been involved in since the last meeting. It seemed like ages since then, but it had been less than a week. So much had happened, so much... As she was finishing up, Luke came through the door.

"Whew! It's nice and cool in here," he said, passing his hand over his forehead. In the humidity, his tousled hair was even wilder than usual.

"Hang on, Luke. I can't talk right now. Executive committee meeting in a few." Allie didn't look up as she worked. "I do want to catch up with you later..." Her fingers kept tapping away at the keys.

Luke tensed up when Allie said she couldn't talk, but his shoulders relaxed at her statement that she wanted to talk later. "Ok, Allie-Cat. See ya." Mollified, he loped back out the door.

Allie continued working on her short report for another few minutes. She looked at the time—eek!—ten minutes to go. A few minutes later, she hit "print 6 copies" and stood over the printer.

"We've missed you on the podium." Ken Henson's voice boomed as he opened the door. Wondering who he was talking to, Allie turned around and saw that Ken was following Tony Bainbridge, who looked peeved that Ken had caught up with him.

"Though that boy, Thomas Whatshisname, did a decent job." Allie winced, glad that Thomas hadn't heard Ken.

"Of course he did a fine job," said Tony, scowling. "He's developing into a damn fine conductor. Now, are you here for a meeting? I was hoping to chat a bit with Allegra here."

"Oh, Tony, the board's executive committee is meeting in about five minutes." Allie gathered the copies of the report from the printer. "It was just added to the calendar this morning."

"Thus, I was unaware of it. Not a problem; I'll just stop back in on my way from doing errands." He slid his sunglasses on and turned to leave.

"Hey, maestro, when will you be back?" Ken's voice followed Tony through the door.

"Soon enough, I reckon," the music director shot back, as he kept moving through the doorway.

"Well, he seems out of sorts," said Ken, "Like he's got a hair across his derriere." He marched into the conference room and pulled out his phone to peruse while he waited for the rest of the committee to arrive.

The meeting had gone well, Allie reflected as she collected the glasses and pitcher of water from the table. True to form, Esther Swift had been nothing but helpful, with various suggestions of things that she and other volunteers could do to help. Ken was grudgingly positive after looking over Allie's report of the activities she had already taken on. Arnold Shimmler was back from his vacation, and in his professorial way expressed admiration for Allie's work and promised to help. And David Brewster's replacement on the executive committee, Sarah Wilder, said repeatedly that she was amazed at how efficient Allie and George were. She didn't actually volunteer to help, though. Probably just as well, thought Allie. She wasn't known for being the type of board member who actively gets involved and lends a hand wherever it's needed.

Allie typed up cursory notes from the meeting, mostly detailing that it happened and who was there. After all, they hadn't really made any decisions, except for Esther's offer of help. After distributing the notes, Allie remembered with a pang that she had promised to talk with Luke at lunch, and lunchtime was almost there. She sat for a minute, trying to think of how to tell him about her feeling that she wanted distance, without causing him sorrow or worse, incurring his wrath. She put in her earbuds and first turned on Taylor Swift's song, "We Are Never Ever Getting Back Together." But that seemed too harsh, and besides, she was not angry, not really. It just seemed like they had grown apart, like Luke didn't understand her. Allie searched through her music for a better song, more reflective of her feelings, and finally settled on "Two Ghosts"[1] by Harry Styles.

Fifty-Seven

Even though it was deathly hot outside, Allie just had to get out of the office and stretch her legs. She decided to walk down to the concert barn to see how the morning's rehearsal was going. She filled her water bottle with ice water and pulled her hair up into a high bun to keep it off her neck. Slipping on her sunglasses, she headed out the door. The humidity was a physical presence, a wall she had to push through. Ugh, she thought, I can barely breathe. Thank god there is shade on the way to the barn. She kept close to the apple trees on her way down the hill.

A wave of cool air washed over Allie as she opened the door to the barn. It was dark, except for the lights on the rehearsing musicians. She shivered as the temperature changed abruptly and a wild combination of sounds hit her ears. Thomas was on the podium, still filling in for Tony. His head was down, his eyes buried in the score on his stand. The motions of his hands seemed tentative, lacking any connection to the sounds emanating from the 60-something instruments onstage with him. Allie wondered what on earth they were trying to play.

"No, no, NO!" Allie saw Ruben leap from a seat in the front row of the audience. He jumped onto the stage and strode to the podium. Allie couldn't hear what he and Thomas were saying, but Ruben's voice sounded angry as he gestured first to the violins and then to the trombones. Allie slipped into a seat in the dark and strained to hear what was going on. Thomas was nodding in response to each of Ruben's comments, but his body language said he didn't seem convinced. Ruben stepped up onto the podium and Thomas stepped off, shaking his head.

"Bar 102, with vigor!" Ruben barked. He raised his hands to conduct, and the musicians prepared to play. The sounds that resulted were hardly more organized than what Allie had heard before. She could see some of the musicians' faces; they were squinting as if trying to figure out what was on the pages on their stand. Ruben was clearly no conductor. His motions were clumsy and hard to follow. After about two minutes, he stopped the players and turned to Thomas, who in the meantime had jumped off the stage and was listening from the front of the audience seats.

"Oh, Allegra, hi," Ruben said, spotting her sitting in the dark near where Thomas was standing. Thomas turned around, found her, and sent her a rueful smile.

"Tough rehearsal?" she murmured.

"You could say that," Thomas replied, too softly for Ruben to hear.

"Thomas, get what I am trying to do there?" Ruben asked loudly. "I want those three rhythms to bounce off each other. It's deliberate, the 3/4 time against the 15/16 time, and the 4/4 time droning in the background."

"Yeah, well, I haven't figured out how to conduct it yet, Ruben," Thomas replied. He shrugged. "That's Tony's problem, anyway. He'll be back for the next rehearsal."

Allie stood up and looked at her watch. "You know, Ruben," she said. "It's almost noon. Why not call it quits for now? Everyone's had a look at your piece; now they can go home and practice." The musicians immediately began putting away their instruments, eager to escape before Ruben or Thomas could ask them to start again.

"Let me know if you have any questions about your parts," Ruben said to the departing players. He scooped up the score and walked toward the door, shooting Allie a grimace as he passed her. "Incompetence," he muttered.

Allie gave Thomas a questioning look. "Hope that was ok," she said.

"Ruben pulled the idea of reading through his piece on me at the break. Said all the parts had been passed out and could we run over the first movement at the end of the morning rehearsal." He shrugged. "I thought it would be no big deal, so I said sure. Now that I've had a look at it, I'm thanking my lucky stars I'm not conducting that piece. 'Concerto for Orchestra'! It's more like 'Concerto for Conductor'!" He laughed half-heartedly.

"Wow, it did sound difficult. Sort of like Charles Ives on steroids or meth or something."

"Ha! Right, like Ives's Symphony No. 4[39]. Only more so." Thomas laughed. "You nailed it, Allie."

"Glad you think so." Allie laughed in return.

"Seriously, Allie, you saved me. If I'd had to muddle through that score any longer, I think I would have lost my mind. And the respect of the musicians, I should add." He shook his head. "I know Tony has already vetted the piece. And god knows he'll be able to figure out how to conduct it. But sightreading the damn thing? That's fucking impossible." He ran his hand through his hair. "But I knew if I said no to the reading, Ruben would have driven me nuts. He's been off the wall ever since Tony agreed to put it on the program."

"Hey, he's excited, right? Don't let him get to you, Thomas. You've got your own thing going, anyway. I mean, you stepped into Tony's shoes at the Friday concert and you were a star. You absolutely wowed the audience. And I know you impressed the musicians, too. I heard lots of great comments."

Thomas looked into her eyes with a serious expression. "How about you, Allie? Did I impress you?"

Allie's breath caught, and she felt her pulse quicken. "Ah, yeah, sure. I was definitely impressed."

"That means a lot to me, you know. Your opinion..." His voice died away, but he kept staring into her eyes.

Allie blinked. What is it about him, she thought to herself, the heat must be getting to me. She shivered.

"I need to get back to the office," she said.

"Are you free after work? Maybe join me for a beer?"

"Uh, ok." Allie turned to leave. "Umm, text me where to meet you."

"Will do. I'll try to think of someplace cool."

Allie waved in assent as she walked to the door. The heat hit her, timed perfectly with the recollection that she needed to meet Luke...

for the reason she had been putting him off. It was not going to be a fun conversation.

Fifty-Eight

The festival's carpentry shop was shady and slightly cooler than outdoors, thanks to an industrial strength fan that was blowing the air around. Luke was bent over a wooden chair he was sanding, his tee shirt streaked with sweat.

"So, lunch?" she shouted above the fan's insistent whirr.

Luke turned around and looked at his watch, surprised. "Guess I lost track," he said. "Where do you want to go?"

"Somewhere quiet," Allie said, thinking about the painful conversation ahead.

Luke seemed oblivious to Allie's somber mood. "Too hot to eat," he said, grinning. "Maybe we should skip lunch and go for a skinny dip at Brewsters' cottage."

"Luke." Allie rolled her eyes. "Let's grab some sandwiches and bring them back to the office. We can eat in the conference room—no one will be using it and George is out for the next few hours."

"Aww, you're no fun." Luke gestured to the chair. "How 'bout if you go grab us a couple of sandwiches while I finish up this little project?"

"Ok, what kind do you want? And a drink? I'll go to the Green Reaper."

Luke's order in hand, Allie got in the old Volvo and headed down the road. The local public radio classical station was playing "Verklarte Nacht" by Arnold Schoenberg.[1] Its angsty chromaticism fit Allie's feelings. She felt nervous. At the store, she absentmindedly grabbed the two sandwiches, a bag of Cape Cod chips, and a couple of cold waters.

"So, Al," Luke said, peering into Allie's face. "How are you? Really?"

She declined to look at him and busied herself setting out the sandwiches on plates, arranging the chips alongside, and pouring the soda into glasses.

"Al?" Luke grabbed her hand as she passed him his drink. "What's going on?"

Allie freed her hand, pulled out her chair, and sat down. "Luke," she started. "Um." She took a deep breath.

"Oh, come on, girl. What the...?" Luke's voice rose. He moved his chair closer to Allie's.

"Keep it down, Luke. Look, I need to talk to you about... well..." She paused.

"About what?"

"This isn't easy." Allie took Luke's hand, the one she had shaken off a few seconds earlier. She looked at him and saw the wariness in his eyes. "Luke," she said, wincing. "We've known each other for a long time."

"Since we were kids, Allie. A very long time."

"Right, we were kids. And I think you're a good person. I *know* you're a good person, I mean. But..." She paused again. "But..."

"But what? What are you trying to say, Al? Come on! Are you breaking up with me or something?" Luke's voice cracked, and Allie's eyes filled with tears in response.

"People change, Lukie," she said in a soft voice. "It's just... I..."

"Oh, Al. What's going on with you? Where did my old alley-cat go?" Luke withdrew his hand from Allie's grasp and rubbed his eyes.

"We're not the same people we were, Luke. I don't know. Somehow, us together... I don't know, it doesn't feel right. I'm different."

"I'm not different," Luke said. "Maybe you are. Maybe you're too wrapped up in your big job, hanging around with conductors and composers." He frowned and pushed away his plate. "So, you don't want to see me anymore? Is that what you're getting at?"

Allie briefly closed her eyes. "Luke, don't get mad. I care about you. A lot. But..."

"But you don't love me."

"Actually, Luke, I do. But not in the same way you love me. I love you as a special friend."

"'A special friend.' Great. So all that great sex we had... done, finished? Meant nothing?"

"No, no, I don't mean... I don't know. I just feel different. Things have changed. Life is more serious." Allie looked down and mumbled, "People die."

"I don't know how to help you with that, Allegra Brewster. Yeah, people die. Everyone dies. It's a fact. You don't have to like it, but it's a fucking fact!" He shouted the last word. Allie flinched.

"See, I don't think you understand..."

"Oh, I understand all right. People who die get in the way of your caring about people who are alive and breathing right in front of you. Al..." His voice cracked. "Where does this leave us? I don't want to be 'a friend.' I want more than that."

"I can't give you that. Luke, I..." Tears trickled down her cheeks.

"Allie, Allie, Allie." Luke reached over to her and put his arms around her. "Alley-cat, it's ok. We'll figure it out. It's ok." He stroked her hair and wiped away a tear with his thumb. He inhaled a ragged breath and held it for a few seconds. "Listen, I'll back off. I do know you love me. And I know you know I love you." Taking her chin in his hand, he smiled wistfully. "Maybe we're not on the same wavelength right now, but that could change."

Allie expected him to kiss her, but instead he dropped his hand and pushed back his chair. "This was a crappy lunch," he said with a half-hearted smile. "See ya around, kiddo," he said, and left the conference room.

Allie surveyed the table. As soon as he had closed the door, she began picking up the plates and carrying them to the kitchen. Without thinking, she carefully wrapped the sandwiches in plastic and placed them in the refrigerator, slid the chips into the garbage, poured out the waters, and set the plates and glasses in the dishwasher. Suddenly, she realized she was humming a tune. It was "Hejira," by Joni Mitchell,[2] from one of her father's favorite CDs. How did the lyrics go?

We're only particles of change I know I know
Orbiting around the sun
But how can I have that point of view
When I'm always bound and tied to someone?

She remembered the electric bass line that threaded throughout the song, winding around Mitchell's singing almost as a second voice. Yeah, she thought, those lyrics said it. They really did. She shook her head as if to clear it, and returned to her desk.

Fifty-Nine

beer at the watering hole maybe oysters 2

time?

6

k see ya

The Hole, as the locals referred to it, was a restaurant built on a rough platform over the water, barely attached to land on the left side. Patrons could see the water below through the spaces between the rough-sawn planks. The furniture was old, mostly rusty metal chairs and round tables. A few umbrellas, labeled Cinzano, offered a small amount of protection from the sun. A covered bar ran along the left side, and customers ordering drinks had to be wary of getting a splinter it they leaned on the counter or pressed their knee against the support. But the Hole was always hopping, mainly because the oysters were fresh from nearby aquaculture farms, and local beers were on tap. Often, musicians and pickup bands would stop in and play for tips, and soon customers would be dancing on the boards.

This Tuesday evening, the Hole seemed a bit subdued. No musicians had shown up. But almost every table was filled and laughter and vivacious conversation flew through the air. Allie looked around for Thomas. The noise and carefree atmosphere surprised her; it was like stepping into a whole different world. A hand went up from the last picnic table, where Thomas was sitting with someone else. Allie made her way through the jumble of chairs and tables.

In a courtly gesture, Thomas stood as Allie approached. The second person at the table turned, and Allie saw that it was Ruben.

"Don't worry; this fool is just leaving," Thomas said to Allie with a smile and a wave toward Ruben.

"Whaaa? Not planning on going anywhere soon," Ruben said. "Not when such beauty arrives on the scene."

Allie rolled her eyes.

"Beer?" Thomas asked. Allie nodded. "Pemaquid draft?" She nodded again, and Thomas headed toward the bar.

"Add one for me," Ruben called after him. "It's a thirsty afternoon," he said to Allie. He interlocked his hands behind his head and leaned back in the metal chair. "How're things in the office these days?"

Allie lifted her chin. "Fine."

"You prepared for George's departure? Or is everything going to fall apart without his guiding wisdom?"

"It's fine. No problems. I've got lots of help."

"What do you hear about the big debut? People excited?"

"If you're referring to your Concerto for Orchestra, not too much." Allie craned her neck and saw that Thomas was still in line at the bar. "We just keep rolling on. One week at a time, like that."

"Yeah, well, I'm so glad I convinced Sir Tony to switch pieces."

"Yeah..."

"I mean, imagine getting another cellist ready to play the solo part. Anne was struggling as it was..."

"She was not!"

"Well, it hadn't come together yet. That was clear."

"It hadn't come together because you hadn't finished the damn piece! Anne was..." Allie stopped and took a breath.

"She was fine, ok? I just am glad that we've moved on to the CFO."

"CFO?"

"Concerto for Orchestra. I think it shows off my abilities to a much greater extent. And Tony will be great with it. I swear, he was a little caught up in the Cello Concerto because he and Anne were banging."

"You are full of shit, Ruben. They definitely were not." Allie stood up. "I'll go help Thomas bring the drinks."

"Hey, easy. I didn't mean to rile you, Allegra." Ruben's words followed Allie as she walked away. She could feel her face flaming. What was with him, anyway? Clearly, he was on some sort of ego trip today.

"Ruben got to you?" Thomas handed one of the 16 oz frosted mugs to Allie as they walked back to the picnic table. "I'll get rid of him as soon as possible." He smiled at Allie. "I made the date with you, not him. He invited himself."

"Guess I can stand it for a few more minutes."

"No worries. He usually gulps his beer down."

As they set the beers on the table, Ruben said, "I stopped the waitress and ordered fries. You guys hungry?"

"Uh, no," said Thomas. "How long are you planning to stay here?"

"Got nothin' to do, nowhere to go." Ruben smiled. "Cramping your style, roomie?"

"Drink up and get your fries to go."

"Guess that's my answer." Ruben laughed.

The three sat in silence for a few minutes. The crowd on the dock grew as more customers stopped in for a beer. There was a steady stream of cars on the road, and a few boats motored in and tied up. Several people gestured to the three empty chairs at the table as if to ask if they were available and were answered in the negative by a head shake from Thomas.

"Popular place," said Ruben, looking around.

Thomas placed his empty mug on the table. "Too popular. Allie, shall we move on?"

She held up her mug, still filled a third of the way. "Give me a minute."

"Relax, man," Ruben said to Thomas. "What's your rush? Nice evening, great company, beautiful woman..."

Allie thumped her mug down. "Finished." She and Thomas got up and walked away, leaving Ruben shrugging his shoulders.

"Whatever," he said, turning and motioning to a group of young women in short shorts and halter tops who were looking for seats.

It seemed weird to be going somewhere with Thomas after her difficult conversation with Luke that afternoon. But she and Thomas were just going somewhere to grab a bite to eat, right? It signified nothing. Still, Allie felt as though she was betraying her longtime friend and lover. She clenched her teeth. Why was this relationship stuff so hard?

"What are you in the mood for—burgers? Seafood? Salad?" Thomas was oblivious to her emotional dithering, luckily. "You know what," he continued, "I'm up for some fried clams. Like from Fred's Eats. You up for that?"

"Oh, sure," said Allie. "I'll probably have a haddock sandwich. But I might steal a clam or two from you." She shot him a quick smile.

"You and Ruben not getting along these days?"

Allie shrugged. "He was disparaging Anne's playing of his damn concerto. His UNFINISHED concerto."

"Yeah, he's been tough to be around lately. Especially as a roommate. If I didn't know better, I'd say he was a bit manic-depressive. Like, he was sort of glum when he hadn't finished the cello concerto, but now he's acting like he's God's gift to classical music with his Concerto for Orchestra in the line-up. I mean, it's great for him and everything, but can't he be a little humble now and then?"

"I agree. And he really pissed me off when he started trash talking about Anne. I don't know, it almost seemed like she was in his way or something."

"Ah, well, the world revolves around Ruben these days. No consideration for others." Thomas spoke the words with disdain. He gave Allie a lopsided grin as he pulled into a parking place at Fred's. "Luckily, he's not here. So we can ignore his annoying behavior and enjoy ourselves."

Allie loved the spartan interior of Fred's Eats. Painted gray concrete floor that was hosed down every night, firetruck red picnic tables arranged in rows, order numbers blaring over the loudspeaker for pickup. Best of all were the black and white photographic murals of fishing boats from the past that adorned the walls. Some of the boats' names were visible on their sterns in the photos, and Allie knew lots of the owners, many of whom were now very old or dead. In some cases, their son or daughter had inherited the business and the boat.

Thomas and Allie stood in line and ordered, then chose a picnic table and sat down to wait. Their conversation was minimal; both were preoccupied. Allie wondered why Ruben had turned into such a jerk, and Thomas was worrying about his next conducting job at the festival. When their order's number was called, Thomas got up to retrieve it from the counter and Allie filled little paper cups with ketchup and tartar sauce and brought them to their table. They ate mostly in silence, munching happily and occasionally exchanging positive comments about the food. When she finished, Allie asked Thomas if he'd give her a ride back to her car at the office and he said sure.

Once back home at the cottage, Allie thought back to the couple of hours she just spent with Thomas. It had felt companionable, not pressured or awkward. It was a relief.

Sixty

As Allie got ready for bed, she noticed two new voicemail messages on her phone. The first was from her dad.

"Allie, just wanted to let you know a couple of things. First off, Hylie has done something terrible and I wanted to tell you first before you heard it elsewhere. This evening, I let Archie out to pee, and suddenly I heard a ton of barking and a volley of gunshots. Christ! I was sure Hylie had shot Archie!"

Allie caught her breath, then let it out with her father's next sentence.

"But then Archie came dashing back to the kitchen door, unharmed. A moment later, though, I heard a crashing noise in the bushes along the stream that separates Hylie's land from ours. I walked out to investigate just in time to see a moose—probably the one you've seen around—fall to its knees and then collapse. Next thing I knew, Hylie came crashing right behind it, carrying his huge automatic rifle.

What the fuck—he killed the moose? Allie couldn't believe it.

"It's not hunting season," her father continued, "and besides, you have to win a lottery in order to kill a moose. So I asked him what he was doing. And he claimed that the moose had charged him and that he shot it in self-defense. I think he was disappointed that the moose had died on my property instead of his. Anyway, I told him to leave, and then I called the police. They've sent someone to take away the carcass." David cleared his throat. "So, anyway, I thought you should know. Sorry to be the bearer of bad news, honey."

Allie decided to send her dad a text.

that's awful —poor moose —hylie is an asshole

Her father quickly replied.

No kidding!

and you should stay away from him dad — he's dangerous with that gun

Oh he'd never shoot a person. I think. Heading off to bed. Maybe see you tomorrow.

I'll be around dad love u

The second voicemail was from Anne's sister, Jennifer. Allie listened to it and heard Jennifer say that she wanted to talk to Allie—tonight—if Allie could call before 11:00. Allie quickly hit the reply button. Jennifer picked up right away.

"Jennifer? It's Allegra Brewster. I got your message."

"Thanks for calling back, Allie."

"What's up? Is everything ok?"

"Ok as much as possible, I guess. Look, I saw some texts I thought you might be interested in."

Allie was puzzled. "Texts? Having to do with Anne?"

"Yes. I had already downloaded the photos from Anne's iPhone and decommissioned it so no one could access her bank info and other sensitive stuff. But in looking at her laptop, I discovered that she also kept her text messages in an app there as well as on her phone. So, curiosity compelled me to see if there were any recent messages from right before..." Jennifer paused. "...And sure enough there were."

"Ok?" Allie realized that Jennifer must have found something interesting.

"That night, she sent a text to someone she identified as 'Agitato.' I couldn't find this name in her contact list on her laptop, so I can't identify him or her. But then there's an exchange that seems relevant."

Agitato? Allie knew she'd heard that musical term recently, but where?

"Let me read it to you," Jennifer continued. "It starts out with a text from Anne, 'I read over the score you sent a few minutes ago. I can't believe you did this.' Then Agitato replies, 'Did what?' and Anne texts, 'Directly plagiarized JMcK.' Then Agitato says, 'Not true.' and Anne says, 'If you come over, I'll play the original composition.' And here's the important thing, Allie: Agitato says, 'Heading over now.' So whoever Agitato is must have been at Anne's cottage after you left. Can you figure out who that is?"

Allie was pretty sure she knew who Agitato was. But she wanted to make sure before she told Jennifer or anyone else.

Sixty-One

"What's this?" Allie set her cup of coffee down and picked up the heavy embossed envelope that lay propped against her laptop on her desk.

As she began to open it, George stepped out from his office. "Ah, you're opening it," he said with a smile.

Inside was a beautiful wedding invitation, hand-lettered and painted with a pale watercolor wash.

"Wow, this is so beautiful," Allie said. "How did you have it made so quickly? Where did you find the artist?"

"Ahem," George cleared his throat. "Actually, I made the invitations. There are so few people invited and it will be such a simple ceremony and celebration, that I figured it was the least I could do."

"But, George, I had no idea you were so artistic."

"They did come out well, didn't they?"

"And I'm honored to be one of the very few guests. Wow, I'm feeling really special here."

"Of course you were always going to be invited, Allegra. In fact, in the beginning, Grant and I were hoping we could hire you to play during the ceremony. But after Anne's death, well, I wasn't sure you'd want to do that."

"Do you still need music?"

"Yeah, we haven't figured that out yet. Of course, musicians are a dime a dozen around here." George gestured to the festival grounds. "But none would be as meaningful..."

"I think..." Allie started cautiously, "I think I could do it." She paused for a second, thinking. "What if I brought in someone else, too? Would that be alright?"

"I wasn't trying to convince you to do it, Allie, if it doesn't feel right."

"No, no, I would like to do it. You've been such a good boss to me, George. I am grateful for all you've done."

"You mean foisting my job off on you?" he said, laughing.

"I mean having faith in my ability to follow in your footsteps." Allie looked at the invitation. "This is coming right up! Next Thursday." She looked at the invitation more closely. "Wait! At my dad's house! He didn't say anything about it."

"That's because we just asked him yesterday. And once he said yes, I immediately got to work making twenty invitations."

"Funny, I did get a voicemail from him last night but he didn't mention it. Although he did say there was something else but then he didn't say what it was."

"We don't need him to do anything special. We're hoping to get married in the field. The forecast is for nice weather, and since we set the time for five o'clock, the sun will be lower and not as hot, we hope. David is just going to mow a path out to the level spot, and we'll set up a bunch of folding chairs."

"Sounds nice." Allie shook her head as if to clear the cobwebs. "You two sure move fast when you make up your mind."

"Hey, when you know, you know," George responded. "Now, I've got a lot of wrapping up to do." He headed back into his office, saying over his shoulder, "Glad you will be playing your cello at the ceremony, Allie. Grant and I will appreciate that."

Hmmm, Allie thought. Thursday was four days away. What could she get together in that amount of time? The Vivaldi Cencerto for two cellos she and Thomas (and the murder victim, Sylvia on piano) had been planning for the Spring fundraiser—that would have been good, except that you need a piano or harpsichord, too, and neither of those would be available out in the field. Then Allie remembered that she and Thomas had warmed up on a Rossini duet for two cellos that was easy enough that they sounded decent without rehearsing. She recalled the first movement, Allegro, was lively and would provide a bit of a grand entrance. That should work. Allie wondered if Thomas was on the festival campus. She decided to see if she could find him.

"There you are, Thomas," she said as she found him studying a score in the green room of the concert barn. Formerly the home of the tractors and farming implements, the green room was now a medium-sized room carpeted with indoor-outdoor green carpeting, a hung ceiling with sound-absorptive tiles, and a scattering of tables and worn out sofas and chairs donated by festival friends. Before a concert, it was packed with musicians, their instruments, and their instruments' cases, but this morning it was empty except for used paper coffee cups scattered around and one lone Thomas, sitting on a pink flowered over-stuffed sofa with a lap full of orchestral scores. He was silently conducting the pieces on the top of the pile with a miniature conductor's baton, his face a study in concentration. That brown strand had slipped down over his forehead and he didn't look up when Allie spoke. She stood directly in front of him and, noticing his ear buds, motioned for him to take them out. He looked up at her, raised his eyebrows, and removed them.

"What's up?" he asked.

"Have you played your cello recently?"

"Why do you ask?"

"Well, remember the Rossini duet we played through in the spring?"

"Of course I do. We were preparing for the ill-fated, murder-riddled, benefit concert. That one?" He smiled ironically.

"Guess so. Yeah. Well, George asked if I'd play at his wedding and I thought maybe the two of us could play the Allegro from that. If you feel up to it, that is."

"The Allegro is pretty short, right?"

"I think it's only a little more than five minutes if we keep it moving."

"Ok, I think I could swing that. Oh, but when's the wedding? I should check my calendar." Thomas pulled his phone out of his pocket.

"Thursday at five o'clock."

"This Thursday? Maybe we'd better try it before we commit to doing this."

"Ok, when can you get together? I've got to work in the office all day..."

"Why don't you come by the cottage this evening? Ruben is going to be out, I think. We can run through it quickly and see how bad it is." They both laughed.

"About eight? That work?" Allie asked.

"Fine, see you then."

Allie quickly returned to the office. There was a stack of papers on her desk and about twenty new emails and texts on her laptop, new things she had to figure out before George was gone for good. Guess I'll be staying late, she thought, but I do need to get to Thomas's by eight. She put in her earbuds and turned on a recording of the Rossini duet.[42]

Sixty-Two

At seven fifteen, Allie closed her laptop and headed to her cottage to pick up her cello, find the music to the Rossini, and grab a bite. She stuck a frozen cheese enchilada in the ancient toaster oven on the kitchen counter to cook while she pawed through her collection of sheet music. Luckily, the Rossini was near the top, with both parts together in its folder. It occurred to Allie that she might need to scan the music so she and Thomas could use their iPads instead. Paper music was a challenge outdoors, where at any moment it could sail away in the wind. And the trouble with using clothespins to hold the pages, reflected Allie, is that when a page turn was necessary, you had to first unclip the clothespin, turn the page, then re-clip the clothespin. Not workable in a performance like George and Grant's wedding ceremony.

She took her cello out of its case and tested the strings. It wasn't too terribly out of tune, which was lucky. She'd tune the cello when she got to Thomas's. She placed the cello back in its case and was about to take a bite of her enchilada when a message beeped on her phone. Glancing at it, Allie groaned.

hey al

It was Luke. She decided not to answer.

wassup?

Shit, she thought. I don't have time for this.

cant talk now. busy

k later?

tomorrow ok?

guess so :(

She took a last bite of the enchilada, gulped down some water, gathered up her cello, the music, and her folding music stand and carried them to the car. Her phone said quarter to eight; she'd get to Thomas's just barely on time.

"So, not too bad!" Thomas smiled as he set his bow down. "I think we can pull this together in one practice session."

Allie was pleased. She had thought they'd be able to get the Rossini ready in time for the wedding, and it was turning out to be even easier than she had hoped. "Let's go through it again," she said. "This time, why don't you take the top part and I'll play the lower part? We need to keep the tempo steady through the sections with the sixteenth note runs? And maybe we could plan to end right at measure 90? That seems like a good stopping place. I think it's about three minutes in—that's probably long enough. And we can always go back to repeat the beginning if we need more music."

"That sounds right." Thomas adjusted his chair. "I hope the top part is easier than the bottom. If I have to play that part, I'm going to need to do some woodshedding. Especially if we want it to move at a fast clip."

"Which we do," said Allie. They played through the first three minutes of the piece again and then stopped and went over a few places where one of them had made a mistake or they had gotten out of sync. As they played, Allie felt a rekindling of the sense of joy that she'd been missing. It felt good to hold her bow, and her fingers confidently took on the quick runs, pressing on the metal strings of the neck. The piney scent of rosin on her bow's horsehairs and the cello's curves against her body brought back all the pleasure she had in making music. Not just listening, she thought, *making*. Thomas glanced at her as they played, winking at a difficult run that she pulled off with ease, and mimicking a look of overly dramatic horror as he began a difficult passage of his own. Their two cellos matched in tone; as they played, they blended their styles so it was hard to tell which player was playing which part.

Finally, they stopped, each breathing heavily from the effort. "Whew, we really clicked on that," said Thomas. "I haven't had that much fun playing for a while." He looked at his watch. "It's 9:30 and Ruben is still out. Want to read something else? I have a nice goopy romantic duet that would be a fun challenge."

"Ok. I don't need to be anywhere super early tomorrow morning."

"Oh, yeah…" said Thomas, as he paged through a large file of music. "I know that piece's in here somewhere. Hey, so how are things going with your new job starting soon? Oh, here it is." He pulled out a couple of pages of music. "Want to try this?" He handed one of the parts of music to Allie.

"Hmmm," she said, perusing the music. "I don't know this, and it doesn't have a title on it. I don't think I do, anyway." She tried to hum the opening bars of the cello 1 part.

"You'll know it when you hear it, I'm sure." Thomas laughed. He counted off a measure for nothing to establish the beat: one, two, three, four, and they started together.

"Hey," said Allie, a smile dawning on her face as she played. "'You can count on me like 1,2,3, and I'll be there. And I know when I need it I can count on you like 4,3,2 and you'll be there. 'Cause that's what friends are supposed to do, oh yeah…''" she sang along. "It's 'Count on Me' by Bruno Mars[1]! My dad used to sing this song to me. Where did you get this arrangement?" She kept playing as she spoke.

"I put it together years ago, before I became a conductor. A friend and I used to play it on the street with a hat out front. I have a collection of similar arrangements we used to play. We could make some decent money, though the weather was often a big factor."

"I know what you mean. Anne and I did a lot of that kind of playing. Just for fun, though. We weren't trying to make any money. And I was pretty young, too."

"It must have been adorable," said Thomas. His eyes met Allie's and held their gaze for a little longer than was comfortable. Then he looked away.

"You know, Allie," he said, "I... Well, I have been impressed by how you've handled everything. I mean, the troubles this spring, and then being appointed the acting director, and then Anne... I... uh... you..."

Allie put her cello in its case and set the bow in its holder on the lid. She looked at Thomas questioningly.

"I think I really screwed up," Thomas said. "I think I was wrong, I mean, I assumed something about you that was wrong."

Allie raised her eyebrows but didn't say anything.

"What I'm trying to say is, I like you and I respect you. A lot. Not sure that came across that time..."

"You're right, Thomas. I'm not the casual hook up type."

He brushed back the hair that had tumbled down his forehead. "Yeah, I know that now. And I'm sorry. I wish I hadn't gotten off on the wrong foot." He looked down. "You're pretty special. Talented, hard-working, a good friend, funny..."

Allie smiled. "Hey, don't stop!"

Thomas stepped closer and took Allie's chin. "Don't stop what?" he asked softly as he bent to kiss her.

It was a short kiss. More than a peck, but less than a smooch. Even so, Allie felt her legs wobble. She closed her eyes and inhaled, then put her arms around Thomas's shoulders and kissed him back, long and hard.

"What have we here?" leered Ruben, as he threw his keys on the table. "Sorry to break up your 'practice session.'" He laughed. "Guess I should have stayed back at the pub for a little longer. Or maybe a lot longer."

Allie and Thomas had pulled apart instantly at the sound of Ruben's voice.

Allie looked at her phone. "It's 10:30! I'd better get going."

"By the way," said Ruben, "I'm still hoping to get that sailing lesson from you."

Thomas picked up Allie's cello. "I'll walk you to your car."

Once outside, he said, "Allie, don't mind Ruben. This premiere of his big Concerto for Orchestra has got him out of control. He's just being an egotistical pain in the ass, that's all."

He set the cello in the back of Pablo and came around to the driver's door. Allie rolled down the window, and Thomas leaned in. "I don't want to rush you, Allie," he said. "But I've felt something for you for months now. I thought you and Lucas were together, though." He gave her a searching look. "Am I wrong about that?"

Allie looked down, then met Thomas's gaze. "You're not wrong. But I..., I'm feeling too wrapped up in other things right now to have a serious relationship with anyone. But..." She closed her eyes.

"I get it. You have a lot on your plate. I can be patient, I guess."

"I've got to go."

"See you tomorrow, Allie. Hey, and thanks for asking me to play with you for the wedding."

"Ok. See you, Thomas."

Allie drove up the dirt road, her insides a hot mess.

Sixty-Three

The next morning, Allie awoke with a feeling of panic. How did she really feel about Thomas? Why did she go all mushy when he came near her? Was it just lust? It was some sort of physical reaction, that was for sure. Ugh. Why did her body betray her? Why can't I just do my work? Romance is the last thing I need right now, she thought. I can live without sex.

Then she sat up in bed. Oh, shit, she had told Luke she'd talk to him this morning. This won't go well, she thought. Maybe the best thing would be to talk in the office. That way, he'd have to keep control of himself. But was George going to be in? Allie looked at the calendar on her phone. Yeah, he'd be in at 8:30 for a meeting with some donors. Perfect. Luke would have to behave and also be quick.

Allie got dressed and gulped down some eggs and toast. As she finished her coffee, she sent Luke a text.

meet me at the office at 8:45

k

he quickly replied.

George's door was closed when Allie entered the office. A low murmur of voices was audible, not enough to distinguish what was being said. She hoped the same was true for the reverse. She didn't want her breakup speech to Luke to be heard beyond her desk.

As she looked over some poster designs that the graphic design firm had sent for the final concert of the season, Allie suddenly remembered what Thomas had said about Ruben. He'd been picking mushrooms. Was he the person who'd left the mushrooms on the cottage steps for Anne the afternoon before she died? Allie remembered Jennifer had tried them and thought they'd made her sick. As these thoughts whirled through her mind, Luke walked through the door.

"Hey, Alleycat," he said, smiling. "How's my girl?"

"Uh, not your girl, Luke."

He folded his arms and made a face. "Damn. I hoped you'd had a change of heart. What's up, anyway, Allie? Where are we?"

Allie considered the man she'd been with on and off for most of her life. She just didn't feel a flutter, certainly not like the way she'd felt with Thomas last night. But Luke was a *good* guy. Honorable. He stood there before her in his torn jeans and tee shirt, a pencil tucked among the brown curls behind his right ear. She had a matching tee shirt at home; they'd bought them together at a concert about ten years before. Thick lashes ringed his brown eyes that were wincing in a pained expression.

"I can't go on like this," he said. "We're... I..."

"I know, Lukey. I know. It's just... it's too much. I'm overwhelmed."

"I told you I would give you space..."

"I think, I think... it's more than that." Allie reached out for his arm. "I care about you..."

"Oh, right," he interrupted, yanking his arm away. "Here it comes. It's the 'It's not you, it's me' bullshit." He looked down, trying to hide the tears that filled his eyes.

Allie's eyes teared up in response. Why did this have to be so hard? "We've grown apart. We're different. We want different things."

"No, Al. That's your interpretation. I just want you to be happy. I want to make you happy."

"To be honest, Luke, being friends—nothing more—is what would make me happy." There, she'd said it.

He sent her a sharp glance. "I don't know, Al, I don't know if I want to be one of your *friends*. Yeah, me and Ruben and Thomas and god knows who else. We'll just all be Allie's friends." He turned on his heel and headed for the door. "I don't think I want to be in that group," he said, swivelling away toward the door.

Ruben and Luke passed each other in the doorway. Ruben looked after Luke's retreating figure. "What group is that?" he asked Allie.

"Oh, nothing."

"Hey, I came in to talk about that sailing lesson. Are you still up for it? The weather looks great. After work maybe? Like, maybe, can you leave at four o'clock?"

George chose that moment to open his office door. Behind him was a couple that Allie recognized as frequent audience members. "Joan and Jacob, this is my soon-to-be replacement, Allegra Brewster," he said to the couple. "Allegra, Joan and Jacob Keller have joined the Conductors' Society. And this is our young composer in residence, Ruben Perrotta," he added, motioning to Ruben. Everyone shook hands and said how pleased they were to meet each other, and the Kellers left the office.

"I heard you ask if Allegra could leave at four," said George. "It is a nice day, Allie. Why don't you take off early and catch up at home this evening? No need to waste a beautiful afternoon."

"Maybe we'll even have time to catch a bite afterward," said Ruben, emphasizing the word bite and wiggling his eyebrows suggestively.

"No, we won't have time for that. I don't know if I'll even have time to go sailing..."

"Aww, come on. Just for a short spin." Ruben made puppy eyes at her.

"Ok, ok, ok," Allie replied. "Meet me at the main dock at the sailing club at four-thirty."

"Super. I'll be there," Ruben said.

"Lucky guy," said George as he returned to his office.

"By the way, Ruben," Allie said. "Thomas tells me you've been out picking mushrooms."

"Huh? Oh, yeah, I do that. Sometimes."

"Did you leave a bag of mushrooms on Anne's doorstep that day before she died?"

Ruben looked mystified. "Me? No, why would I do that?" He pulled at his shirt, as if he were suddenly overheated.

"Hmm, someone did. Anne's sister ended up taking them home and cooked them a few days later. The weird thing is, they made her sick. So, was someone trying to poison Anne?"

Ruben cleared his throat. "I know nothing about that," he said. "Well, I better run. See you at the dock at four-thirty." Ruben practically ran out the door.

Strange reaction, thought Allie. Was he guilty? Did he know Anne suspected he was plagiarizing the Joyce MacKenzie piece? Allie felt pretty sure Ruben was the person Anne had labeled Agitato. She pulled up the folder with Ruben's application to become the composer in residence. Maybe there was something there that would either confirm or dispel her worries about him.

> I have considered Philip Glass and John Cage my musical predecessors. I had the honor of meeting Glass at a symposium in 2005 and have met him several times since. His influence has permeated my life. Like Glass, I've explored Buddhism and I've also become an avid mycophile.

Mycophile? Allie stopped at that word. What did it mean? She decided to look it up.

Mycophile, noun, my·co·phile : a devotee of mushrooms *especially* : one whose hobby is hunting wild edible mushrooms.

Allie snapped her laptop shut, nausea gripping her stomach. She didn't need to see any more.

Sixty-Four

Allie hauled in Calliope's mainsheet and headed upwind toward the sailing club dock, weaving her way between the similar small boats bobbing at their moorings. She could see Ruben waiting for her at the end of the dock. He looked small, hugging himself against the breeze's chill. Allie had considered cancelling the sailing trip, but doubt had displaced her previous suspicions. Why would Ruben have done such an evil thing? It didn't make any sense. Anne's death had postponed the premiere of his concerto; that certainly wasn't good for him, was it? In the ensuing press coverage of Anne's death, his concerto had been largely ignored, unlike the expected critical acclaim he would have received if she'd been alive to perform it.

Anne. The thought of her friend's painful death struck Allie's heart like a knife yet again. I have to get to the bottom of this, she thought. I need to know who did it—who murdered Anne and simultaneously killed the joyful spirit of the SummerFest. Thinking of Ruben's enthusiastic attitude toward his participation in the festival, she couldn't imagine he had anything to do with the tragedy. She waved to him, but he didn't unwrap his arms to wave back.

As she brought Calliope alongside the dock and grabbed a post, Ruben seemed oddly tentative about getting aboard as the sails flapped loudly in the wind.

"Are you sure you want to go for a sail?" Allie asked. "It's a bit windy, but it should be fine with two of us in the boat for ballast. But if you don't feel like it, we can sail another time."

"No, we're going today. I mean, I want to stick to the plan." He stepped into Calliope and chose a seat across from Allie. She handed Ruben a blue collar-like device with nylon straps.

"If you're ok to go, here's an inflatable PFD to wear. Personal Flotation Device, that is." Allie held onto the dock post with one hand and pointed to the PFD she was wearing with the other. "You put it on like a jacket, sort of." she explained. "See, put one arm through here, and then the other arm through there."

Ruben struggled with it for a minute but then succeeded in getting the PFD on. Following Allie's directions, he buckled the belt strap and tightened it.

"How does it inflate?" he asked. "Automatically?"

"No, see this little tab. If you find yourself in the water, pull on the tab and the device will immediately inflate. But for now, push that little tab up out of the way so it doesn't catch on anything. You don't want it to inflate if you don't need it." Allie laughed. "Did you ever have to wear the old kind of orange life jacket? God, they were uncomfortable. I had to wear one once, and I felt like I was getting choked."

"Never wore one."

Allie pushed Calliope away from the dock, and the boat heeled as the wind filled the sails. "Could you let out on the jib sheet, Ruben? We're heading downwind."

Gripping the gunwale, Ruben looked around the small cockpit. "What?"

"Just pull up the line that goes through the chock there and let it out a bit. The rope there. Until I say stop." Allie pointed to a small rope threaded through a spring-loaded device with teeth that held the rope in place. "We'll be on a run for a few minutes, so we want the sails out as far as possible to catch the wind."

It took Ruben several tries to loosen the jib line and let it out, but eventually the jib was set to Allie's liking. She had let the mainsail out so far that it was almost perpendicular to the boat, way out over the water. The breeze filled both sails. Although Calliope steamed along, the sailing was deceptively calm on this tack. With the wind behind them, it felt less frantic, and the boat didn't tilt. The sun was warm. Ruben visibly relaxed.

"I brought two sodas, if you want one," said Allie. "There's water, too. You can get pretty dried out in this wind."

"It seems to have died down, though," said Ruben, as he reached for a ginger beer.

"That's because we're in front of it. It only seems calm. If I were to swing up to face the wind, we'd be heeling right away. In fact, keep an eye on the boom." Allie put her hand up on the wooden spar that held the bottom of the mainsail stretched over the cockpit. "If the wind should shift suddenly, that baby will come flying across the boat, crashing into anything in its way. You don't want that conking you in the head!"

Ruben shrugged.

"So, um," Allie started. "Did you want to learn something specific or just want to go for a friendly sail?" She fiddled with the line from the mainsail, looking down at her fingers.

Ruben looked at her, then scanned the cockpit. "How far out can we get?"

"It depends on how much time you want to spend and what the wind does. Why? Do you have something in mind?" Allie glanced at her watch. "I do have to get back for a phone call at 7:30."

"Ok." Ruben didn't match Allie's uncertain smile.

"We can get pretty far going downwind. But then it takes longer to return against the wind. You know, we'll have to tack—zig zag back and forth, that is—we can't head directly into the wind." She took a breath. "So, maybe 30 minutes out? That will get us to Sisters' Island. And we'll have more than twice that to get back."

"Not many other boats out this afternoon," said Ruben, surveying the harbor. "Have you had much time to sail lately?"

"No, between George leaving and Anne's death, I've been super busy." Allie paused. "Anne's death was such a shock. "

"Yeah. Too bad about that." Ruben played with the rope in his hand, then looked up. "Wonder why she did that. Commit suicide, I mean."

"I don't think she did." Allie stared up the length of the mainsail. She was keeping track of the wind to avoid an inadvertent jibe that would send the boom flying over the cockpit and possibly crashing into their heads.

"And something else.," she said. "I saw that you have written about mushrooms. You kind of fashioned yourself a protégé of John Cage, following in his mushroom hunting footsteps."

"Yeah, a long time ago. I admired him. I wanted to be like him. So what?" He leaned forward.

She looked directly at him. "You did leave those mushrooms at her door the afternoon before she died, didn't you."

"What if I did?"

Allie was surprised at the tone of belligerence in his voice. His eyes had narrowed, and he was scowling.

"Anne's sister found a series of text messages Anne wrote to someone the night she died." Allie slid down the bench, moving away from Ruben. Her voice quavered, but she continued. "I didn't understand it then, but now I think I've figured it out. She thought you plagiarized the fourth movement of the concerto, didn't she?" Allie's breathing was shallow and quick.

A sudden wide smile transformed Ruben's face. For a moment, Allie thought he looked like the old Ruben, the fun-loving and generous friend. But she didn't trust that smile anymore. She detected a false undertone and stayed on guard.

"Allie, you're just too damn smart. Who else would have thought to research my writings from ten years ago?" He slid a little closer along the seat. "And that fucking fourth movement—I couldn't get a handle on that and the clock was running. Then I remembered Janice MacKenzie's composition for cello and piano from 1970. She was my composition professor in grad school, you know. Brilliant composer, so-so teacher. I learned a lot more by studying her work than by listening to her lectures. Boring!" He sniggered. "She couldn't do self-promotion for shit. Her early compositions are practically unknown. At least, so I thought."

A small powerboat overtook Calliope, passing too closely. The boat's wake rocked the sailboat, and Ruben clutched at the side of the boat, the gunwale, turning to watch the other boat zoom ahead. While he did that, Allie tried to press record on the iPad surreptitiously.

"What are you doing!" Ruben glared at her.

"I..., I was checking our location on the chart. See? There are some rocks near here." She held out the iPad with the chart displayed, hoping that Ruben wouldn't notice her finger was covering the red dot signaling a recording in process. "We need to turn around soon."

"No. Keep going." Ruben's voice was low and imperative.

Allie positioned the iPad as if she were reading it, in actuality aiming the microphone toward Ruben. Looking at the chart, she said, "So Anne figured out that you had stolen Janice MacKenzie's composition. That must have..."

"I was fucked! If she told anyone, it would end my career!" Ruben stopped shouting and calmed down. "Anne was ok, you know. She was a fine cellist. But I couldn't let her ruin everything. I had no choice."

"So, what? You killed her?" Allie was shocked to hear herself say those words.

"No, she killed herself. The police said so."

"You know that's not true."

"Look, she invited me to come to talk to me about the fourth phase that night. So I did. And she was yelling at me about plagiarism and Janice MacKenzie and stuff. It really, really pissed me off." He looked off over the water.

"And, then what?" Allie prompted.

"What did she expect? She left a god-damn loaded gun sitting on the counter!"

"So you picked it up and shot her?"

"Not like that. I mean, that would have been stupid, wouldn't it?" He smiled. "There were some rubber gloves sitting right by the sink. And Anne was so engrossed in finding the recording of MacKenzie's piece on her laptop—which I had on right my phone," he laughed, "that I had time to stick my fingers in the gloves, pick up the gun and walk around in front of her."

"But she was lying down on the couch—that's what RuthEllen Cox told me."

"True. I persuaded her to do that. Along with pointing the gun at her. Told her to lie down and close her eyes and I'd disappear. I said I'd own up to it all. I'd stop trying to pass off the MacKenzie piece as mine." He clearly was proud of his ruse.

"And she believed you."

"She fell for it hook, line, and sinker."

Allie closed her eyes for a moment, imagining Anne in such a dangerous situation. Now she herself was in a similarly precarious position. She tried to think, her heart pounding in her ears.

"So why are you telling me this, Ruben? You won't get away with it. You are trapped here on this boat with me and you don't know how to sail."

"Oh, I have a plan," he said. "And you know, if Anne hadn't accused me, if she'd kept her trap shut, she'd be alive. It's really her own fault that she's dead."

"That's not true. You killed her, Ruben. You shot her! *You* are a murderer!"

Ruben's response was eerily cool. "It's really a shame that you're so emotional and obsessed with this. Curiosity killed the cat, you know. I really hate to have to do this." He picked up a loose piece of rope, stood up, and lunged toward Allie.

Sixty-Five

As Ruben stood up, Allie quickly pulled the tiller toward her, causing the boat to veer. The boom came flying over the cockpit and thwacked Ruben in the jaw, knocking him backwards. He cried out as he landed on the floor of the cockpit, his head glancing off the edge of the seat. He appeared dazed but conscious. Allie quickly retrieved one of the oars stored under the seat. She held the tiller with one hand and raised the wooden oar with the other. "Stay down," she shouted, "Or I'll hit you with this."

Ruben rubbed his head and looked confused. There was blood on his hand. "Did you do this? Did you?"

"Stay down! Don't move!" Allie waved the oar threateningly. What should she do next? The powerboat whose wake had rocked them was a speck in the distance, and there were no boats to be seen. She grabbed the whistle attached to her PFD, letting go of the tiller for a moment. Maybe if she blew it, someone on shore would hear and would raise an alarm. Three sort blasts, three long blasts, and three short blasts again. S.O.S. She blew the whistle again as she saw Ruben struggle to rise up from the cockpit floor.

In the midst of Ruben's menacing approach, Allie forgot to watch the wind. A sudden gust of wind sent the boom crashing over the boat once again, this time catching Ruben in the shoulder and sending him off balance. As the small boat rocked, he tried to grab onto to something to steady himself, clutching at the jib sheet and pulling it out of its chock. Relying on the tension of a line that suddenly was loose, Ruben lost his footing and pitched over the side with a loud splash.

It all happened in a second. Ruben's head disappeared underwater. Allie threw a floating seat cushion near where he went in, and in a moment his head popped up, his arms scrabbling for the cushion. Allie turned Calliope around to face directly into the wind, which stopped the boat, sails flapping madly.

In a panic, Ruben sputtered. "I can't swim. You are going to drown me! Help! Help!"

"Pull the orange tab. On your PFD. Your life vest. Pull the orange tab!" Allie shouted over his cries for help.

Ruben yanked on the tab and his PFD inflated, pushing him onto his back with his face well out of the water. With the sails still flapping wildly, Allie tossed him a rope, the other end of which was secured to a cleat on the boat. He pulled himself to the boat and attempted to grab the gunwale, but again Allie threatened him with the oar. "Stay in the water," she ordered in her fiercest voice. She hoped he didn't notice that it was still shaky. "You're fine." Digging into the canvas bag with her free hand, she tried to locate her phone while keeping an eye on Ruben in the water.

Just then, she saw the Harvey Hancock's lobster boat zipping through the water toward Calliope at full speed. It quickly covered the distance and slowed as it neared the sailboat. "Allegra Brewster, is that you?" shouted Harvey. "Do you need help?"

"Watch out!" Allie shouted back. "There's a man overboard on my starboard side." She pointed toward Ruben, who was thrashing around in the water. "He has on a PFD, but he can't swim. He's dangerous—he's a murderer, he murdered Anne Kirschner, and he threatened me. Please take him in. And call Chief Knowles and ask him to meet you at the dock."

Harvey was not young, but he was bigger than Ruben and burly from years of lobster fishing. He hauled Ruben into his boat as if Ruben were an extra heavy lobster trap. "No funny business now, mister," he said. "Go through that little door to the cabin. You'll be warmer." Ruben followed Harvey's directions and ducked below, too confused to put up a fight. Harvey closed the small metal lock that hung on the door, ignoring the pounding that started when Ruben figured out he'd been imprisoned. The fisherman turned to Allie. "Shall I give you a tow?" he asked.

"No, thanks. I'd rather sail back. I'll call the police so they can meet you at the dock." Allie turned Calliope slightly away from the wind and trimmed the sails. It would take her a while to get back, time enough to calm her shaky breath and think about what had just happened. She picked up the iPad and pressed play on the recording. Ruben's voice sounded eerily weak and petulant without his threatening physical presence. It was all there, his unmistakable admission to the murder of Anne Kirschner.

Allie looked at the musical choices on the iPad. They were limited; this device was mainly used for navigation while sailing. Something relaxing, she thought. A phrase from a song came into her mind, "Oh, the canvas can do miracles, just you wait and see..." That was a song her father liked; maybe it was on the iPad. Yes, "Sailing" by Christopher Cross.[44] She cued it up and trimmed Calliope's sails. "If the wind is right, you can sail away—find tranquility..."

Sixty-Six

As Allie neared the sailing club docks, she saw a contingent of people waiting for her. Lined up to catch Calliope as she came to the dock were her father, Chief Knowles, Harvey Hancock, Luke, Thomas, and George. They all started shouting at her as she got within range.

"Wait! I can't hear you!" Allie yelled. She expertly piloted the little boat to slide alongside the dock, as several pairs of hands vied to catch her. "Just hold on—I'll throw you the lines. I'm ok, I'm ok," she said.

Once the lines were secured, Allie jumped onto the dock, holding the canvas gear bag. Her dad engulfed her in a big hug. Pulling away, she turned to the assembled audience. "I'm fine, everybody. No need to worry." She looked at the group and singled out the police chief. "Did you get him?"

"Yes, we have him at the station. But on the way, he claimed he's completely innocent. He said you went 'mental' on him." The Chief looked questioningly at Allie. "That true?"

Allie reached back into Calliope's canvas bag and pulled out the iPad. "It's all here. I recorded it." She handed the device to Knowles. "But I think you'll find some other proof as well, back at Cormorant Cottage."

"Naw, we thoroughly searched that site."

"I bet you didn't happen to check the inside of a pair of rubber gloves that were there. I think you'll find several sets of DNA in them: Anne's, mine, the cleaner's, probably the new renters', but most importantly, Ruben Perrotta's. He used the gloves to handle the gun."

"He's a piece of work," said Harvey. "He almost busted my cabin door. I'm gonna have to replace it."

"Yep, we had quite a tussle getting him into the squad car," added Chief Knowles. "I called your dad—figured he'd want to be here when you got back." He pointed at George, Luke, and Thomas. "Don't know where they came from."

"I was here at the sailing club already," said Luke, "and I saw Harvey bring him in."

"And I was in the festival office talking with George, and when I heard you and Ruben were going out on the water, I got alarmed. We both hurried down here."

"Quite a feat of detective work, Allie," said David Brewster. "A bit dangerous, though."

Allie suddenly felt a little dizzy. She leaned on her father.

"You were right, Allegra," said George. "You insisted Anne didn't kill herself, and you proved it."

"I'd better get my boat out to the mooring," said Harvey. "Glad I could help out."

"You were amazing, Harvey," said Allie.

"Aw, it was nothing."

George spoke up. "If you're alright, Allie, I'm going to head back to the office. I was just packing up my stuff, so you can move in tomorrow. It's really your office now."

Luke held Allie's arm for a moment. "You're something else, Alley-Cat. I'm gonna head off. See ya." He looked her in the eyes for a bit too long, then hurried to the parking lot.

Thomas pointed to George. "He's my ride, so I guess I'm going back to the festival office with him. Glad this turned out the way it did, Allie. It might not have. I guess we all know that Ruben was more dangerous than he seemed."

"No kidding," said Allie.

"Allie?" Thomas said. "I'm really glad you're ok. I was afraid..."

"Hey, maestro, let's get going and let Allegra have some space," George said as he walked toward his car. "By the way, you two, I'm assuming that you won't be up for playing at the wedding so soon after this shock."

Allie's eyes met Thomas's. "I think it will be fine," she said to George.

"Ah, yes, spoken like a professional. 'The show must go on,'" George said.

As the others walked away, David Brewster turned to his daughter. "Let me drive you—you're probably still in shock after all that." He gave his daughter another hug. "Where to, Agatha?"

"Agatha?"

"I'm calling you Agatha from now on—like Agatha Christie. You've solved two murders in the space of a few months."

"And that's the end of it. My career as a sleuth is over. Home, Dad. Just drop me off at the cottage."

IV: Finale

"Music is the breath of life. It connects us all, heals us, and makes us feel alive." *—Jennifer Higdon (American composer, b. 1962)*

Sixty-Seven

The sun shone on the strings of Allie's cello and the escaped locks of her hair as she played the first Bach Cello Suite from memory. The wedding guests made their way down the path David Brewster had mown through the field and took their seats in the clearing. David walked with the other guests, escorting George's mom and holding a leash connected to a well-behaved Archie with his other hand. Beyond the mown area, tall grasses danced in unison in the gentle breeze, creating a wavelike motion across the open acres. Thomas sat to Allie's right, perusing with a serious expression the Rossini duet one last time before they would have to play it together.

Finally, everyone was seated, and Allie could see Grant and George waiting expectantly at the edge of the field. She smiled at Thomas, and the two of them launched into the beginning of the Rossini with a triumphant flourish, as the two men walked down the path.

Allie's mind wandered as the ceremony began. From her seat off to the side, she could watch the guests and the two celebrants. Tony was there, wearing a flowered bowtie and a seer-sucker jacket. His eyes looked sad, though his face wore a faint smile. Had he been in love with Anne? Perhaps so. Allie looked down, hoping to squelch any tears that formed at the thought of Anne. How she wished Anne could be here; she would have loved to see such a joyous occasion, even if she didn't share Tony's affection. Thank goodness, Allie thought, that Anne's sister and two kids now knew that Anne hadn't deserted them. Her death was still a terrible tragedy, Allie thought with a sharp pang, squeezing her eyes shut, but somehow it was better knowing that she hadn't done it to herself.

Allie's attention returned as the two lovers recited poetry and promises to each other. First, Allie recognized a Shakespeare sonnet:

> *"...Let me not to the marriage of true minds / Admit impediments. Love is not love / Which alters when it alteration finds, / Or bends with the remover to remove: / O, no! it is an ever-fixed mark, / That looks on tempests and is never shaken; / It is the star to every wandering bark, / Whose worth's unknown, although his height be taken."*

And then came a poem by Robert Frost:

> *"Two such as you with such a master speed / Cannot be parted nor be swept away / From one another once you are agreed /That life is only life forevermore /Together wing to wing and oar to oar"*

It was so romantic, she thought. Although, she shuddered as the mention of oars reminded her of the confrontation with Ruben in Calliope. A flash of white in the sky caught her eye as a bald eagle swooped over the field. She glanced at Thomas and saw he was looking at her intently, a slight smile on his lips. He raised his eyebrows in a questioning look, and Allie felt her cheeks flush.

After the ceremony, the newly married couple and their guests ambled back on the path toward the Brewster farmhouse, where wine and beer and appetizers had been set out under an enormous maple tree. Three young nephews of George and Grant carried Thomas's and Allie's music stands and cases, so the two of them walked back together, unencumbered.

"It was a lovely ceremony," said Thomas. "I've played at many weddings, but this was special. For a number of reasons."

"Yes. Perfect. And they deserve each other. They seem so happy."

"You seem happy, too. Are you happy, Allie?" He moved a little closer and entwined his pinky finger with hers.

"Am I?" she said. "Can I be, after what's happened?" She looked at Thomas. "Is that even possible? Maybe. I guess maybe I am, a little," she said. "Yes."

Afterward

This novel contains discussions about suicide. If you are feeling suicidal, please get help. Know that you are loved, and the pain your death would cause is beyond your imagining. For immediate help in the United States, call or text the national suicide prevention hotline at **988**.

If you're interested in stopping our country's senseless gun deaths, there are advocacy organizations working for sensible gun regulations in the United States: EveryTown.org, Giffords.org, SandyHookPromise.org, and BradyUnited.org.

Acknowledgements

I had a crew of early readers—some of whom are musicians and others who are careful readers—who saved me from making a fool of myself. Carole Zalucky, Julia O'Brien-Merrill, Kristen Fox, Katherine McCreary, Francine Rondina, Patricia Winning, and Margaret Johnston all generously provided insightful comments and corrected egregious errors. Any mistakes you found while reading are mine alone, of course.

A shout out goes to Maine Writers & Publishers Alliance, whose recognition of my earlier book, *Dissonance: A Novel of Music & Murder*, as a finalist in its 2024 Maine Literary Awards (Crime Fiction) gave me a boost of confidence that helped me complete this sequel.

Counterpoint's cover designer, Bailey McGinn, continues to make visual what exists as imaginary. She is a delightful collaborator; just the person you'd like to meet for coffee and chat with for hours. Rick and I had that happy experience this past winter.

Daughters Jenna and Nita and granddaughter Madeline continue to provide enlightenment on current culture as I muddle through the writing and editing process.

And there's Rick, my partner in all things creative. I hope he already knows how much I rely on his support and encouragement, but there's no harm in repeating it here for you to read.

Counterpoint Playlist

1. Schubert, Franz. String quartet No. 14 in d minor, "Death and the Maiden"
2. The Bangles, "Walk Like an Egyptian" by Liam Sternberg. From the album, Different Light.
3. Mozart, Wolfgang Amadeus. Piano Sonata No. 17 in B-flat, K. 570
4. Grieg, Edvard. Piano Concerto in A minor, Op. 16
5. Dvorak, Antonin. Symphony No. 9 in E Minor, "From the New World," Op. 95, B. 178 (1893)
6. Adams, John. "Naïve and Sentimental Music"
7. Trainor, Meghan. "All about That Bass"
8. Alanis Morissette, "Ironic."
9. Keyshia Cole, "Confused in Love" from the cd Calling All Hearts.
10. Traditional Irish tune, "Out on the Ocean"
11. Claude Debussy, "Les Nocturnes."
12. Andreas Vollenweider, "Cosmopoly"
13. Mendelssohn, Felix. "Song Without Words," Op. 109
14. Wagner, Richard. "The Ride of the Valkyries" from his opera, *Die Walkure*
15. Antonio Vivaldi. Chamber Concerto in A Minor, RV108
16. Mendelssohn, Fanny. Piano Trio, Op. 11, Finale. Allegretto moderato.

17. B-52s. "Your Own Private Idaho."
18. Newcomer, Carrie. "Sanctuary" from the album *The Beautiful Not Yet*
19. Ravel, Maurice. "Le tombeau de Couperin," 3rd mov't, Menuet.
20. Britten, Benjamin. "War Requiem," Opus 66. I. Requiem aeternam.
21. The Best of Victor Borge https://youtu.be/x6EfWmHDLbU
22. Bartok, Bela. "Concerto for Orchestra." [needs accents]
23. Copland, Aaron. Hoe Down from "Rodeo."
24. Glinka, Mikhail. Overture to the opera "Russlan and Ludmilla."
25. Fauré, Gabriel. "Requiem."
26. Bach, Johann Sebastian. Two and Three Part Inventions (BWV 772-801).
27. Ravel, Maurice. Pavane pour une infante défunte (Pavane for a dead princess).
28. Barber, Samuel. *Adagio for Strings*.
29. Tchaikovsky, Pyotr Ilyich. "Symphony 5 in e minor, Op. 64, 2nd movement."
30. Tchaikovsky, Pyotr Illych. Symphony #5, 2nd movement.
31. Shostakovich, Dimitri. Waltz No. 2 from "Suite for Variety State Orchestra."
32. Bach, Johann Sebastian. Cello Suite No. 1 in G Major, BWV1007.
33. Prokofiev, Sergei. Symphony No. 1 in D major, Op. 25, Mov't 4 *Finale-Molto Vivace*.
34. Adele, "Set Fire to the Rain"

35. Brahms, Johannes. Hungarian Dances, arranged for orchestra by various composers.

36. Tina Guom "Relaxing Cello" YouTube.

37. Bach, Cello Suite #2. Emmanuelle Bertrand, cello (YouTube)

38. Harry Styles, "Two Ghosts"

39. Ives, Charles. Symphony No. 4.

40. Schonberg, Arnold. "Verklarte Nacht."

41. Mitchell, Joni. "Hejira" from the album of the same name.

42. Gioachino Rossini, Duetto in D Major, "Allegro."

43. Bruno Mars, "Count on Me" from his album, Do-Wops and Hooligans.

44. Cross, Christopher. "Sailing."

Made in the USA
Columbia, SC
17 July 2025

60860156R00148